So This Is College...

The Other Side of An HBCU

Darlene Cunningham

Copyright

www.darlenecunningham.com

ISBN 979-8-218-09559-8

Cover Art by Darlene Cunningham

Edited by Darlene Cunningham & Align Editorial

Printed in the United States of America

Dedication

To Howard University Class of 2012 and 2013

Content Warning

Trigger Warning: Oedipus Complex, Drug Use, Campus Violence & Abandonment by a Parent

If you have experienced any type of trauma, proceed with caution

Acronym Dictionary

A Building = Administration Building

SOC = School of Communications

SOB = School of Business

COAS = College of Arts and Science

HoChi = Howard China (Chinese Takeout spot)

Founders = Library

TSA = Transfer Student Association

Locals = Native Washingtonian

Bison = Howard University Mascot

HUH = Howard University Hospital

Playlist

Playlist

Ladies and Gentlemen **Saliva**

Diary of Jane **Breaking Benjamin**

Numb **Linkin Park**

Crazy Bitch **Buck Cherry**

I Don't Like the Drugs **Marilyn Mason**

Iris **Goo Goo Dolls**

Holy Ghost **Bar Kays**

Emotional Rollercoaster **Vivian Green**

So Cold **Breaking Benjamin**

Did my Time **Korn**

Bones **Melanie Fiona**

Spotify Playlist for So This Is College...

Contents

Welcome to Howard

Stepping onto the yard, Diane took a few minutes and deep breaths reflecting on how her life had changed. At twenty-seven, she's considered an adult student, but she still saw herself as a child with adult responsibilities. With the difficulty of growing up in a toxic home, Diane had to figure out what was and was not normal. A healed adult is what she strived to be. Hopefully, by attending the illustrious Howard University and surrounding herself with various Black people from diverse backgrounds, she'd be able to navigate her new life as an adult.

As a little girl, Diane remained in a constant state of confusion and always wondered why things fell apart around her. She had no one. No one to teach her, mold her, or encourage her passions, hopes, and dreams. In a home with a family that showed no love or compassion, she was absolutely alone. She existed in a state of numbness. Wiping a tear and taking another deep breath, Diane continued to reminisce on her life. She had to be observant and watch how people in and out of her life moved in various situations, how it affected those around them, and the consequences of those choices. Raising herself had been hard, but she had no choice.

Diane's mother, if you want to call her that, worked hard to provide her basic needs. She consistently reminded her that she would not mistreat her physically or verbally, but it would be the only commitment she could make. A drug addict? An alcoholic? Neither. Just a woman who allowed life and those around her to dictate who she was. She gave up and accepted it. They lived in the same home, ate, watched television, and cleaned the house together with little to no words being exchanged. Her mom did just enough to keep her alive and not much else.

Diane's dad came around occasionally, but maybe he had other obligations that meant more than being a consistent father. Diane believed he wanted to be a better father than the one he had. His dad was in and out of his life, mostly out. With Diane, she really believed he gave all he knew how to give. She was his only child and gathered that he never wanted kids because he knew he wouldn't be a fully involved dad. She never asked what happened between him and her mom. Diane had suspected her mom got pregnant to keep her dad, not realizing being pregnant was the quickest way to have a man run.

She didn't know what seemed worse: being around a parent that didn't show any emotion or being around a parent that attempted to give you all he had with his intermittent visits. She remembered the promises of showing up. Sometimes he did and sometimes he didn't. She learned to live life with little expectations, so she'd never be disappointed again. Believe who people show you they are the first time. When he came around, he showed her some affection, not much, but it was what it was. He gave her the basics in the beginning, hygiene, caring for her clothes, properly washing, and telling her to ask for what she needed and not to be ashamed of it. All the things a girl growing into a woman needed to learn. The things he taught her through his actions meant the world. Her dad never compromised what he wanted for someone else. If he sensed he deserved it, he wouldn't stop until he got it. Diane learned this would serve her well with this new endeavor.

Working hard in high school, Diane maintained a low profile and a high GPA. She wanted the future she wanted, unlike her mom. Diane planned on being the master of her universe. She would make sure of it.

She worked part time at a grocery store while in high school and saved every penny to help fund her college education. After graduating high school at the top of her class, she got a few scholarships that totaled about ten thousand. It was not enough to afford Howard and live during the summer and winter breaks. So, Diane enrolled at community college and used the grant money to pay for her first two years. She saved the scholarship money to finance Howard. After graduation, she took a full-time job as a receptionist while continuing to live with her mother to save. College is and always will be expensive, and loans are a last resort. It took four years before she had enough savings to apply to one of the most prestigious HBCUs in the country. Maintaining her high GPA at community college paid off, it allowed most of her credits transferred. Now here she was at the illustrious Howard University as a junior.

The sororities and fraternities gathered at their respective trees, laughing, scrolling, and having a good time. The Divine Nine exuded groupthink in their various colors. Crimson and Crème, Pure White and Royal Blue. Sororities and fraternities are great for volunteering and parties, but other than that, what's their value? Diane understood they helped allow other Blacks to have a sense of belonging when white students outnumbered Black ones at PWIs. Their impact changed Jim Crow and the civil rights era laws, but once Blacks started getting more and more pieces of the pie, their influence seemed to diminish. Sororities and fraternities are mostly exclusionary. Classism at its finest. Being judged, so maybe one day you'd be able to join us so we can judge others together in the name of sister or brotherhood.

Diane knows she is being a little harsh. There are plenty of young men and women who need to belong or have a group of people that have their backs. Especially if they grew up in a family like hers. So, she guesses it depends, but it isn't her ministry; not anymore.

The rest of the campus seemed more individualist. The Fine Arts majors comprised actors, singers, musicians, artists, etc. On the steps in front of the Fine Arts building, they danced and sang to the beat of their own drum. It seemed as if everyone accepted everyone, regardless of the uniqueness of character or dress.

Students sat under the Caribbean tree adorned with flags from Haiti, Jamaica, and Trinidad and Tobago. Patois and various dialects from their home countries filled the air. Diane didn't recognize many other countries' flags on the tree. The women wore hijabs and some men, turbans. Based on her research before attending, Howard had a far reach. Everyone looked for a place to belong, and it is one place to find your tribe.

Diane looked around one of the country's most prominent HBCUs, and contemplated this step toward becoming mentally, emotionally, and financially free. In the words of Kanye before he became white, "Everything I'm not made me everything I am."

As she entered the *A* building, Diane quickly realized the "Howard Hustle" is a real and frustrating thing. They informed her she would be enrolled in the College of Arts and Science (COAS) as an English major instead of being admitted as a student of the School of Communications (SOC) to which she'd applied.

"That shit ain't happening!"

Diane is not about to let Howard dictate what her path should be.

She understood everything the provost said, "Your powerful essay impressed the School of Communications so much they suggested you enroll in the College of Arts and Science."

Etcetera, etcetera. She stopped listening after a while. Aggravated, it took an hour and a half to advocate for the School of Communications, but she walked out of the building down to the SOC and got her new schedule for Radio, TV, and Film (RTVF).

Back up the hill to COAS, she confirmed she was an English minor. Then she had to go back to the *A* building to confirm Financial Aid, only to realize there was a medical hold on her account.

"This shit was for the birds."

Diane walked down past the bookstore and almost to Florida Ave. to the medical center/school clinic. The nurse explained she had to get immunized all over again because, at her big age, the ones she took at eighteen were no longer valid. By the time she walked back up the hill to the *A* building to confirm her medical hold had been removed and all her grants and scholarships had been accepted, she wanted to fuck somebody all the way up. The attitude she'd gotten from the staff had her wanting to put in work. Hot, hungry, and tired, Diane had successfully conquered enrollment.

"Shit! I still have to find my dorm and move in. Ugh. Fuck the Howard Hustle!"

She thought as she walked back down the hill to the residence hall to get her dorm assignment.

The West Towers housed honors and adult students, which meant she had more freedom than the incoming freshman at Tubman Quadrangle. Diane walked through the entrance, passing the front desk where the Residential Advisor or RA sat. RAs from each floor rotated manning the front desk throughout the semester. Diane took notice of the students mulling about in the lobby area. Fine ass dudes in every color of the black rainbow. Light, bright, damn-near white to blue-black. Tall, short, thin, thick, locs, Caesars, and fros. Both lips pop in appreciation. She patted herself on the back for the free condoms the clinic provided that she'd helped herself to when she got vaccinated.

The women are stunning. From the most natural naked faces to faces beat to the Gawds, rocking everything from thrift store finds to Teflar bags and ice so cold it left a chill in the air. BBWs, thick and thin, "French Vanilla" to "Chocolate Deluxe" all together conversing. Braids, locs, fresh perms, and cuts, laughing and living their best life. "I definitely belong here."

Diane pushed the up button on the elevator to get to her floor. She noticed a scrawny white guy rushing to get in before the doors closed. He stood next to her and smiled. Dianne's not shocked to see a white guy at Howard. It's just she didn't expect to see one so soon. "I'm Dominic, but everyone calls me Dom. I'll be the RA on your floor."

Diane was hoping the elevator ride to her floor would be fast. She didn't like small talk, especially to people she wasn't familiar with. Dominic seemed nice enough. However, he was white at an HBCU. That meant one of two things: He was an Ally or an Opp. She rarely had any interaction with white people, and she proceeded with caution. Knowing she'd need to have a friend in "high" places, and he was an RA, so she placed a smile on her face and engaged.

"Oh. Cool. I'm Diane, room 612."

"You'll be right across from the elevator, so be prepared for the noise, but it's not too bad."

Dominic seemed nice, but Diane is not used to conversing with anyone. She had no real social skills. The little she had came from her father, and he was a man of few words. It's not like she had little to say. She loved to express herself, but it's limited to writing and being behind a microphone. Here at Howard, she was going to have to learn to adjust.

"Also, if you need a plug, I got you."

"Cool. Where you from? Why Howard?"

This is a question every student asked and answer for at least the first month at Howard. After the first month and for the rest of the year, it's "What's your name, class and major?" It was a quick way to determine whether you had commonalities or not and if you should continue the conversation.

"I'm from Cali and I want to be a civil rights lawyer. Howard has taught some of the greats, so...."

Howard did have a history of producing top talent in all areas of study. The law school and Fine Arts department produce the more recognizable names such as Letitia James, Louis Berry and, of course, Thurgood Marshall. Dominic, explain he wanted to advocate for the legalization of cannabis for every state in the US.

"I ain't mad at that. Nice to meet you, Dom."

Stepping off the elevator, he grabbed her arm. "What about you?" Diane hated discussing herself with anyone. She was so emotionally detached. She prepared herself for this as much as possible by masking. Diane believe if she transformed into a bright cheery person then it would hide her lack of emotion.

"What about me?"

"Where are you from? Why Howard?"

Thinking about it before replying, "A small town in Virginia called Radford. You may wonder why I didn't apply to Virginia Tech or the state school, Radford University. Two reasons: I didn't want to have to fight for my life at a PWI. Figuratively and literally."

Stepping off the elevator, she made her way to her door. She turned to Dom laughing.

"And as for the second reason, I'm here for the niggas. Strictly for the niggas."

They both pause with serious looks on their faces before bursting out into laughter. Masking works every time. Diane had to mask until she became more comfortable expressing her emotions. As much as she hated to admit it, she was exactly like her mom and hoped that by being removed from the situation, she the potential to unlearn the behavior.

Dom reached out his hand and palm a small baggie into her palm.

"You and I are going to be good friends." He said, walking down the hall to his door.

Diane entered the suite. It surprised her to see it's more like an apartment and less like a dorm room. The entry gave the appearance of a small foyer. The kitchen area housed a full-size refrigerator, a small countertop, and a sink. Regular size cabinets up top and at the bottom, to the left a bathroom. Everything in there also looked standard size. In front of her, a large room, seemingly the same size as the entryway and the bathroom combined, it had a large bay window that took up most of the wall. Diane planned to put a loveseat right under it. A five-drawer dresser, desk and chair, and an extra-large twin size bed completed the spacious bedroom. The closet, if you want to call it that, is big enough to hold toiletries and some bins.

"Yep. This is my shit right here."

Dropping her bag on the bed, she walked to view the room next to the bathroom. The other bedroom is a little smaller than hers, but her roommate should be able to fit a chair by the window, which appeared standard size.

"She'll be alright."

Her room claimed, Diane sat on the bed and sighed. She remembered she had to bring her shit up and get organized.

"Let me find one of these niggas to help me with this shit."

"Hi! Welcome to the West Towers at Howard University. How can I help?" The girl at the front desk said as if she wanted to leap into Diane's arms.

"Hi. How can I get one of those cart things to move my stuff?"

The perky girl scrunched her face with a look of disappointment, "Ah, sorry I just gave the last one to that guy."

Pointing to this lil light skin skinny dude with enough ice that said he came from money but didn't have to be flashy with it. He had a nice little fro, pretty smile, and semi blemish-free skin. Kind of short, about five seven and had on these nice fitting jeans. At this distance, it looked like he held something heavy in them. It's a big reason she preferred shorter men over tall ones.

"You can ask him if you two can share if you helped each other move into your respective rooms." Stepping away from the desk heading his way, Diane threw over her shoulder.

"Thanks."

Jared stood with a group of his Kappa brothers when he noticed a thick lil' something looking at him, smiling. She was about five feet five inches in a yellow sundress that did not hide the stomach he would love to squeeze with both hands and bury his face in. Her hair's shaved on both sides with a shoulder length mohawk and skin the color of toffee. His dick bricked up thinking about bending that fat ass over and burying himself deep inside all that goodness. Women always stared at him, and he used it to his advantage. His player days behind him, he wanted someone long term. Fingers crossed; it'd be her.

She walked over to him. He noticed she had on a pair of dark-blue Atoms that made her dress pop even more. Unless you recognized Atoms, you wouldn't know Atoms. She walked up to him, smiled a greeting to his boys.

"Hey, can I talk to you for a minute?"

He dapped up Kenny and the other guys as he moved toward her. She jerked her head away from his ear-hustling line brothers and he followed.

"Sup, I'm Jared."

"Your voice deep as fuck for you to be so lil. I ain't mad at it, though."

Chuckling, Jared smirked. "You about to be mine."

Diane looked him up and down as she ignored the comment. "Um, I wanted to know if you'd be willing to share the cart. I need to move my stuff into the bigger room before my suite mate comes up. It sounds fucked up, but it is what it is. Right?"

She folded her arms under her chest and leaned on her left side. The look of exasperation marred her face. It gave Jared enjoyment, watching her squirm as she waited for an answer.

"What's your name?"

"Oh sorry—Diane."

She said. He took her extended hand but didn't shake it. Jared rubbed between her thumb and index finger with his thumb without letting go.

"Yeah, I got you lil momma. You ready to do this?" Nodding her head, she removed her hand from his and walked out onto the courtyard. He followed.

It took about an hour of walking back and forth from their cars to their rooms to get everything moved in. Thankfully, the campus police didn't ticket anyone for parking by the courtyard. "Lil Light Skin" had one of his line brothers (LB) assist him with moving into both rooms. Diane rolled luggage and was grateful that his LB gifted her with a futon as a seating area for her room. She was a little envious that "Light Skin" had a single suite to himself. His family definitely had a coin to pay six thousand for a single for the semester. As they moved, she frequently offered to do more, but he refused. He said her being there was enough.

He and Diane conversed as they moved everything in. She learned he came from old money and lived in DC all his life on 16th street NW known to native Washingtonians as the "Gold Coast." The Gold Coast is mostly composed of affluent Blacks. His great-great-grandfather started the United House of Prayer for All People, Rev. "Sweet" Daddy Grace. Light Skin didn't even believe in God, but acknowledged his gratefulness for all his grandfather had taught him about his great-great-grandfather and their legacy.

"So, where you from?"

"Virginia near Virginia Tech."

"Oh, you one of them corn-fed country girls, huh?"

"No, I grew up in the city. Well, what's considered a city for Radford?"

Light Skin licked his thick lips while perusing her body.

"That's corn-fed country to me, lil momma. Come on, let's organize your shit so your suite mate really won't have shit to say about getting into the smaller room."

He thanked his LB, dapping him up as he walked toward the elevator.

Working in tandem over the next hour, both sweaty but energized, they finally had a finished room in front of them. She was thankful to Light Skin but couldn't remember his name, which is sad with all the conversing they'd been doing over the last couple of hours. After the initial introductions, names weren't needed. Diane wanted to pay him back somehow. Light Skin vacuumed the room. He opened the bedroom door, turned to her.

"Well, I think we have everything. The kitchen and bathrooms are clean. Candles and air fresheners doing their thing. I guess we're done."

They stared at each other, waiting for one of them to say or do something. She parted her lips, about to ask for his number, when the door to the suite opened.

A tall girl, about five eight or nine, walked in, caramel-complected skin with a weave hitting her ass. A cocoa-colored woman with a beautiful smile and flawless skin followed. Jared had to admit her suite mate was gorgeous.

He noticed Diane seemed unhappy as her face scrunched. Not in a hateful way, but in an“ Oh” expression. Shorty bad, but not what he wanted.

Diane had to admit her suite mate is gorgeous. She assumed Light Skin's entire mood was about to change. Bracing for it, Diane understood societal beauty standards. Men chose someone like her roommate. Ready for the fuckery, she internally rolled her eyes but placed a smile on her face and held out her hand to this "bitch".

"Hi, I'm Kim, this is my mom."

"Hi, I'm Diane. And this is..." looking over at Light Skin with flushed cheeks.

"Jared." Jared said without blinking or caring that Diane didn't remember his name.

"I put my stuff in this room, but if you want it to switch, I'm cool with whatever." Diane appeared nice and appeasing, hoping Kim wouldn't ask for the bigger room.

"No." Kim said, "I'm cool with the other one. Are you done with the cart? I want to go to Target, but I also want to keep this in my room to bring my stuff up, since the front desk is out."

"Yeah, I'm done. I'm about to hop in the shower, so have at it."

Kim and her mom took the cart, moving it into her room and headed to the elevators to go to Target for whatever else Kim needed. Target stayed packed with kids and parents purchasing last-minute items for college. They had a long wait ahead of them. Diane turned and waited for Light Skin to make an excuse to walk out with this bitch and her momma, but he surprised her when he walked back into her room and sat on the futon.

"Yep, this nigga getting fucked today."

She said to herself as she bit her bottom lip to hide her smile. Jared opened his legs. He began a slow perusal of Diane's entire body as she walked into the room.

This the type of nigga that saw Diane as a challenge. He thought he could "teach" her some shit.

"So, you trying to hit the shower with me?"

"Yeah, I can get wet. I don't have a change of clothes, though."

"I'm a big girl. I'm sure you can fit a pair of my sweats and a Howard T until you get to your room. Wait, how old are you? I'm not tryin to catch a charge."

He laughed. "I ain't no lil ass nigga. I'm twenty-six and how can the willing press charges?"

She walked into the bathroom with a smirk on her face and he followed.

Jared stood and watched as Diane undressed. She slipped her sundress over her head, which left her standing in her undies and bra. Diane didn't do girdles, spandex or none of that form fitting shit. What you see is what you get.

Diane unsnapped her Savage Fenty bra. It fell down her arms, and she removed it. Before she could reach the waistband of her panties, Light Skin licked his thumb, gently grabbed her left tittie, gliding his thumb over her nipple.

"Yeah, this nigga knows what he doing," whispering to herself as she closed her eyes and leaned her head back. He repeated the move with her other breast. Jared paused his movement and Diane looked at him.

"Let me see what that dick is about. Take that shit off."

Diane said, coming out of her panties. She stepped into the shower and turned the water on.

Adjusting the temperature to her liking, Diane turned and faced him. Jared waited until he had her full attention before he unbuckled his belt and jeans. He's not a skinny jeans type nigga, so as soon as his belt opened and unzipped the zipper. His jeans fell to his ankles. Saliva gathered in Diane's mouth as she swallowed, thinking.

"This nigga is about to fuck my whole world up."

She licked her lips when his dick poked out of his boxer briefs and bounced a little. She swallowed again. Ladies, y'all can have them tall niggas. Short niggas are the ones that will stretch that pussy outta shape. One word. Girth.

Diane started massaging her jaws. Jared's thick ass dick is about to beat her mouth up. Jared smirked and grabbed the monster between his legs and squeezed, releasing pre-cum.

"Don't get scared now. Imma make sure you don't forget a nigga name again", he said as he massaged up and down his dick.

Diane moved toward the back of the shower, allowing him to step in. He got under the spray and his body looked even better wet. As a big girl, you think you would swallow a lil nigga up only to find out they will fuck up your life. He stared at her with such intensity she became a little self-conscious. Light Skin had tattoos down both arms and on his chest. This nigga is about to show her the insides of hell. Well, Diane ain't no bitch, so she squared her shoulders, walked toward him and got on her knees, ready to put in work. Jared watched as Diane got under the spray, not caring she'd fuck up her hair. Moistening her lips, she took in the tip of his dick and sucked on the head while stroking the length of him with both hands. Diane understood dick and the tip of a penis are like the clitoris. If you focus on that, he'll shoot like a street sweeper. It saved her jaws from damage with such a thick dick. If she didn't take her time, she would get lockjaw.

Jared placed his hands on the top of Diane's head for balance as he looked down to appreciate the softness of her hair. He gripped tighter as she started licking the head. She placed her thick lips on the tip, popped it out, and repeated the motion. It sent tingles down his spine. Jared threw his head back and moaned.

"Got damn, you got all that work and just on the tip?"

She focused on the tip while keeping her lips moist and tight, sucking like a Hoover. Once ready, she opened wider and slid down, slowly adjusting her jaws for the girth as she took him all the way in her mouth. When his tip tapped the back of her throat, she contracted her tonsils and, just like she imagined he would, he unloaded his clip.

"Got damn girl! Shit! Git yo ass up here. Let me slurp that fat pussy."

Diane stood almost face to face with Jared. He pressed forward until her back hit the shower wall.

Jared lifted Diane with the back of her knees secured in the crook of his elbow. He kept a hold of her as he kneeled and placed her legs on his shoulder. Once facing her pussy, he took a minute to just look at it. It glistened as the aroma of coconut wafted in his nostrils. Her pink bud poked out as he admired the thickness of her pussy lip. Jared almost nutted from the sight. He gripped her thighs, leaned forward, took her entire pussy in his mouth and sucked her labia, clit and all. Diane bucked from the sensations. He suckled and licked her shit like it a sour Apple Jolly Rancher.

"This pussy taste so good. I could suck this mutha fucker all day."

Diane started climbing the walls when Jared stuck his tongue in her. He looked up, grabbed her wrist.

"Where the fuck you think you taking my pussy? I'm signing my name on this shit."

He dove back in, licking, sucking and tongue fucking her. Diane swore she saw Satan as her eyes rolled to the back of her head. Light Skin mumbled "Un huh" as he took her clit and sucked on like a pacifier. Diane's legs trembled; her orgasm was seconds from erupting. On the verge of fainting, he pulled away and eased her down. She could not believe what he did.

"Don't look sad lil momma, imma let you buss. Save that nut for this dick."

Her feet hit the floor as he turned her, so she faced the shower wall. Jared tapped her legs, indicating he wanted her to open wider. She complied. He ease in from behind inch by inch until her wet pussy sucked him in. Jared started slow stroking her kitty, trying to hold back his nut. Her pussy was wet and pulsing as it continued to suck his dick further in. Diane had tears running down her face, wondering who taught this nigga to fuck like this and where to send the "thank you" card. Jared's meaty dick was a tight fit, and she creamed a little with every pump of his hips.

Jerking her out of her thoughts, Light Skin asked at the shell of her ear.

"What's my muthafucking name, Diane?"

She couldn't formulate a complete thought. The deeper he fucked, the more her walls contracted around him. She tried, but didn't utter a word. Her pussy is being a straight whore. Jared slapped her ass when she didn't respond.

"Who ruining this pussy for the next nigga?"

Finding her voice as her whole-body shook.

"J... J... Jared."

She whimpered. Jared began pounding into her with the force of a sledgehammer. His dick, slick with her juices as sex, permeated the air. Diane had her hands on the shower wall to prevent her head from contacting the tiles. Jared bent at the knees, coming through with the upward stroke. The grip he had on her waist was going to leave bruises, but she did not care. Diane stiffened as her orgasm crawled down to her core.

"You about to cum on this dick?"

Jared stuck his thumb in her ass. Diane exploded.

Diane didn't realize she'd blacked out. His breath on her ear gave her a chill.

"What's my name?" D

iane attempted to raise her head to answer, but failed. With eyes closed she hoarsely whispered, "Jared".

"Good girl. I put my number in your phone. Holla at me when you recover."

She didn't bother to ask how he got her ass in the bed. She was just thankful for it.

The loud crash jolted Diane out of her sleep. Flinching as she rose from a sore and satisfied ass, she smiled, thinking of Jared. She got out of bed, pulled a long t-shirt over her head, went into the bathroom to handle her hygiene.

Diane noticed Kim on the floor, struggling with what looked like a mini bookshelf. "You need some help?"

"Yeah, if you don't mind?"

She walked into the room, sat crossed-legged and helped Kim assemble her bookshelf. Working in silence for the next few hours, they folded clothes, placed area rugs, and organized her books. Kim scrutinized Diane.

"So that nigga left you with a wet pussy and a hangover, huh?"

Shocked but impressed by Kim's blunt comment, she blushed, biting her bottom lip, remembering the way Jared worked her over. It would've been something she'd say if the roles reversed.

"Yeah, his lil short ass held some major weight."

They both looked at each other, then burst out laughing. A friendship formed at that moment and remained that way.

"So, where are you and your mom from?"

"Detroit."

"It's so cold in the D, how the hell we s'pose keep the peace."

Diane sang as Kim laughed.

"Yeah, but if you're not working for the casino, then you ain't working. I'm majoring in accounting so I can get with a major firm here in the city. I'm trying to move my mom out of Detroit. My momma stuck in her ways and not big on change. Imma keep trying to get her out of the D, though."

"Yeah, I get that, but it's cool you want to have better for your mom."

Diane did not know what it's like being a kid with a proper parent. The relationship with her mom is nonexistent and on the verge of being extinct. She hadn't heard from her since she text her mom and dad, letting them know she made it safe. In their eyes, their job as parents was done.

For the rest of the late afternoon/early evening, they worked together to make sure the suite had a homie vibe by hanging curtains at both windows, placing rugs throughout, and adding utensils and bath supplies to the space. Both Diane and Kim were ready to call it a night and decided they'd explore the campus a bit in the morning.

Chapter 2

Campus is just as he'd expected. Kids walking around, jumping Double Dutch, and kicking around those little bean bags, enjoying the start of the weekend before classes. This is an exciting time for Professor Resto. He's one of the most popular professors on campus and there is always a mile long list of students who wanted to be in his poetry class. Part of the reason is his half-Latino, half-Black heritage. He only stood at five eight with coco color skin and hair that hung slightly past his chin. His Nuyorican accent he picked up from living with his Puerto Rican Abuela as a kid from the Bronx also added to his appeal. Being exoticized was just as bad as colorism. He never acknowledged the flirtatiousness of his female and sometimes male students. Happy to see them out, enjoying each other, he hoped the happiness remained through the end of the semester.

Resto is a forty-year-old accomplished poet and author. He isn't interested in being a father figure to any of the young kids that entered his classroom. Eighteen to twenty-year-old are still kids in his eyes.

"Get a job that pays to do what you love. Keep said job so you can fulfill your passion and not risk being falsely accused of inappropriate behavior by one of your students."

A motto he lived by. He ignored the stares and plethora of numbers left on his desk and inbox. Resto always made sure that during office hours he met with the students two at a time or that the other professor he shared the office with was present. Students at that age were learning how to make life choices without the watchful eyes of their parents and often made poor decisions they later regret. They'd either learn from it or continue doing it because it felt grown. Yes, he is a teacher, but a teacher of poetry, not relationships or how to navigate life experiences.

In COAS, Resto checked the mailbox and reviewed the syllabi for the two classes he'd be teaching this semester. It's important for students to immerse themselves in indie authors who gave their all to a craft that gave them little to no recognition. His list of materials consisting of authors, poets, rappers, and musicians. Music is poetry, just in motion. As an artist, it's difficult and could be most of your career. If you didn't struggle at some point, you weren't doing it right. He understood a struggle. He'd struggled for the first half of his life. His Abuela raised him since his mama was too strung out to care he existed until her death.

His papi hadn't been a constant in his life, but he attempted to be involved. He remembered Papi picking him up on Saturdays and riding the six train to the zoo, park, or the local library. Why his Papi would choose those places? Resto assumed it was all he could afford, which was little to nothing. All he cared about was the time spent with him.

Resto could never imagine what it took for his abuela to bring home a drug-addicted toddler and give him everything he needed to become a man. She raised a well-traveled college graduate who became a successful author and worked at one of the most prestigious universities in the country. To the average person, it may seem Resto had it all, and he did. Almost. If only he had a mama who'd left him more than the occasional shakes that he still experienced as an adult. One of the many effects of using drugs while pregnant with him. Resto couldn't maintain a stable relationship with women because of the relationship he had with his mama or lack thereof.

Every woman he'd ever bedded had to answer for his mama's sins. Things would be great at the beginning, like all relationships. However, Mama always showed up when things appeared too perfect. Resto would become suspicious of the women or find comfort, and that closeness he desired from women in men. Men showed up. Men stayed. Like his father did, but regretfully, he still never had a mom.

Men gave him hugs that didn't cause him to tense or flinch. Their kisses that evoked safety and comfort. Penis allowed him to forget his mama and remember the closeness he and his papi shared. Not sexually, just the time they spent at the zoo or hours in the library buried in books. When he missed his papi or needed to forget his mama, he turned to men. He could be soft, innocent, and childlike in bed.

Before he became honest about his proclivities, Resto would get caught cheating. He did not intend to deceive or misrepresent himself to the women in his life, but to protect them from the things they wouldn't be able to accept or understand. Resto tried introducing a few women to his proclivities, and in each situation, it backfired. Currently, he's taking a break from serious relationships. He allowed himself to become fully immersed in his lifestyle, hoping to find a woman who would learn to enjoy it as much as he did.

He shook himself out of his thoughts and prepared for Monday.

Diane declined Kim's offer of walking around the campus together. She wanted some alone time to really immerse herself and embrace this journey. Diane could have taken the shuttle up the hill to campus. However, that would defeat the purpose of familiarizing herself with the city and the culture. She not only wanted to experience her fellow Bison but also the local Washingtonians.

Diane would've regretted her decision to walk if she'd worn different shoes. She patted herself on the back for deciding on her Atoms instead of heels to look cute. The hill to the yard is as brutal as she remembered from the other day. Diane tried to slow down and pace herself to absorb her surroundings, but she's a fast walker. The weather was weathering, and her skin was popping in the sun. With her head held slightly higher than normal, she took in her surroundings.

There were eateries such as Potbelly, Starbucks, and Mickey D's en route. A popular Jamaican spot Negril and she'd also heard stories about HoChi (Howard China) which is a few blocks from the School of Business (SOB). There is also a Banneker Recreation Center across the street from the main entrance of the school. It housed an indoor gym, an outdoor track and pool. Howard had an indoor pool, track and field and a gym on campus, so Diane would never use Banneker, but it was nice for the neighborhood to have one. It gave Howard students an opportunity to mingled with the locals if they chose.

As a big girl, Diane knew she could not stop in the middle of that long hill leading to campus, but once she reached the top, she stopped and looked down at her iPhone as if replying to a text to catch her breath. Don't get it twisted, she exercised. However, that hill ain't no joke, and it tested her limitations. She leaned on the wall that held the name of her school and took a few minutes to bask in the thought that she'd accomplished something most people wouldn't be able to afford. All the fighting, stress and struggle, she did the muthafucking thing! Overcome with emotion, she almost missed the "What's good, shorty?"

Looking behind her, she saw some random licking his lips and squinting while rubbing his hands together. It took everything in her not to burst into a fit of giggles.

"How you doing Ma? What's good?"

Diane Couldn't believe this fool is approaching her looking like a straight predator.

He's a decent-looking man with medium brown skin, nice teeth, but he had on a pinky ring and a long sleeve shiny shirt. He moved like a predator plotting an attack.

"Is his hair in braids? I'm sorry. No man over the age of twenty-five should wear braids. Transition to locs, my nigga."

Diane continued to look at her phone while starting to walk away. Knowing she had to play it cool because male fragility is a muthafucker. Things may get outta pocket and Diane's not equipped to fight a grown ass nigga.

He perused her body, moving his head up and down like a pump jack while walking closer.

"Yeah, this nigga a fucking crazy."

She thought, backing up a few steps.

"I'm trying to see if I can take you out? Get to know you better? You new here?"

Stepping further away, Diane turned on her heels. "Naw, I'm not new here."

Diane lied. "I don't think I have time to go out like that. You know, focusing on my studies n shit. I'm late. I need to go meet up with one of my professors."

Speed walking from the guy, she acted as if she couldn't hear him calling her all kinds of fat bitches. Niggas will always show who they really are when you turn them down.

A thin girl with weave down her back and some Jackie O shades walked toward Diane. She slipped an arm in hers. She pretended like they were friends meeting up.

"Girl, these locals be lurking. Always try to walk with someone when you tryin to mind your business. Especially at night."

With a nervous laughter, Diane nodded her head in understanding.

As they continued to walk arm in arm, Diane introduced herself. "Hey, I'm Diane transferring junior, Radio, TV, and Film."

"I'm Keisha Senior, Accounting."

Keisha seemed friendly, but she didn't want to form relationships with people who wouldn't be in her circle for long, however she didn't want to be rude. Diane wanted to make connections that would assist her with navigating all things Howard and beyond.

"Thanks for helping me out back there. Creepy as fuck."

"It's a mixed bag with the locals. Some are cool, some think you have money because you go here and will try to use you and the rest. They hate Howard students. Oh, and another thing, never call them locals to their face. To them, it's like calling them nigger with the hard er."

Listening as Keisha rattled on and on about all things campus life Diane appreciated and learned a lot, but she just wanted to get away from her and finish exploring the campus on her own. Diane blindly followed Keisha as she continued chatting. She looked up and realized they'd stopped. Both stood in front of SOB. The building is a beautifully designed structure in the shape of a canyon. Thanking Keisha for her help and advice, Diane beeline it back toward the main yard. She also noticed on that side of the campus stood Aldridge Theater, Crampton Auditorium, the athletic dorms and, off in the distance, the football field.

COAS isn't the most popular building at Howard, but it faced the yard. Fine Arts is at her right and to the left Founders Library. Diane sat on the steps with everything in view. She leaned her head back to soak in some sun, calm her thoughts, and rest in the moment. She realized there is no place she'd rather be.

The month of September is still warm, and she wore a White T paired with a cute flowing skirt to catch every breeze. Not too crowded on campus, she sat and enjoyed the way the wind skated along her legs and thighs as her skirt blew up slightly.

A shadow cast over Diane. She opened one eye to find out who she'd have to curse out for interrupting her oneness with Mother Nature. Her mouth dropped and suddenly became as dry as the Sahara as she looked into the most beautiful face she'd ever seen. He had wavy hair to his neck, cafe mocha skin, and a smile that had her lips shaking. And not the ones on her face.

"It is a beautiful day, isn't it?"

He looked too old to be a student but too young to be an old ass professor. Good genes. It had to be a professor. Diane wondered what he taught and did she have time to enroll in his class.

"You, okay?"

"Ah Oh yes, I'm sorry. It is a gorgeous day. I'm glad we can have such beautiful weather before the grind of college life takes over."

He walked down the steps toward the yard. Diane lustfully followed his movements with a smile plastered on her face.

Turning to face her, Resto observed the thickness of her toffee color thighs. He imagined burying his face between them and licking until he got to the center.

"Yes, I agree. Enjoy the rest of your afternoon."

Diane wanted to run back to the dorm and rose herself down at the thoughts of Naughty Professor, but the more rational part of her brain told her to stay focused. But shit that Professor! Is he a professor? He is sexy as fuck! Diane had no idea what it attracted her to short, medium built men. Well, she did, but damn, he is fine!

"I hope I don't be slutting myself out too much this semester."

Diane laughed at that lie. She gave herself permission to be sexually open in college. It was all a part of the experience.

The yard had gotten crowded since she first sat down. People congregated in various spots, just like the day she arrived on campus. That's her cue to head down to SOC and take care of her schedule. Standing, wiping the back of her skirt free of debris. She picked up her crossbody and placed it over her head, careful not to disturb her perfectly twisted out mohawk and walk toward Founders Library. The library isn't her final destination, but you had to bypass it to get to the SOC.

Chapter 3

Jared thought he saw Diane walking across the yard. He recognized the sway of her hips and the Atoms on her feet. He jogged to catch up to her.

How he became enamored with her country-sounding ass he had no clue but wanted her to be his. She didn't trip like some women. He hadn't heard from her at all after putting her ass to sleep. Usually, he'd get a call the next day for another hook-up. He got close enough to confirm her identity. Jared slowed his steps and admired the way her skirt lifted every time she took a step. Those thick-ass thighs with faint stretch marks had his dick bricking. He picked up his pace a bit and put his arm around her shoulder. She jumped a little until she saw it him.

"Say my name."

"Hey Jared." Diane giggled. "Hey Diane, how was the rest of your night?"

"Cool. I helped my roommate get her room together and just chilled. What about you?"

"Gravy. Had your scent on me until this morning."

"Ewww, that's so nasty."

"If it's nasty, why you blushing?" With a shrug of her shoulders, she sighed. They walked in silence for a bit people watching and glancing at each other.

He moved his hand to her lower back. "Where you going?"

"I want to check out the school of C, walk around a bit, and daydream."

"Can I show you something before you do that?"

"What?" Jared took Diane's hand and led her to the side entrance of Founders.

"Have you heard of the stacks?"

Diane shook her head in confusion.

"The stacks are where all the older books are housed. They have a few desks scattered about, but it looks scary as shit. Like a horror movie could be filmed down there."

They entered the side entrance as Diane glanced at him skeptically.

Once in Founders, they slide their IDs over the sensor at the turnstile and walked through another set of doors into the lounge/study area. Founders Library is hot as hell year-round, and the steps are brutal. The entrance is like walking into a museum. Encased books, photos, and relics from Howard's founding days and throughout the years on display.

He guided her to the main hall. There were wooden round tables and chairs throughout and off to the far corner cubicles with computers on them. The librarian sat at this large circulation desk, checking in books. Jared guided her to the left, past the circulation desk, and took the stairs down one level. Diane looked a little creeped out and got nervous when they arrived at an old school elevator that had a gate. Jared slide the gate to the left and reached for her hand and they stepped in. He pulled the gate closed and selected one of the metal buttons that protruded out, not flush like newer elevators. The bottom floor selected; Diane jumped a bit when the second set of doors slid close.

"This shit looks like an elevator from the thirties. I'm jive nervous." Jared kissed her cheek and assured Diane she's safe with him.

The elevator jerked to a stop when it reached the basement level. The doors slid apart, and Jared opened the gate.

"Come on."

Diane stepped off the elevator and looked around in awe at the stacks and stacks of books. You could easily get lost between the shelves in the enormous space. The bookcases were metal and looked as if they'd been there in the seventies. The books needed a good dusting, but it didn't take away from their antique beauty. Rows and rows of shelves that seemed to reach the ceilings. Diane grabbed one book and noticed the publication date was from 1910. In awe, she turned slowly in a circle, looking upward, marveling at the history before her.

The area seems dark even though the lights above shine down like sun peeking through clouds. The rows and rows of books made it seem like a dungeon. There's a small window with very little light every fourth row, but she couldn't confirm if it's tinted or just dusty.

"Jared, what are we doing down here? These books look fifty to a hundred years old."

"Some probably are, and most of them are black books by our people." Moving closer to her.

"Two beautiful Black people about to fuck surrounded by Black history."

"What?!"

Diane's eyes grew wide in shock at his words. He grabbed under her skirt, cupping her ass, pulling her flush against his chest.

"I can show you better than I can tell you, lil momma."

—

Diane bit her bottom lip as Jared kissed her gently, inserting his tongue in her mouth. She reciprocated as he massaged her ass while slightly spreading her butt cheeks. Jared deepen the kiss, sliding hands down her panties as his fingers glided in between her parted cheeks, teasing her asshole from both sides.

"Yeah, I'm going to slide my dick right between them juicy cheeks. My dick needs to be squeezed by them muthafuckers."

She giggled and pecked at his lips lightly. "Boy, ain't nobody ever been back there, and you have to be something special to gain entrance."

"Oh yeah?"

"Yeah."

Slowly kissing her lips Jared pulled back unzipped his jeans all while looking into her eyes. She didn't break the stare as he pulled out his dick, allowing it to swing from side to side. Jared tapped her inner thighs as he got on his knees.

"Spread them muthafuckers, so I can suck this pussy."

"Jared. Anyone can walk by and see us."

Diane said as she backed close to the dusty window, leaning on the windowsill but still not parting her legs. She leaned forward a bit to see if she saw anyone. Turned on but scared, she bit her lips pensively.

"I'm not going to let anything happen to you. Trust me. I've always got you, lil momma." He said as he pushed her on the window.

Diane took Jared at his word, looking down at him and that heavy anaconda resting on his pants at his knees, and opened her legs wide. Kneeling, Jared slid his fingers over Diane's lower stomach.

"I love that you don't wrap your shit up all tight in them spandex shit. I need access to my pussy."

He slid a finger in either side of her panties and gently began splitting her lips open. Closing her eyes, Diane's head fell back on its own accord as his fingers sent a shiver down her spine. Moaning, she barely spoke.

"I'm not ashamed of my body."

She said as Jared drove her crazy by slowly sliding his fingers up and down her panty covered lips.

"Diane, you may or may not believe me, but I'm about to make you, my wife. I know we just met and need to get to know each other better, but my mind is made up. You're it for me."

Jared pulled her panties down and off one leg. He stared at her pussy.

Diane's juices felt like a light rain as her legs trembled. She didn't know how to respond to his comment, so she didn't respond at all.

"That rose bud is peeking out at me like she ready. Damn, your pussy is so pink and juicy as fuck. I just could rub these lips all day and watch that mutha fucker cream down to your ass."

Jared is so nasty, and she loved it. He worshipped her twat like an undiscovered masterpiece. He slowly grazed his finger over her clit, outer and inner lips. As he slipped his fingers gently inside, he moved in languid circles around as if spinning cotton candy. "Hmmm," Jared whispered, his face so close to Diane's center that if he stuck his tongue out, he'd hit the bullseye.

Jared stuck his nose in her pubic area and licked her clit.

"Awe fuck!" she screamed.

"You like that?"

He asked as he licked. Stop. Lick. Stop. Licked and stopped. Totally different from the pounding she received the other night, Diane's arousal to increase tenfold. Jared moved his mouth to her lower stomach and nibbled while still sliding his fingers along her labia.

Diane creamed so hard a puddle gathered on the floor. Legs trembling, she buckled over with an ache exploding in her stomach.

"Holy fuck nigga. Fuck. Fuck. Fuck."

She didn't understand how the things he did made her feel like she was floating. The nibbles and light touches drove her crazy. Jared slid both thumbs into her pussy while kissing up to the bottom of her stomach. He slow stroked her with both thumbs as he licked and sucked her stomach.

"What the fuck is this nigga doing?"

"This nigga about to fuck up yo whole life. That's what I'm doing."

Diane's brows creased, trying to suppress an orgasm, not realizing she spoke out loud.

Jared placed her thighs on his shoulders so he could be up close, and personal. He buried his face deep in her pussy. Diane leaned back on the window as he literally tongue kissed her down there. She braced herself on the windowsill as Jared gave that ass a good thrashing. He gulped her shit like some Henny. He tried to lick every crevice of her walls a climax rocked her body. And did. He squeezed her clit between his thumb and forefinger as he continued his assault on her fat ass pussy. Her clit pulsed as her walls contracted around his tongue.

Diane's pussy taste so fucking good that Jared's stomach clenched while he tried to suck her soul from her body. He removed his face from her pussy and looked up to see Diane's glazed-over eyes watching.

"Your life is officially fucked."

"Yes, the fuck it is."

She moaned. Jared placed his index and middle finger in Diane's gushy center, circled and flick her walls as he simultaneously sucked her pearl. Diane almost flew off the windowsill. She screamed at the top of her lungs and had no control over the octave or durations. Diane's voice died down as he nibbled at the remaining tremors from her.

"I have never ever," before she could finish her sentence Jared stood and said, "You never ever will unless it's me."

Diane attempted to jump off the windowsill. He paused her movement. "Where are you going? We ain't done."

Tapping his dick on her stomach, smearing the pre-cum over it.

"I forgot to ask, but I hope you on something? If not, I'm about to put my baby in you."

He took his dick, slowly slid it into Diane's pussy, and pushed in and out at a torturous rhythm. She began moving in tandem with his strokes.

"I'm on the pill so you can nut all day in this. Ain't nothing coming out but your dick and sperm."

Jared lifted her legs to her chest as he held on to the side of her waist, massaging it softly as he pumped in and out.

"Fuck." Diane moaned with her head to the ceiling, wondering how his touches make her so wet? Her juices slid down the crack of her ass. Diane pushed as Jared pushed, causing goosebumps to pebble all over her body.

"Damn nigga. You deep in this pussy. You gonna make me cum before I'm ready"

Lifting his head from her neck, "I can't help it. Your pussy's in control, not me."

He increased the pounding as his orgasm hit him in the spine. Diane fucked him back as much as she could with the way he had her restrained.

"Get in the pussy nigga, dig this shit out!"

She encouraged as her lower half started shaking. Jared looked up as Diane grabbed his head with both hands.

"Look at me! Put them fucking lips on mine. I want your breaths when we cum."

She parted her lips, resting them on his, but they didn't kiss, just breathed each other's air as they both exploded. "Oh, my fuck..." was the last thing she heard from Jared before she passed out.

Jared nutted so hard in Diane that his knees buckled. Not knowing or giving a fuck how long they held that position. He looked up to see her smiling at him.

"You're mine. I don't care what the fuck you say, you're mine. I need you to really hear me and understand this is it for me."

Both stare at each other for a few more minutes. He wanted to confirm the message was received before helping Diane in her panties and off the sill.

"I have to go back to my dorm before heading to SOC."

"Naw lil bit, that's in you the rest of the day while you handle your shit." Grabbing her hand, they made their way out of Founders. Jared kissed her cheek, and they parted ways.

Diane was thankful the School of C went downhill and not up. As she walked, her legs felt like al dente noodles. She is going to have to be very strategic in dealing with Jared in the future. He's the type of guy who wanted to be a couple. Jared's funny, family oriented, had money and the sex is mad good, but she just began living the life she wanted to live and didn't want to complicate it or deter herself from the endgame. The right connections ensured she'd secure a position that will lead her to being comfortable and not have to worry about needing anyone's help to survive. Also, there were too many men on this campus to only be test driven by one. She didn't give any thoughts about a long-term relationship, marriage, or children. Neither for nor against any of it. Diane shrugged it off.

"Yeah, Jared needs to calm all the way down."

Diane reached the bottom of the hill and walked around to the front of the building. In the grassy area of the roundabout, she came face to face with Cathy Hughes School of Communications. She took a deep, cleansing breath with her eyes closed to summon the spirit of those that came before her.

Diane swung open the doors. The first thing that greeted her were all the greats that got their start at Howard university or worked at WHUR, the radio station that used to be owned by the University. Pictures of John C. Johnson, Cathy Hughes and the original Quiet Storm host himself, Melvin Lindsey, were on the walls at the main entrance. These were some of the bests in television, radio and print media. Students were walking up, and down the halls, taking it all in the same as Diane.

She spent the next hour in the guidance office, going over her class schedule with her counselor and registering. As a transfer student, she didn't have to take any of the General Ed courses. Her schedule was major & minor adjacent. Radio Production, script writing, Shakespeare and Creative Writing. Diane wanted to take poetry instead of creative writing since script writing and Shakespeare involved a dense workload.

School schedule all set; Diane entered the busy common area. She walked down the hall as students milled about, making small talk. She realized she'd only met but Kim and Jared so far. Neither of them had the same majors. Kim is in SOB, and she did not know about Jared. She thinks she remembered him saying pre-med. Diane decided that she'd attempt to get closer to Kim and Jared in case friends were scarce. She wasn't social at her high school and community college is just that. You really didn't make friends. Most students were adults with families. They came to class and went back home like high school. She also had a job and no time to develop long-lasting friendships.

Diane set off to find the school's radio station, which, according to her map, is in the basement. The production and editing rooms were on the third floor, so she started from the bottom. She made her way through the double doors and down the stairs. Once in the hallway, she saw a crowd gathered like they were at a kickback. The glass wall had a mural with the call letters WHBC and a logo of a dude in Howard sweatshirt rocking a gold chain and a snapback. The music coming through the speakers is loud. Diane stood back, observing the students congregating. They were young. She didn't mind it, but she didn't want to converse with anyone in the eighteen to twenty-year-old group, knowing they'd have nothing in common. Not that she is old, but twenty-seven is a huge difference maturity wise when compared to eighteen- and nineteen-year-olds. Yeah, she definitely had to get better acquainted with her roommate.

Diane made a beeline back to the stairwell, jogging up the three flights to the production and journalism floor. Once she reached the top steps, she realized she shouldn't have jogged up. It's as if she'd pissed herself, but it's just Jared. As a bigger girl, people assumed she's outta shape. The gym saw her three times a week, and she had no health issues. It's funny how people are fatphobic but not thinphobic. There are a lot of anorexic women out here. People don't see being fat as a disease and treat it much differently than anorexia nervosa. Doctors never want to test you for illness when you're thin but let a fat person walk in their offices. They run test and swear all your aliments are because you're fat. Diane had no health issues, but every doctor's visit, they tested her for everything under the sun as if they want to prove that being fat meant you're sick. She did her fair share of walking, so she's not winded. Just leaking. Diane found the ladies' room; she cleaned up as much as she could.

"I really am going to have to be careful with Jared's ass. He's developing "delusions of grandeur" she thought, shaking her head as she exited the ladies' room.

Two rooms that mimicked the radio station downstairs just on a smaller scale were down the hall from the ladies' room. Through the large picture window, she saw a huge production board taking up most of the space, a mic and monitor. Diane continued down the hall and opened closed doors along the way. She opened a door that had an "on air" light above it. The sign wasn't lit, so she opened the door. It's more of a booth than a full room with a production board, monitor and mic setup. She nodded in approval. Closing the door and walking to the opposite end of the hall, she smiled at the other students doing the same thing. The hallway seemed as if it would go on for miles. Not just in SOC but all the buildings at Howard were enormous. She came upon an entryway that stated she'd entered the journalism department. The first room she entered was the length of three classrooms. On both sides, with one long table lined with computers. Perfect for wanna-be reporters or writers to tell their story.

Excited at the possibility of accomplishing all her goals, Diane whispered a quiet thank you to the universe for realizing her dreams.

Chapter 4

Professor Resto couldn't figure out what it was about the young woman on the steps, but he couldn't stop thinking about her. She's obviously a student, but she seemed different. He didn't like the way he fixated on her beautiful face, but he couldn't look away. The sun had caused her toffee-colored skin to glisten, and her lips were full with a slight indentation on the top one. His dick to stirred. He'd never gotten excited about a student before. As he said, children didn't appeal to him, but she is no child. This is all women, and he took notice. Resto captured her medium brown orbs only for a moment, but that was enough. Her eyes spoke of things that were naughty and nasty. He'd be lying if he said he didn't want to fulfill every single one. Resto wanted to sink his teeth into every fleshy part of her and suck until he absorbed her aura. That's what she was giving off, an energy stronger than any he'd known before. He wanted to be consumed by it.

"Fuuuck!"

He had to stop thinking about her or it could not only get tricky, but dangerous. There's too much at stake, too many people could get hurt, and he didn't want to cause that to happen.

The keys hit the table with a clink. He walked to his fridge and grabbed a beer, gulping it down completely. Grabbing another, he walked to his living room and dropped onto the couch, staring into the void. He didn't remember getting in his car, the drive home, or opening his door. The only thing on his mind was her.

"Fucking Her."

He realized she's the exact image of his mama.

Stepping out of COAS with imaginary blinders. Resto hoped he could make it to his car without having to converse with a colleague or potential student trying to get an override signed to get into his overflowing classes. But before his foot could hit the first step, there she was, looking like Her. The woman who'd been a part of his dreams since he was a teenager. Mama.

The woman who still haunts his memories to this very day. It wasn't healthy, it's a demented obsession, but he couldn't help it and he couldn't stop the dreams. It didn't matter what he took or who he was with. He'd fixated on the type of person she was his entire life. Carmen was a beautiful woman in the pictures his abuela shared, but they weren't enough. Who was she?! What was her personality? Did she laugh a lot? Smile? Read and write as he did? Did she enjoy cooking, eating, and going out? Was she mean, angry, in pain? These are things a picture couldn't answer for him. He'd longed to learn about her, Carmen, his mom. Who was she authentically? It'd gotten so bad that obsessing about his mother became a part of who he was.

Life with mama in his dreams had been the best and worst times as a kid. No son should experience the things he did in those dreams. It wasn't normal, but the shame of it had prevented him from seeking the help he desperately needed. The first time it happened, he thought it was his twisted way of being loved.

At fifteen, he had his first dream. T*he toffee-colored, fluffy hair thick woman was on top of him. He remembered opening his eyes, "Mama?" Resto reached out and grabbed her. She was so soft. Was he was on the brink of madness? She seemed so real. He squeezed and rubbed her as she looked down and smiled at him. "That's a good boy, Hijo. Just like that." Resto moved his hips as he continued to rub and caress her as if he could force the feelings to continue forever. It was a mixture of euphoria, lust, and love.*

She caressed her breast while sinking down on him with a slight moan. His mama repeated how much she loved him and would never leave him again. He jerked awake with his dick in his hand and cum running over his fingers. Once Resto realized what happened and what he did, he went into the bathroom to shower, turning the water on as hot as he could stand it. He allowed it to wash away the dirtiness and the tears of shame. He stood under the spray until the shower ran cold.

After that night, the dreams continued. It almost drove him to insanity until he leaned into the feelings and accepted them just as he did other things in his life he couldn't control. Every night, sometimes twice a night since he was 15, the dreams tortured him. Once he stopped fighting them, he became more curious, trying to decipher the meaning and what his mama was trying to tell him. Even though they were sexual, he assumed that's because he's a virgin. However, once he lost his virginity, the erotic nature of the dreams increased. He enjoyed and looked forward to seeing her in his dreams. Sometimes it was nice and slow, very emotional for him. Those nights often ended in tears and on other nights, the violence was palpable. The rage sometimes scared him more than realizing he'd ejaculated from sex with her. Sighing, Resto got up and headed toward his bedroom as another night with mama awaited him. Maybe this time the woman he saw today would replace her.

The first few weeks of school were uneventful. Resto hadn't seen her since that day on the steps of COAS. He was also disappointed she hadn't replaced his mama in his dreams. However, thinking of her while he was with his mama made the dreams seem less twisted.

He entered his office surprised at the group of kids congregating around his desk. He was not accepting any additional students. This shit was ridiculous. The administration always told students to request an override from the professors when a class was full. There were a certain number of seats for a reason and instead of saying no to these elitist brats they sent them to the various departments. Professors were forced to deny them or give in to the whining and crying that only presented themselves when a student wanted to get in a class or get a better grade.

Sighing, the uncontrollable shakes started. The one and only thing his mama left from the enormous amount of drugs she put into her system while she was pregnant with him. The only thing that kept them under control was alcohol or reduced stress. When he couldn't drink, he'd control the rocking and the leg movement by walking around when it started, but with the students lurking about, he'd be in full-on epileptic mode by the time he got everyone out.

He cleared his throat loud enough for the students to quiet down.

"If you are here to get a seat in one of my classes, they've been filled. Yes, the extra seats that were reserved have also been filled. This is the end of the second week in school and you cannot expect me to review what assignments you've missed that you can't make up. Attendance and class participation, which is a large part of your grade, cannot be made up. So even if you are allowed in, which you will not, you will automatically start my class with a C. I would suggest being more proactive next semester and signing up for my class earlier. Also, before you hang around to beg, the answer is still no."

Students began trickling out of his office looking on the brink of tears or flat-out rolling their eyes at him. He didn't care as long as they left his office. Resto began pacing back and forth to relieve the involuntary movement, and after a few minutes, the shakes subsided. He turned to take a seat at his desk and took a calming breath before preparing for his afternoon class.

Diane was rushing around rearranging her class schedule for the last week. Desperate to track down Professor Resto to get into his poetry class. She couldn't drop Creative Writing until he signed off. She had to be a full-time student in order to keep her scholarships and grants. He was like a nocturnal animal, only available in the afternoon.

"Ugh, this mutha fucker better let me into his class. I know that!"

She approached, noticing his office door was slightly ajar. Lightly tapping on the door, Diane didn't wait for an answer before entering.

"Excuse me, I'm looking for Professor Resto?"

Resto was in his office sitting at a round desk littered with books and paperwork. Organized chaos is what he likes to call it. Classes were going well, and he was optimistic about the semester. The students varied. There were some hidden gems that were naturally gifted and few that were taking his class because they assumed poetry would be an easy A. That group usually got more than they'd expected and the rest left with C's that were dangling toward a D if the class was a week longer.

The knock on the door startled him and he rolled his eyes, figuring it was a student trying to get out of an assignment already. Student-athletes were notorious for preemptively giving excuses for why their next few assignments would be late. After a deep breath, Resto turned and received a gift from the heavens above. Her. That toffee color skin, those medium brown eyes, that hair, and last, that muthafucking body. Resto's dick bricked and had to get himself under control for two reasons. She was a student, and she looked like his mama. Resto couldn't, in reality, fuck his mama? Even if she was her doppelgänger.

Diane thought the rumors she'd heard about Resto were true. He was fine, but weird as fuck. She noticed the slight tremble in his right arm but tried to focus on his face instead. His skin was a gorgeous cocoa-colored tone.

Dominican, she wondered as she appraised the rest of him. Medium length hair with a nice lil curl pattern. He didn't have Big Dick Energy, but his height had her thinking there was an eighty percent chance that his shit was thick. Then she remembered he was the guy from a few weeks back as she was sunning herself on the steps of COAS.

"How can I help you?"

Pausing her perusal of him, she looked up.

"Oh sorry. I wanted to know if you could sign my override form for your poetry class. See..."

Resto listened and comprehended most of what she was saying, but his focus was on how much she resembled mama. Almost as if she reincarnated into a drug free version of herself. He was desperate to learn everything he could about her.

"Diane?"

He reached out, taking the form and looking back up at her.

"Why do you want to take my class?" Clearing her throat.

"Well, I am taking three writing dense classes and wanted to drop one for something... lighter. Wait! That sounds shallow. It's just that I also need to complete an internship for my major and don't want to stretch myself thin. I promise I'm not slacking, just setting myself up for success."

She rushed out. Resto had to turn away and used signing her override form as an excuse. If he'd watched her mouth move any longer, his dick would've been placed in it and he would've been fucking those thick-ass lips.

She had on a halter dress that was mid-thigh. Her titties were pushed so close together, her cleavage looked like they were levitating. Every time she spoke, they jiggled. His dick was on high alert. Shit! She was sexy as fuck.

"So you're not an English major?"

"No. Radio, TV, and Film. I want to, I don't know, make money doing something I love. You know? And as much as I love writing, I love music more."

Professor Resto made her kind of nervous. Yes, he was fine as fuck, but creepy. Was his dick hard? Damn, it was fat from what she could tell. But why did he have to be an ole ass professor? She was not doing anything to jeopardize graduating. And she didn't want this nigga to think she would fuck for grades. He was staring blankly at her, almost like he was caught up in a daydream. Crazy dick is good as fuck, but it's also crazy.

"Professor Resto?"

"Oh yeah, sorry. Here is your override. I'll be emailing your syllabus and the assignments you missed. See you in class."

Diane bounced up and down without her feet leaving the floor. Resto imagined pulling the top half of her dress down to slap her titties, adding to the current jiggle.

"Thank you so much Professor, you won't be disappointed. I promise." Turning on the ball of her feet, Diane walked out.

Resto noticed she had hips, not too big of an ass, but enough for him to bury his face in.

"Shit!"

How was he going to get through this semester with, Her?

There were nice looking men on campus but Diane had to be careful not to entertain anyone younger than twenty-four. Howard labeled her an "adult" college student. They made it clear where she fit in.

Howard dubbed anyone over the age of twenty-one an adult student insinuating those under that age still needed a certain level of supervision and to distinguish predatory behavior. College is a business and Diane understood that the institution had to protect themselves as much as possible in case anything happened to someone on their campus.

Back in her room, she noticed Kim was home. “Hey.”

“Hey.” Diane leaned on the door. Noticing how Kim had her head buried in a book like she was trying to fall in.

“How were your first few weeks so far?”

“This trigonometry class is kicking my ass! All my other classes are cool, though. How about you? Your schedule is straight now?”

“Yeah, but my poetry professor is weird as fuck! He signed my override though, so it’s whatever.”

“Have you been able to meet anybody our age since you got here? I mean, it’s college, but I’m not trying to be around all the lil as kids doing stupid shit.”

“I get that. They don’t have the responsibilities we do and some of, not all, are immature as they should be, but not who I’d want to be around.”

“Agreed. TSA is having a lil kickback...”

“What’s TSA?” Diane asked.

“TSA is the Transfer Association for the students who came from other colleges, usually older students who transferred from two-year colleges and started school late.”

"That's what's up! Do you mind if I roll with you?"

"No. It'd be cool. We can have each other's back. I don't smoke like that but I drink..."

"It's cool. I don't smoke on the regular but if someone offers I might take a toke and I only drink beer or wine, so we should be good."

Instead of driving, they decided it'd be best to take the shuttle to the house where the kickback was being held. Kim and Diane were both thankful that Howard provided a shuttle for students to travel throughout the neighborhoods in the vicinity and in some areas of Maryland. It was great to see the historical houses, small parks and people walking around. Students and native Washingtonians were mixed on the subject of gentrification in the city formally known as "Chocolate City." The Howard students heard the stories of "old DC" and were grateful crime had decreased. Kim and Diane discussed how if they really wanted to get ratchet they could walk the few blocks to Florida Ave and take the train or bus to immerse themselves in the real culture of "Chocolate City."

Jared told Diane about the nineties in DC and how the neighborhoods were all Black with a sprinkle of Caucasian. They had neighborhood watches where the drug boys on the corners were being watched by the older ladies in the neighborhood. No one ever reported anything. It was more of a symbol. You can make your money but don't fuck with our houses, cars, or block. He talked about how the corners of Petworth, LeDroit Park & 14th Street NW were where drug boys did their thing. The prostitutes hung out on M. St. NW between the upper echelon and regular folks to capitalize on the most sales. It was crazy because a lot of police had apartments in that area back then according to Jared.

The ride took about fifteen minutes, giving Diane and Kim time to familiarize themselves with each other. Diane really enjoyed Kim's company. Kim was slim, tall, with pecan skin that could use a good facial regime, or maybe it was stress. Her weave was laid and long. Diane gathered Kim was on a mission to find a man to marry and make her a kept woman. You can tell she was done with the struggle.

Diane couldn't blame her; however, she was taking a different route to freedom. Diane and Kim discussed how it was difficult growing up in an environment with no emotional or mental support to assist you with navigating the things in life that girls growing into women dealt with. You grow through those experiences that meant you were learning and healing. Being happy and confident in who you were authentically was something neither of them got consistently. That brief trip down memory lane helped them realize that even though they were very different people physically and mentally they both had the same struggles, hopes and dreams. They were also both worried that the healing was only beginning. Agreeing that sometimes that shit was painful.

Diane had found her people when she entered the house that apparently a group of "adult" students shared. It was wall to wall niggas and females.

"Girl, this is what I'm talking about!"

"Right! I'm trying to get chose."

Kim laughed as they walked toward the kitchen for a drink. "Kim right?" A girl said as they approached the makeshift bar.

"Hi Alyssa. This is Diane. She is also a transfer student. From VA."

"Hi." Diane said, reaching out her hand. Alyssa came around the counter and hugged her. "Hey girl! It's good to meet women our own age."

"That's one of the main reasons we throw these kickbacks at the beginning of every semester. The "Young Adults' can keep these dorm room parties. We grown over here."

Laughing, Diane agreed and instantly vibed off of Alyssa's energy. "So, where are you from? What's your major?"

"Journalism and I'm from the M. I. A babeee!"

"Okay go off, Sis," Diane said as Alyssa popped her lil booty. She was model thin and had enough energy for four people. A shorter girl walked up behind Alyssa and started smacking her on the ass, egging Alyssa on as she bucked harder.

"Hey, I'm Jennifer. Acting major from Cali." Jennifer introduced herself and was just as outgoing as Alyssa.

"I'm Diane."

"I'm Kim."

"Nice to meet you.", they both said at the same time. Being nosy, Diane asked, "Did you two know each other before?" Jennifer is slim, thick with a natural that was curly and falling below her nose.

"No, we meet at orientation and just hit it off from jump."

Alyssa looked at Jennifer, cheesing. If Diane was the messy type, she'd say Alyssa and Jennifer are fucking each other.

The girls purchased a few drinks and moved from the bar area to the living room. It had been cleared of furniture, making for a nice size dance floor. As the drinks kicked in, they began dancing with each other, laughing and enjoying the music. Walking up to the group holding out a J Dom spoke.

"Hey ladies, want a hit?"

"Dom!"

All of them said in unison and Diane wondered how everyone's associated. She remembered he was the RA on her floor and it was the adult dorms which she found out later all of them lived except Jennifer. She had off campus housing but spent most of time in Alyssa's room since she didn't have a roommate. They passed the blunt around a few times before the group dispersed. Some left with guys asking to dance and some headed back to the kitchen for refills. Diane remained on the dance floor, moving to the music, high as fuck, in chill mode. She hadn't heard from her momma or daddy since she left and was maybe not okay with it but resolved to the idea she was on her own. This was the reason she didn't partake too much in smoking. It made her reflective and melancholy.

A hand move around her waist, turning, she came face to face with a pair of light brown eyes on the darkest skin she'd ever seen on a person.

"Are those contacts?"

Pearly whites smiled back at her, "What? Dark skin men can't have light eyes?"

"No. That's not it at all, no offense, it's just damn, you're beautiful."

"I've heard a lot of compliments, but beautiful hasn't been one of them. Sexy as Fuck, Fine as Fuck, Big Dick Energy but never beautiful."

"Sorry didn't mean to offend, however I'm standing ten toes down on that statement. You're beautiful."

They began swaying slowly to the music even though the DJ was playing a 90s hip hop set. "Beauty" had the type of looks that made bitches fight. He was dark skin, light eyes medium to stocky build six feet and sexy as fuck.

"Yeah, I could definitely see myself fighting a bitch over this nigga."

Diane allowed her head to roll back as Beauty began kissing along her neck and rubbing on her ass. She could tell he could give the killer head by the way he was working his tongue up and down her neck. It was like they were in sync or both were just high as fuck. The slow swaying turned into winding and Diane clasped the long dick he was holding.

"Yeah imma fuck this nigga" whispering to herself. After a few minutes, Beauty slid his hand in hers and led her to a door leading to what she assumed was a basement. Turning to find Kim to make sure she was good, Diane saw her smiling in some dudes' faces with a drink in her hands.

"You good ma?"

"Yeah."

He led them downstairs and there was a small living area and three doors, all closed.

"This is my room. Are you comfortable coming in here with me? I wanted you to understand my intention is to suck the shit out of your soul, put that bitch back and suck it out again." Throbbing at his statement, Diane's clit almost jumped out of her panties.

"Fuck yeah, I'm comfortable. Condoms?"

"Always. Come on."

Diane opened her mouth as Beauty placed an edible on her tongue. At least she thought it was an edible or a Molly. Her eyelids fluttered open.

"Hmmm what is this?"

"Molly. You are good with that?"

Nodding with a smile, she allowed the M to hit her system as he pulled the dress over her head. Beauty removed his shirt, slapped her thigh, and laid back on the bed.

"Come stand above my head." Diane took off her sandals, afraid to mention she was a little nervous about what was coming next. Hopefully, the Molly would work its magic quicker than things were moving along. Biting her lower lip, Diane asked, "Are you sure?"

"Yeah, I'm sure."

She climbed on the bed and stood with her legs on either side of him above his head. He reached up, grabbing her stomach, and massaged it for a bit, then dragged his hands lower. Beauty moved her panties. He tapped her thigh again. "Lift." She did, and he took them completely off one leg.

"Why you up there looking down at me?"

He asked and went back to massaging her stomach.

"Come down here and sit on my face."

"You know I'm a big girl, right?"

"Naw really? Bring your ass down here, so I swallow that pussy."

Beauty held onto Diane's ankles as she squatted above him. His hand moved higher to her knees than the back of her thighs. He slapped them as a sign for her to keep going. Once she nestled on his face, Diane grabbed the headboard for leverage. Beauty moved his hand, grabbing and massaging her stomach, which seemed to make her wetter. Silently cursing as he placed his mouth over her entire pussy and sucked.

"Holy fuck!"

The M had kicked in and Diane sensed every fucking thing. This nigga had his lips around her clit, labia and all. Beauty literally tried to snatch her soul. Diane's pussy was leaking like a faucet. Tingles were all over her body.

"Nigga! Got damn!"

She screamed as her legs began trembling.

He slapped her stomach and pulled down, causing her pussy to fall deeper in his face. Beauty stuck his tongue in her pussy, stroked, then pulled it out. Diane creamed on his face when he repeated this. He didn't stop once her orgasm subsided; he took her clit in his mouth and sucked it like a pacifier. Screaming her second orgasm, Diane's eyes rolled in the back of her head and she fainted forward.

Diane woke up to Beauty slapping her stomach while he was still laving at her shit. She assessed his slick out face. She couldn't have been out that long.

"You alright ma? I lost you for a minute."

"Yeah, I'm good. I'm about to give you my credit card." Laughing, Beauty moved her on her back on the bed.

"Naw, I'm just a head nigga, ma. Your shit taste so fucking good and juicier than a mutha fucker."

"Thanks?"

"You ready for me to put this demon in and really fuck up your life?"

Not giving her a chance to answer, he slid in. She was so wet, and he was as thick as Jared, but the length of him almost fucked her cervix up. Thankfully, he was aware of his length and took his time stroking the shit out of her. It was like his dick had a mind of its own as his head hit all of her walls before going back to the bullseye, her g spot.

"Fuck girl. This pussy is good as fuck! She gushy gushy got damn."

Grabbing her hand in his Beauty look into her eyes as he stroke her to bliss. Diane couldn't decide if it was the sex, the J, the drinks, or the Molly.

Her entire body was sensitive as fuck. A puddle gathered at the base of her ass as her pussy pulsed. No one had ever been there, but this nigga could hit it the way his dick had her in a trance.

They couldn't take their eyes off each other as he stroked, and she pumped her hips.

"I got that pussy marinating huh."

Smirking as he gripped her hands tighter in his.

"Fuck I'm about to nut and don't want to yet."

Pulling out slowly just so the tip was barely in, "Fuck girl, you got me thinking about killing that next nigga for real."

He slide back in and pounded the fuck out of her. He was reckless with that shit. Diane wanted to tell him to stop and keep going. It was hurting so good.

"Take this dick. I'm fucking this shit up."

Beauty said as he pounded harder, gripping her titties hard as fuck for balance. Diane would have bruises on her breast in the morning. She wanted to cry. He was gripping them so hard but the beating he was putting on her pussy kept her mouth closed about the pain. He continued pounding as Diane's orgasm hit her in the stomach. Her legs started shaking again, and they both came at the same time. She screamed like he was killing her.

He bent down and covered her mouth with his. All she tasted was pussy and liquor.

Chapter 5

The buzzing sound woke Diane. Something prevented her from being able to move. Lifting her head, saw she and Beauty were in the same position they were in last night after he collapsed on top of her. Barely grasping her phone with her fingers as it ranged. She answered before the call dropped.

"Hello?"

"Bitch! Where the fuck are you?"

Kim sounded frantic on the other end. Diane couldn't be mad at her for the attitude or volume.

"Kim? I'm so sorry I didn't realize I was going to be gone for so long. I popped a Molly and went to hell. Then this demon sucked my soul outta me."

Diane's laughing died in her throat when she realized Kim wasn't reciprocating.

"Look, I'm sorry Kim. I honestly passed out after. I didn't mean to scare you. Let me make it up to you. I'll come home and make us breakfast or brunch or lunch, depending on what time it is now. Please don't be too upset. I'm really sorry."

"It's okay. I was worried something bad had happened to you. We've only known each other a few weeks, but you cool people, so..."

"I get it and I feel the same way. When I get in, we'll talk and come up with a system for going out and leaving with someone. Sound good."

"Yeah, see you when you get here. Dirty ho. Fucking at first sight." There was a pause and then both Diane and Kim burst out laughing.

She checked the time on her phone. It was 11:30 in the morning and time for her to get the hell out of this nigga house. Diane was able to push Beauty off her, but not without waking him up.

"What's good, ma?"

"Nothing, I'm about to get dressed and head out. You good?"

"I'm better than good."

"Don't be out here sharing my shit in these streets." Moving so she could get up and get dressed.

"Yeah alright."

She stumbled twice, trying to walk over to get in her dress and panties. Laughing with a wide-ass grin on his face like he did something last night. He did, but she'd never admit it to his face.

"You want me to drive you to your place? You look like you need some help."

Grateful for the offer Diane accepted because she really didn't want to take the shuttle looking like she'd been fucked into oblivion, which she was.

"If you don't mind, yeah, that'd be cool."

Jared was outside, back from breakfast with his boys when he noticed Diane getting out of some nigga's car looking well fucked and satisfied.

"What the fuck was she playing at?"

Walking toward her, Diane noticed Jared.

"Awe fuck. I do not want to see him right now smelling like a bag full of used sex toys and bad breath."

Increasing her speed while looking down, she tried to avoid eye contact with him. Jared was not having that.

"I know you see me, so don't even try it."

About a foot away from him, Diane stopped and looked up with embarrassment as she tried to exude bravado that she didn't have.

"Hey, Jared. I can't stop right now. I'm meeting Kim for brunch."

"That nigga fucked your world up, huh? Yeah, you look like they split your shit wide open."

He said with a smirk that seemed like disgust more than humor. Diane opened, closed, then open her mouth again, avoiding his eyes.

"Jared, don't be disrespectful. I didn't do shit to you for you to be talking to me crazy."

"You got it. I'm not trying to be disrespectful. A nigga hurt, though. I thought we were trying to get to figure this out and shit, but hey we ain't make no commitments right. I hope you strapped up?"

With her head down Diane whispered. "I did."

Leaning closer with his hand to his ear, "Huh, I can't hear you?"

"I did!"

"Oh, I was about to say cause I've been nuttin all in that raw as fuck. Who else you fucking bareback?"

"Nobody." She whispered hoping no one was paying attention to their interaction.

"Speak up you an English minor, use your words."

Diane looked around and thankfully not too many people were out. His frat was far enough away but still ear hustled.

"Nobody Jared. Why you bugging out? I mean, we cool, and I like you, but I'm single as fuck right now. School just started and I'm enjoying myself for a minute."

Jared shook his head and turned to see his boys. They looked as if they wanted to find the dude she came home with and fuck him up. He shook his head no and focused back on Diane.

"You right shorty. Why I'm tripping? I was feeling you too thought we kind of had some shit in common."

"Was feeling me?" Diane cocked her head mean mugging him.

"Man, look shorty. You out here being kind of reckless. Don't let that shit suck you in."

"Look I hear you and for real, I was smoking, drinking, and popped a Molly so I was just... feeling good."

"So that nigga drugged you?" He stepped closer to her but stopped. He hated she smelled like sex. Sex they didn't have together.

"No. Jared. Listen, I like you, but you right we aren't tied to each other and until we commit, or if we commit, it is what it is. I hope we can continue to become familiar with each other, but if you can't handle the talking phase, then I understand. Won't like but I understand."

Jared realized he had no say right now, but he wanted to let Diane know he was serious about them.

"I'm not saying I want to be married or some shit but I like you. A lot. I thought I made it clear what I wanted. I don't be fucking around like that, especially raw. I just want to make sure you strapping up with them other niggas 'cause I'm nutting in mine every time."

"You make it sound like I'm fucking a bunch of dudes."

He threw up his hands in a surrender stance. "How do I know?! Huh? I don't know shit. Look man, just go chill with your girl and I'll holla at you later."

"Alright. We cool?"

"Yeah man, you good."

Jared watched her walk away with an ache in his chest. He wondered how she had him twisted in knots so soon.

"Fuck!"

Diane blew out a breath as she walked in the building, happy that Jared didn't get any closer to ask for a hug. The look on his face kind of hurt, but she shrugged that shit off. Yeah, she liked him, but she just wanted to just be before locking in or committing to anything but her classes. Period.

"Lie to yourself, bitch. You feel bad."

She thought to herself as she got on the elevator to her floor.

When Diane got to her floor, Kim was escorting out the same guy she saw her with at the party last night.

"I guess we all fucked at first sight last night."

She walked to the bathroom to shower with a smirk plastered on her face.

After devouring brunch, Kim and Diane sat on her futon and talked about their game plan for going out and hooking up. She and Kim cleaned the apartment together, studied a bit, organized their schedules, and prepared for classes tomorrow. Both were upset with themselves for letting half of the day get away from them because of the debauchery on Saturday night. By nine o'clock, exhaustion set in and they both turned in early.

The next few weeks flew by. Kim and Diane had heavy workloads, and both were glad they'd set up a time to study together. Even though they had different majors, having someone just as focused was enough to keep each other on track. Diane had been texting with Jared more often now, trying to keep the budding friendship growing even though they wanted different things from each other. Jared seemed to take it all in stride. He was a Chem/Pre-med major, so his schedule was just as hectic, and texting seemed to appease them both.

Kim had some group projects and was pulling an all-nighter in the iLab which gave Diane the dorm all to herself to push out the script for her script writing class. She thought she would like this class more than she did. Scriptwriting was more nuanced than she'd expected. Every single detail from the door opening, the actor walking, if the scene was out or inside, including the dialogue, had to be written into a script. This shit was for the birds if you weren't interested in making a movie, which she wasn't. But whatever Howard required for her to graduate, she would do it.

Diane heard someone knocking on the door and got out the bed. She figured it was Kim, maybe forgetting her key or something. Door unlocked and left ajar, Diane sat back down. It was hella late on a Friday and school was in full swing, so no hanging out tonight.

"So you just gonna open the door for anybody?"

"Jared? I thought you were Kim and also I wanted to get my thoughts down before I forgot."

Jared purposely stayed away from Diane for two reasons: he needed to see if missing her would hurt as much as when his mom left him and his dad. An also, he wanted to give her time to think about what it's be like if he was gone. Thinking back a few weeks made him want to gag. He didn't think Diane realized how strong the aroma of sex was coming off her that day. Part of him wanted to vomit, and the other part wanted to punch her in the face. He was being irrational but Jared was a fall-hard-and-fast type. Knowing what he wanted when he wanted it and getting it, no questions asked. But Diane was playing hard to get, and he had to move differently or risk losing all of her. That wasn't happening.

Posted in the doorway, he watched her type away and smiled at how cute she looked, concentrating on the keyboard without lifting her head.

"What? I feel you staring at me."

Pushing off the door, Jared walked toward her. He turned her chair to face him, bending down to get eye level.

“I was watching you work in this grandma gown you got on.”

The gown looked like something a grandma would wear silky with the ruffles on the sleeve and around the neckline. On his knees, Jared pushed her legs open as far as they would go in the desk chair and slid his hands under her gown. When he reached her waist, he realized she didn’t have on any panties.

“What was you really doing in here?”

“Nothing boy, I like the way the silk caress my skin. It helps me write.”

Jared sat on the futon and motioned for her to come to him. Diane got up, closed her bedroom door, and walked between his parted legs.

“How are your classes going? I heard that if you couldn’t make it through organic chemistry, you might as well changed majors.”

“I don’t have shit to worry about then, just got a B on my last exam.” Jared said, sliding his hands up her dress again.

“No more talking.”

“K,” she whispered as Jared moved his hand over her ass around to her stomach. He moved one hand between her legs, using his middle finger to part her lips and pushed to his knuckle. “Uh shit.”

"Quiet." Pressing her lips together, she moaned.

"That's it."

Jared fingered up and down in her pussy until a nice flow came down. He eased out of her and told her to step up on the futon and place her hand flat on the window. Even though they were six floors up and faced a parking lot, Diane was worried she'd be seen. Diane shook off the big girl fear and complied with Jared's request.

Jared placed her knees on the back of the futon and buried his face in her pussy. She wanted to curse but grunted instead, as she remembered he had said no words. He began working her clit over and moved his hands to hold her ass cheeks. His tongue wasn't as magical as Beauty's but it was a beast just the same. He stuck the middle finger he had in her pussy into her asshole as he slowly pumped it in and out of her. She placed her hands on the window for balance as her pussy muscles pulsed around nothing.

"Damn baby, this shits good."

He continued to focus on sucking her clit and pumping his finger in her asshole. It was like he wanted to see how fast he could make her cum. "Aaahhhhh" Diane yelled, and she collapsed face forward into the bay window, trembling at the nut she just bust.

Jared moved her off the futon, taking her gown off and pushing her down on the bed.

"I'm about to fold and fuck you. I'm not stopping until I want to stop. I'm not asking for shit. I'm just going to take it. You good with that?"

Diane laid back on the bed and said, "Do your worst."

Jared picked the gown from the floor. He placed both of her hands above her head and tied them. He wrapped Diane's arm from the elbow to her wrist in the prayer position.

"Not one word."

He said, standing to his full height removing his shirt, pants, socks, and shoes. Jared stood before her, completely naked and hard as a brick. Closing her eyes and laying her head back between her wrapped arm, Diane wished he wasn't on some get back from the Beauty incident.

"Put your feet on the bed and bust that pussy open for me."

She placed her feet flat on the bed, Diane spread her legs as far as they could go. Jared stood at the front of her opening, stroking his dick, committing everything to memory. The smell of her arousal, the translucent cum seeping out of her, the thickness of her lips and that bud poking out like the bud of baby's breath. He could've just stood there and stroked himself until he came, but he needed to make sure she understood without speaking a word that all of her was his.

The longer Jared watched and waited, the more nervous Diane became. She raised her head and met Jared's eyes. There was something sinister there, and she was both aroused and scared. Head back on the bed, she waited. As her clit became more engorged. Her body continued to pour a steady stream of lust from between her legs.

Jared bent down, never ceasing the stroke of his penis, and licked from her ass to her clit. He latched on and sucked. Diane's scream got trapped in her throat as her eyes bulged almost out of their sockets. The orgasm that hit her had her life flashing before her eyes. Jared placed his hands on the back of her thighs mid-orgasm to her chest. He observed her pussy contracting as her clit remained engorged. He sunk his dick deep into her walls. Another orgasm hit her before the last one crested and Diane fainted.

Her body was limp, but he held her thighs to her chest as he swerved, his hips hitting her walls repeatedly.

"Fuck!"

He wondered how could anyone's pussy could be this fucking fantastic. Her shit pulsed around his creamed covered dick.

"Fuck!"

The smell was strong. It was a cross between a Sweet Tart and Mangoes. Jared closed his eyes and focused on reciting the Periodic table so he would last. He wanted to fuck her all night if he could and had a Molly in his jeans if he needed it. That shit makes everything sensitive and heightened while keeping your shit brick for hours. He continued to recite the

Periodic table as he admired her pretty pink pussy that contracted every time he pumped in and out.

"RH Radium, Pd Palladium."

Diane opened her eyes, realizing she'd passed out, but Jared hadn't stopped. He was still fucking the shit out of her. She looked up at him and her stomach clenched at how manic he looked. He'd opened up the floodgates and the end of the waterfall was at the base of her ass. She orgasmed.

Jared smiled. Diane opened her eyes. She couldn't push back because of how tight he'd locked her down.

"Fuck, this shit's so fucking good baby"

"I thought I said no talking."

He slowed his pace almost to a stop. Diane pressed her lips tight. He stroked and banged in and out of her like a power driver. Her legs started shaking. Jared was going to bust soon, so he fucked her faster and faster as Diane passed out again. While blacking out, she squirted. That was all Jared needed. He pumped one last time nutted.

Waiting until his sperm wouldn't leak out, he got up, popped a Molly and started stroking himself while thumbing her pussy.

"I'm about to imprint my soul on your ass."

The Professor

It was Monday. Diane hadn't gotten out of bed since Saturday morning except to pee and drink. Jared left around 10 a.m. Sunday morning and true to his word, he'd fucked her all night into the morning. Weak from lack of food and too much sex, Diane got out of bed and hobbled to the bathroom. She passed Kim's closed door and wondered about her weekend. They had a rule about closed doors. She'd text Kim later to check-in. Diane was afraid to look in the mirror and when she did, it surprised her at how bright her face looked. She turned on the shower and stepped in, grateful to be well-rested and relaxed. All her classes were in the afternoon, so she could take her time getting ready. The school year was in full swing and students were deep in their studies.

Diane's first month was done, midterms were around the corner and so was homecoming. Howard's homecomings were infamous, and she was ready! It was also time to pull out her fall clothing and start planning what she's going to do and where she's going to stay during Christmas break.

"Home is not where my heart is."

In COAS, she headed upstairs to her poetry class. The heavy smell of smoke almost choked her as she took her seat. This class didn't have individual desks, but long tables with chairs. Professor Resto was walking in when one student said out loud.

"Who is smoking cigarettes in the building?"

Resto placed his books on the table, looked up at the class.

"That would be the chair of the English department She has been at Howard since smoking in buildings was legal. I don't think anyone has told her that's changed or she doesn't care."

Resto was five minutes into class when the door gently opened and a student walked in. He apologized for being tardy, handed him a document while stating he was involved in a fender bender but wanted to sit in on the class to see if he would be interested in taking it next year. Resto took the paper.

"Christopher? Go have a seat."

It irritated Resto that the student came in late. Shit happens and students could sit in classes to determine whether was something they'd take the following semester. It was the fact he sat next to her. Resto couldn't focus, which would be a problem if he hadn't committed his lessons to memory. He rattled on and on about cadence in poetry. The internal dialogue him drove him crazy.

"How the fuck did she know this guy? Were they involved? Who the hell was he? Her entire body language changed, like she couldn't sit still. Were they fucking?"

He became so pissed his shakes started. Twenty-five mins into class, he dismissed everyone and took a seat as quickly as he could in order to control the shaking.

Diane looked down at Resto as she approach the front of the class. Professor Resto, "Is everything okay?"

"Everything's good. I decided it was such a nice day that you guys should enjoy the weather a bit in between classes."

"Oh, okay, I'm really enjoying it so far. I'm excited about the poetry we're all working on. Mad cool."

Nodding, Resto wanted her to continue to talk. She soothed him. What's that scent she's wearing? Brown sugar and Mango? Damn, she smelled so fucking good.

She'd been invading his and mama's dreams lately. It was like having mama overload and his desire for her was increasing by the day. If the opportunity ever presented itself, he was definitely going to take it. He would destroy her.

"Hey, Beauty. You ready?"

"Yeah, let's go. Your class was pretty cool. I might take it as an elective next semester. Thanks for allowing me to sit in."

They walked off, and Resto was pissed.

"What the fuck is a beauty?"

Frustrated, he tried to calm his breathing. Thankfully, this was his last class of the day. He gathered his things and decided it was time to go home and relieve this ache.

When he left out to the building, he saw Diane laugh at something Christopher said to her. He'd gathered a few clues about who she was through her poetry, but nothing substantial enough to know if she was like he'd imagined mama to be. He paused and just watched how she looked when she spoke to this guy. Her eyes, the twitch of her lips, the slight turn of her body toward him, the way her hand held onto the crossbody coach.

"Yep, she definitely fucked him. Shit!" He whispered yelled to himself as he continued to the parking lot.

At home, beer in hand, Resto just wanted to forget. Forget Her and his mama. Forget women. He sent a text knowing this would give him the release he needed, and hopefully, mama wouldn't show up tonight. After a quick shower, Resto decided a towel would do since he would be naked soon. He heard the doorbell ring at the same time his phone sent a text notification. Resto walked to the door, with the towel wrapped around his medium size frame. He didn't flaunt his frame, especially at the University but in the comforts of his home, he was always on display. He opened the door and turned, grabbing a ponytail holder from the counter. He may trim his hair but never cut it all off.

His visitor, he called Wood, came in and closed the door. Resto noticed the smile on his face and knew he was going to forget, if only for a few hours. Wood was nothing like her or his mama. First, he was a man. Second, he was the color of midnight, and he didn't haunt his dreams. Wood walked into his bedroom smirking, knowing Resto would follow. Wood sat on the bed as Resto stood in front of him. He bent down and kissed his lips gently and slowly as his tongue parted Wood's lips. This was exactly what he needed, the touch of a man. Falling to his knees, Wood unwrapped the towel and kissed the tip of Resto's dick. He slowly licked, then sucked it into his mouth.

"Fuck, that's good."

Once fully engorged, Resto grabbed his head and began moving him up and down his shaft. Eyes closed, his mama was there, sliding up and down him as her juices flowed to his pelvis.

"Ah fuck yes. Just like that."

Resto didn't worry about what he'd said. He'd been with him enough times to be aware of his kink. Wood moved his head up and down faster. Slowly his mama disappeared and the feel of a man's mouth urge his nut forward. Resto wanted to savor the moment a little long, so he slowed his pace and eased him off his cock. Standing and making eye contact, Wood kissed Resto just as gently as the last time.

"What do you need?"

"I need to forget."

Resto crawled on the bed, got on his knees, spread his legs, as he laid his head to the side and stretched his hands above him. Wood massaged his ass as he licked and tongue fucked Resto's asshole. He wrapped his hand around Resto's dick, squeezed softly as Resto let out a moan.

"Don't stop, please don't stop. Make me forget."

He stood while still working Resto's dick up and down in a gently. Once hard, he held his cheeks apart while easing the head of his dick in Resto.

"That's so nice. Do you love me?"

Wood didn't respond and continued to ease the head in and out, opening him up more. Once he was fully seated. He reached around and grabbed Resto's dick and slow stroke his dick as he fucked his ass.

Resto smiled as Wood buried himself in his soul.

"Yes, just like that. Fuck, you're so good. I like it nice and slow. Go deeper, as deep as you can go."

Resto felt a smooth hand sliding up his back to his neck. He reveled in the feel of it. His body shook when suddenly he embraced a rough pull on his hair. Wood pushed further until his pelvis was flat against his ass, grinding against him while stroking his dick with one hand and massaging his balls, pressing into his perinea with his thumb.

"That's it! Yes! Oh, fuck! I'm going to cum!"

He gave one hard grind, squeezing Resto tighter and pressing harder. Resto let out a scream as he shot his cum so hard he had droplets on his chin. He continued to slow stroke Resto until he was drained. Wood eased out of his ass and walked into the shower to remove the condom and finish himself off. Resto didn't allow anyone to release in him even with a covered dick.

On his way from Organic Chem to the cafe, Jared couldn't believe what he saw. Diane standing there chatting it up with ole boy that dropped her off that day. She was acting like he wasn't just balls deep in her twenty-four hours ago. He closed his eyes, inhaled, then exhaled. They were just talking, a friendly chat catching up. She looked well fuck though.

"Just calm down. She knows better." He thought to himself.

Jared grew up knowing nothing but privilege. His grandfather was a man of God and preached at the same church his great-great-grandfather started for "throwaways". The people no one wanted to come to their house of worship, ruining their church's good look and name. It was one of the many reasons he didn't believe in religion. DC churches were just as classicist as the neighborhoods. The Gold Coast, Georgetown, Chevy Chase, and DuPont Circle are the crème de la crème. SE from the Anacostia subway to the Maryland line. H Street NE past Union Station down to Nannie Helen Burroughs to the Maryland line and SW the area which now houses the Washington Nationals. Before gentrification, the section eighters, drug fiends, and dealers all occupied those areas with a few older folks from the seventies who were now retired government workers and refused to give up on the neighborhood or couldn't afford to move.

Jared fully understood and knew about those neighborhoods from hanging with his grandfather. He knew how grimy it could be, but he didn't realize how corrupt religion was until he was about twelve years old. His grandfather had done something good for the city, starting The House of Prayer for All People.

Prostitutes, dope fiends, the homeless, and anyone seeking God could come as they were to find Him. Jared loved going to the various areas of the city, embracing the people, the environment, and the culture. His grandfather instilled in him that no man was better than the next and that just because you are doing better doesn't mean you can't fall hard and fast to the bottom.

"Do you think our people want to be in the positions that they are in? No, they want a better life, but when you are raised from birth that this is it and never had a positive word said to you or are treated worthless, then you not only begin to believe it, you act it."

He looked up at his grandfather and allowed those words to sink in little by little until he fully understood what he meant.

Howard's campus taught him about the different types of Black people in this world. We definitely were not a monolith. You had kids who grew up in wealth as he did, the kids of celebrities and artists. The middle-income kids whose parents had a high enough credit score to take out loans to assist with their education and not leave their children in decades of debt. And the kids who got in on a wing and a prayer with grant money loans. Every semester, they had to reinvent ways to keep themselves fed during the semester.

One thing Jared hated the most was the way almost all the Howard community referred to the residents as "locals". It wasn't just the word, but the way they said it. Turning up their noses like being knee-deep in shit. Jared made sure he called anyone out on it and told them not to say that shit around him. He, along with a good percentage of students, were originally from DC. Hell, Taraji P. Henson was a "local" that graduated from Howard and look at her now. He understood students wanted to differentiate themselves from the native Washingtonians, but what he didn't understand was why their reference had to have such a negative connotation to it.

Jared spent the next few weeks focusing on studying for midterms. Some professors understood homecoming was around the same time, but others didn't care, scheduling exams, quizzes, and mandatory group projects during the festivities. Howard's homecoming wasn't just a weekend thing. They have events for seven days, not to mention all the parties and pussy. The exact reason he was putting in the hours. It's the most epic time in Howard's history and he was not missing out. He also needed to figure out how to enjoy himself while making sure Diane did nothing reckless. They were just friends, and he understood that. He wanted her and didn't want anyone to touch her while he was shooting his shot.

It was something about how she wasn't disrespectful, but she was the type that wouldn't pull back from talking to other guys while they developed what they were trying to develop. She understood what it meant to date and do her until she committed herself to one person. To this day she hadn't, so he couldn't do a damn thing but leave her alone or wait. He wasn't checking for any other women and knew it was selfish of him to ask her not to entertain anyone. The most he could ask for that she agreed to was no barebacking with anyone else. Jared hoped that by continuing to dick her down on the regular, giving her just enough space, and treating her like an independent woman, she would cave and "submit" to him. Laughing at that thought.

It was going to take a lot for a woman like her but "If I could tell her what to do I can tell her what to do but if I can't tell her what to do, I can't tell her what to do." Jared was all for women being their own person, but he also loved having control "respectfully" over her. He wanted it willingly handed over, not by force, but because she wanted it.

Chapter 7

Diane had immersed herself in writing, writing, and more writing. She was so thankful that she'd switched her schedule or she wouldn't have been able to enjoy homecoming, which was happening next week. She and Kim had become fast friends with Alyssa and Jennifer. Their classes were different, but they had come together three times a week study or write papers. The best place to study wasn't the iLab or Founders, but the Allied Health Library. Howard built the library for dental and medical students, but other students came to make use of the private study rooms. The windows were floor to ceiling and gave you a fantastic view of SOC or Georgia Ave, depending on which side of the building your room was located. The girls had music going, food scattered, and good old-fashioned girl time.

Nakia also came to hang out from time to time since she was a nursing major and had a valid reason to be in Allied Health. At first, Diane thought she was Bougie, but after getting to know her, she was just naïve and privileged. She was cool once she loosened up. Nakia's dad was in the military and her mom was a government worker living in the suburbs of

Pennsylvania. Her father added money to her account for groceries and incidentals. She said she never had to budget or check her balance before spending. Money was always available. Nakia would just swipe her card and keep it pushing. She reminded Diane of Jared. The only difference was Jared had some street knowledge Nakia was clueless. Diane should introduce the two, then maybe Jared would ease up a bit more. He was giving her the space she needed while getting to know each other better, but in between studying, classes, and hanging with friends, he hadn't blown her back out like she needed. Jared didn't believe in quickies, so if he couldn't give it his all, she didn't get it. The only reason she remained "faithful" if you want to call it that is because there wasn't an opportunity.

College was about experiences and Diane felt as if being in a relationship this early in her collegiate career would hinder some of those experiences. Maybe in her senior year or even after graduation, she would be open to exploring what she and Jared could be, but not right now. Diane was hoping she and her heart stayed in sync because if that traitorous bitch fell in love, it would be all over for her. She thought about how she would handle seeing Nakia and Jared together. Would she be jealous? Would she still fuck Jared on the side and not care? One question is, would Jared fuck her if he was with someone else and how would she feel about it? The better question is, how would she feel if he said no to her?

Sunday morning, Diane and Kim woke up and got dressed for church service at the chapel. Neither one of them was religious but felt it was necessary to take part in all the homecoming activities since this was their first one at Howard. Besides, they heard the various fraternities, sororities, and student promoters would be in attendance and they wanted to not only find out where parties were. They wanted the lit parties. Diane got an invitation from Beauty for a house party at his tonight, so they planned on staying up all night and then going straight to class, hungover and all. She wore a pair of navy slacks, a mock turtleneck and a red blazer paired with some red pumps. She figured she might as well show school pride while fake praising the lord.

The shuttle showed up on time to take them up the hill. Neither wanted walked in heels nor have sweat stains. They made it to the chapel twenty minutes late, and it was packed! There were a lot of locals in the church, along with students. The various organizations sat together, so Diane and Kim sat with the Transfer Student Association (TSA) with Alyssa, Jennifer, and Nakia. Jennifer and Alyssa were attached at the hip, giggling with each other. Nakia was talking to Dominic, who Diane found out was a transfer student as well. Waving at everyone as they sat, the pastor stood to begin the sermon.

Lost in her thoughts, Diane marveled at Andrew Rankin Chapel's history as she looked around the structure, pews, and windows. Named after President Andrew Rankin and completed in 1896. Ancestors such as Frederick Douglass, Mary McLeod Bethune, and Benjamin E. Mays have graced these walls and sat in the very pews she occupied. Martin Luther King Jr. even preached here. She silently asked for their guidance and help for the school year. Diane never really got emotional however, at that moment her heart opened up. She allowed herself to feel everything she needed to heal from her past and move forward into her future. A better future.

Diane felt a finger wiping away a tear she hadn't realized fell. Looking up as she opened her eyes and saw Jared standing above her.

"Hey. You okay?"

He whispered, not caring he was getting stares from some parishioners. Diane shook her head from side to side. Jared, not giving a fuck, reached for her hand and lead her out of the main hall.

Diane didn't know where Jared was taking her, however, she knew she wanted to stop the sadness that came as a part of grieving her past. He opened the door and gently nudged her inside. She saw a desk covered with papers and a huge bible, various robes on a hanging rack in different colors, pictures, and statues of Christ.

"You brought me in the fucking pastor's office?!"

She couldn't believe it. Jared laughed as he closed the door, leaning on it as he did.

"Yeah. Why you scared?"

"No, not scared, but I don't think we should be in here."

"What are they going to do to Daddy Grace's grandson?" He said as he walked over to a fearful Diane.

"What's going on? You good?"

"Yeah, I was just releasing some things to the ancestors so I don't have to carry them anymore." She moved papers around on the desk, avoiding eye contact with Jared.

"You know I'm here for you Diane. I can be that ear, shoulder, or arms you need whenever you need them. You, my Lil yeah yeah."

With glistening eyes, she giggled. She didn't want to digest the feelings that came with his statement. Diane turned to face the window. It had some tint, but not too much. She could see the benches that were placed by the steps leading to SOC.

"I'm not a Lil anything." She didn't mean to say it but her emotions were everywhere.

"Yes, you are."

Jared said as he grabbed her by the waist. He pulled her shirt out of her pants and unbuttoned them. He pushed her slacks and panties around her ankle.

"Don't you ever say no shit like that again and let me hear you. You got me fucked up."

Caressing her lower stomach with one hand as he slid his other to her pelvis, he tugged on the hairs at the apex of her hood. Diane let out a soft "kay". He continued to play with her as she rocked into his hands.

"Jared. We are going to get caught, then they are going to kick us out of school."

"Sssshhhh, stop worrying."

He slid his fingers along her clit, through her folds, and backup.

"Yeah, that pussy shedding tears too."

Diane leaned forward, placing her hands on the window. With her eyes closed, Jared made quick work of dropping his pants and boxers. His hand massaged her ass as her pussy left a trail of wetness down her inner thigh.

"Yeah, baby. My pussy is ready for me."

Diane was aroused, sad, and nervous at the same time. The more Jared played the less she cared about getting caught or her past.

Impressed with the way Diane's body was responding to his ministrations, Jared sucked on her neck. He wanted his mark visible.

"That's it, baby. I apologize for neglecting you, but we had to be on our responsible shit with the school. Jared's back and I'm about to make this fatty scream my name. You ready for me to dig up in these guts?"

Diane said nothing but quickly nodded her head. Jared rubbed his dick up and down her pussy, which was bent at the perfect angle. He eased in. Having to take a moment to gain control as his stomach did flips remembering the feel of being inside of her. Jared needed to make sure she got fucked regularly to the point of exhaustion so she wouldn't be able to fuck anyone else for the next seven days. He was no fool and understood girls got down just like the niggas did during homecoming. He was going to do everything in his power to prevent Diane from slutting herself and his pussy out.

He reached her cervix and started grinding in her nice and slow. Her walls were gripping his shit tighter than a fresh set of braces.

"Fuck girl. You trying to make me nut."

Knowing the pastor was going to take his time and show off since it was the start of homecoming week, Jared wasn't worried about anyone coming in and if they did, oh well. He was not stopping until Diane bust at least three times. His grinding increased to slow pump as he held onto her stomach. He loved how that shit felt. It seemed to make his dick harder when playing with it.

"Shit girl. This pussy going to have me killing niggas this weak."

She moaned and pushed back. Jared was blowing her fucking back out. He pressed a hand on her back. He dipped and stroked her pussy with more speed. His dick was coated creamy white. No lubrication needed if a nigga knows what he's doing. Jared never had to spit on a pussy and if he ever considered it, he would stop. That was his signal the woman wasn't into him and he would never be hard up for pussy that didn't want him.

"Uh fuck!"

Diane bit her lip as he continued his upward stroke. His cream drenched balls had him fully aware she was about to bust. As he grabbed her neck. Jared pushed her face flat to the window and whispered in her ear.

"This ain't a request or a plea, but a command. Nobody getting in this pussy but me for the next seven days."

Jared stroked her a little faster. He started fingering her clit with the other hand.

"Answer me Diane."

He pushed harder. "No dick but mine for the next seven days."

He paused his stroke with his finger waiting for an answer. Diane's knees were shaking like a crackhead going through withdrawals and she would say anything to get that nut.

"Ah fuck please Jared Please." She begged.

"Please what, huh? You didn't just hear what the fuck I said? No dick but mine for the next seven days. I don't give a fuck where I am or what time it is. If you want dick, contact me." Jared said as he stroked once with his hand and dick.

"Okay no, dick, but yours for the next seven days. Oh, my fucking God, please fuck me."

Diane raised her voice in frustration. Jared picked up speed and continued his upward stroke while fingering her clit. Diane's first nut came hard, but Jared didn't stop to give her time to recover. He continued pumping, putting his thumb in her ass while continuing to stroke her clit. Diane's face stayed planted on the window. Her first orgasm was edging just as the second grabbed her in a chokehold. Her vision blurred as tears ran down her face, legs shaking so badly she would've collapsed if Jared hadn't caught her.

Just as the second orgasm subsided, Jared moved. Diane stood on shaky legs in an attempt to straighten her clothes. He had other plans. Jared got on his knees between the windowsill and Diane.

"Jared, what are you doing? I'm trying to get myself together. I can't even get myself together."

Face to face with her pussy, Jared spoke to it.

"I'm about to fuck up your life."

He dove into her folds. Jared sucked on her lips while his tongue went deep, diving into her pussy. Diane's stomach clenched, her toes curled, and her body seized as Jared and latched on her clit. She convulsed. She came so hard her eyes hurt.

Jared stood between her and the window with her juices on his lips. He smirked.

"Feel better momma?"

"Not yet."

Diane said as she lowered to her knees and swallowed Jared to his pelvis. Jared let out a hiss as Diane slob on his knob like a corn on the cob. Nasty as hell, he thought as she swallowed his dick like it was coated in butter and ranch dressing instead of her juices. Jared urged the tingled at the base of his spine to come down as he grabbed the windowsill standing on the tip of his toes. Diane tapped his leg, easing up on her suction. She looked up at him.

"Where you going?"

She took him back in and suctioned even harder.

Without warning, Jared yelled. "Fuuuck" as he shot his load to the back of her throat. She swallowed. Jared dick, still hard, got his bearings as he moved his hand behind her head and began pumping.

"Take all this shit."

Diane sucked faster as Jared continued to pump. His orgasm was seconds away.

"Fuck. I swear I will kill a nigga behind you." He hollered as he came.

The door swung open, and the pastor initially smiled when he noticed it was Daddy Grace's grandson, stopping to say hello. That's until he noticed Jared holding the head of a young lady at his pelvis. Jared's grip tightens on Diane's head so she would be embarrassed at being caught in the act.

"I'm sorry, pastor. I meant no disrespect. Can you give me a minute to escort my girl out? Then we can speak?"

He hoped and prayed the pastor would allow him to get Diane safely to her friends before he went in. And yes, Jesus, he looked like he was going to go in. The pastor looked down and the back of the young lady's head that Jared still had a firm grip on.

"You've got five minutes to escort her out and if I were you, I'd set aside the next hour and a half for that conversation."

The paster back out and close the door. Jared looked down as Diane looked up. With her mouth full of dick, Diane burst out laughing.

Kim looked Diane up and down, shaking her head.

"Bitch where the hell you were looking like you got fucked so good you saw Jesus?"

"And did!"

Kim shook her head with a smile.

"Hell bound in a hand basket cause I know yo nasty ass ain't gon' have draws to put gasoline on."

Diane couldn't help but to laugh at Kim cracking on her and it was just what she needed.

"You ready to get a home nap and plan out our party schedule?"

"Sure am."

They said their goodbyes to the other ladies and headed back to the dorms.

Chapter 8

It was a struggle to wake up for her classes on Monday. Diane was sore from the session she had with Jared, and the air literally pulsated. Homecoming was going to be a literal vibe. Diane and Kim went to the medical center and stocked up on condoms. She promised Jared she wouldn't fuck anyone during homecoming, however; she needed to have protection in case she got drunk, or high and reckless. Diane knew who she was and what she enjoyed. College was the place she planned on indulging before real life took hold again. She focused on school and getting her work done, but she also wanted to explore more things than just books. It took her a long time to build up her confidence and to accept who and how she was. Once that happened; she explored her sexuality more. A late bloomer, her first sexual experience was when she was twenty years old. He was twenty-five. He took his time and taught her a lot, but she wanted more. What that "more" was, Diane didn't know but hoped to find out this during this cycle in her life.

Jared was the only one going bareback in her and she was faithful. Birth control ensured he didn't become a father, and she damn sure wasn't trying to be anybody's momma. Besides, she had no intentions of becoming a one man woman, but she could try to be "committed" for seven days.

Not that Diane was against relationships, she didn't want the commitment of a relationship to deter her from the college experience. She needed to experience whatever it was she needed to experience and learn the lessons she needed to learn, then find a life partner to share and continue to grow with. She didn't believe in the patriarchal roles of society and understood systems are in place as a form of control. There was no pressure to get married, have kids, or own a home, so being in a relationship wasn't a top priority for her. She always danced to the beat of her true authentic self and that would not change because she developed feelings for someone. Yes, she had feelings for Jared, however; she didn't want to act on anything until she was sure she would be able to fully commit. Right now, she was going to focus on drinking, smoking, and enjoying her roomie. Kim walked to her door.

"You ready to fuck up homecoming?"

Laughing at her roomie. Diane stood. "Hell to the fuck yeah!"

Jared walked into the house party his boy wanted to hit up. He wasn't feeling it but figured it'd be a good warm-up before the frats kick their shit off. The music was jumping, and he immediately began bobbing his head and rapping the lyrics. They were some fine ass girls up in here tonight; he thought as he looked around.

"Hey man, what's up?"

Jared heard someone greeting his homeboy Kenny, "Ain't nothing. You got it. Let me introduce you to my boy Jared."

Turning to see who he was about to dap up, Jared realized it was the dude he saw Diane fucked up a few weeks back.

"Jared, this is Christopher. Chris this my boy Jared."

"Whad up man?"

"Ain't shit. Make yourselves at home. It's liquor in the kitchen and if you need gas or into Molly, get at me. I'll have my boy hook you up."

"Bet! Good looking."

It pissed Jared off that nigga was friendly. He hoped Diane had that act right for homecoming. He didn't want to have to beat a nigga ass. Jared and Kenny mingled and danced with a few women. The crowd was alright, but nothing like the frat crowd. They had locals and students at their joints. The women were fine as fuck, but his dick only jump for one person and it didn't look like she was here.

"Yo Jared, I'm about to slide in this piece upstairs. You good til I get back?"

Smirking at his homeboy, he nodded. "Yeah, I'm good at going handle business."

The girl he pulled was bad as fuck. Her dark skin was glowing with her hair up in an afro puff. Jared was damn near salivating at her ass in the beige leggings she was rocking. Shorty knew what she was doing. You could see the plumpness of her pussy in them things. Yeah, he was stuck on Diane, but he wasn't blind.

He mixed some Henn and Coke into a red cup and watch the crowd of people mingle with each other. That's when he saw her and Kim across the room with some girls, laughing and drinking. Jared thought about approaching her but decided not to. Technically, he wasn't her man. Besides, it was homecoming, and no one wanted to be boo'd up.

Watching Diane, Jared almost missed the girl backing her ass against him. He grabbed her waist. She wasn't big like Diane but she was working with a nice size butt. The way she had her ass on his dick told him she wanted to fuck. Jared danced against her as he watched Diane laughing with her friend. He immediately got hard remembering her wet pussy. She was wearing a skirt that barely covered her ass and some tights with some type of flowered design all over them. It hurt him that she slept with Chris. Maybe he should fuck shorty and get Diane out his system. Jared palmed her ass and slid his hand around her waist, just above her pelvic area.

"Damn girl, you throwing that shit like you want a nigga to do something?"

"Naw baby, just dancing."

She smiled back at him. Realizing she was a tease, she focused back on Diane. He saw Chris pass a J to her as he caressed her cheek with the back of his hand. He slid his hand and cupped the pussy of the girl twerking on his manhood. She was wet and her pussy was fat, but Jared couldn't get his lick back like that. He wanted one woman and one woman only. Just because he was a man didn't mean he couldn't control himself. Even though he and Diane were friends, it was homecoming, and they had an understanding. So he was going to let her chill.

His boy came back about thirty minutes later cheesing like shit.

"Nigga, did she take your soul?"

"Naw man never that but she mutha fucking tried."

Laughing he handed him a cup, and they went back in the crowd to rub against some shaking asses.

Thank goodness Jared didn't walk up to her at the party. Diane hoped he wasn't going to be breathing down her neck. He needed to trust her to be responsible and let her have a good ass time. She and Kim popped a Molly and now puffed on some bomb as gas. She would not be any good tomorrow. Thankfully, her first class started at 11 a.m. That meant she'd be able to get a few hours before classes. She couldn't stay up that long and live on no sleep until the afternoon. If her class was at eight, she'd Red Bull and Advil it and be okay.

She remembered Beauty behind her. Diane must have been deep in thought not to notice his aroma. She turned around, clasped the blunt he offered, gave it a hard pull before passing it back. Diane stared at him as she held the smoke and slowly exhaled, blowing the smoke in his face as she close her lips over his. He inhaled the smoke at the same time his tongue found its way in her mouth. Beauty resembled a satisfied pussy and a good night's sleep. He pulled back and clasped her neck.

"What's good Ma? You alright?"

She leaned in and kissed him again.

"And am. This party is a whole vibe and the perfect way to start off the festivities."

Chris slid his hand down Diane's arm.

"You want to come downstairs for a few minutes? You look good in that skirt."

At her ear, he licked.

"I would love to spread you out and feast on that sugary goodness between your legs."

Beauty placed his lips over hers and blew the smoke into her mouth. Diane inhaled.

"Yeah, we can go talk."

As she blew out the cloud of smoke. Diane knows she shouldn't go downstairs with Beauty but Molly had her believing just because she headed downstairs didn't mean she would fuck him. Her stomach fluttered a bit at the thought as she followed Beauty downstairs.

Seated crossed leg on the bed, Diane sipped on something Beauty called blue juice, listening but not hearing a word he said. She set the cup on his dresser and laid back with her feet touching the floor.

"I'm zooted as fuck. Man, that's some good weed, or maybe it's all the shit I've been taking since I got here."

Diane closed her eyes and dozed off. After a few minutes, Beauty placed his hands on her knees and spread her legs. Diane was too high and comfortable to move.

"Beauty, what you doing? We're supposed to be talking about school, life, and other shit. Come up here and let's talk some philosophical shit."

He said nothing, just pulled her tights down and panties to the side. He leaned forward covered her clit and sucked. Diane tried to close her legs but Beauty held them apart with such force one move and they'd break. The sucking sound, along with the flick of his tongue, had her middle clenching.

"I'm not supposed to fuck anybody for the next seven days. I promised him. Uhhhh shit. Fuck nigga. Who taught you how to eat, naw suck a pussy like that?"

Relaxed Diane gave in and allowed her orgasm to build.

"Beauty. Shit. We shouldn't."

He still said nothing, just slurped harder. The orgasm sent chills through her body.

Jared noticed Kim sitting on the couch talking to some dark, short nigga, but he didn't see Diane. He walked over and with a nod of his head.

"Sup. Kim, where's your girl?"

He noticed Kim's eyes were half closed. She was gone gone.

"Daine downstairs with that nigga. She calls him Beauty because she said that nigga is beautiful."

Jared didn't like the smile on her face or the twinkle in her eyes.

"Alright, good looking out."

He turned to the dude, hugged up next to her.

"Can you chill with her until I get back? I want to make sure her and my girl leave together."

Not waiting for an answer, Jared made his way across the room and down the stairs. He saw Kenny, made eye contact, and threw his head in Kim's direction. Kenny nodded back and made his way to her. At the bottom of the stairs, Jared saw three doors, but only one had a light shining through the cracks. He walked over, prepared to fuck a nigga up. He pushed the door open so hard it banged against the wall. Diane laid halfway on the bed with that nigga Chris's face first in her pussy knocked out. Jared shook his head and blew out a loud breath in disappointment. He tried to calm himself down so he wouldn't catch a charge for murder. Jared had to remember she's not his, but she made a fucking promise. He flexed his fist, got his emotions in check and prepared to take her home. Before he made the next step, Jared heard Diane mumble.

"I promised him seven days. I can't fuck you cause I promised him seven days."

In that instance, his entire mood changed a little. She remembered him. High as fuck, she remembered. After a few moments, he wondered, "If she remembered then why this I nigga had his face in her pussy?"

He walked over and grabbed the dude by the collar and yanked him from between her legs. Chris fell back on the floor. He turned on his stomach and dozed off without opening his eyes. Jared walked in the bathroom coming back with a soapy washcloth and cleaned between Diane's legs. He pulled her skirt down while he helped her to her feet. Diane lifted her head.

"That's so fucking good, but I can't. I promised him seven days, and I didn't have any condoms. I forgot to bring any."

Jared's blood pumped in his chest and wanted to jump up and down. She didn't want to fuck this nigga and even high remembered her promise. Upright now Jared grabbed her face.

"Diane it's me Jared."

"Jared?"

"Yeah, it's me."

"I kept my promise?" She smiled with that same goofy smile Kim had.

"Yeah, baby, you kept your promise. Come on, Kim's upstairs. I'm going to help you up and take y'all home."

"Okay."

Jared and Kenny got Kim and Diane in his car and drove them back to the Towers. Kim's a smiling, giggling mess and Diane's, half in and half out of it of consciousness, mumbling random shit. In front of the West Tower, Jared got Diane out of the car, picked her up, and carried her to the elevators. Kenny helped Kim since she's able to walk. He picked up on the attraction between the two, but that's his boy's business.

Laying Diane on her bed, he took off her shoes and undressed her. He walked to the bathroom and then the fridge grabbing two bottled waters. Jared lifted Diane's head, gave her two Advil, and made her drink the entire bottle. He sat the second on the dresser. Once he had her covered, he walked to Kim's door to see if his boy's ready. Before he could knock, he heard the bed knocking against the wall and Kim.

"Damn nigga, you going deep."

Jared shook his head, turned back around, and got into bed with Diane. He realized he'd have to look out for Diane for the next seven days as much as possible. Homecoming is a reckless time at Howard and everybody partakes in the destructive behavior. Kim and Diane quickly fell into that category.

Diane woke up with a full bladder and a sore body. It was the combination of hard partying and church sex with Jared. After handling her business and washing her hands, she popped two Advil and sipped water from the sink. She stretched as she walked back toward her room. Diane knocked on Kim's door.

"Wake up hoe! We got class. We can't fuck up. It's midterms. I'll be back in five minutes."

She heard Kim grunt loudly through the door.

"Why you so loud early in the morning?"

Diane laughed as she headed back in her room. She noticed a lump in her bed as Jared lifted his head, looking up at her.

"What are you doing here? Not that I mind, but I can't remember shit."

Jared explained how they arrived at this point as Diane walked around the room packing her crossbody and getting her outfit for the day together.

"Thank you, Jared, and I'm really sorry about how you found me. I was out of it and never would lie to you or purposely break a promise."

"Yeah, I get it. It's homecoming."

Diane paused surprised he wasn't upset. She admired his lean body and tatts.

"So I need to get ready for class. You trying to take a shower with me? One less thing to do when you get back to your room to get ready?"

Jared got up and wrapped himself around Diane. "We may not have time for fucking, but can you slob on this knob as a physical apology?"

"Nigga, da fuck. We got time. I'm about to snatch yo soul."

She had been surprised. Diane made it to class at 11:20 had a weed hangover and hunger pangs. Both are a bitch. Weed hangover's left you high adjacent, lethargic, and nauseated. There's also the urge to throw up, but only gags ever came. An alcohol hangover, you'd throw up and be ready to go in an hour with proper hydration. A weed hangover, you just had to wait that bitch out. Diane needed sleep, but it'd have to wait until after class. She realized as she sat at her desk that Jared's boy woke Kim up by blowing her back out, and she wasn't mad at it.

Chapter 9

After class, Diane headed to the cafe. She needed some food, bad as hell. She almost lost it in her Shakespeare class. How the fuck can a class be boring and exciting at the same damn time? After drinking some ginger ale, taking an Advil, and some water, Diane felt much better. She got all of her Chickfila down and headed to Starbucks for some coffee before her poetry class started and maybe a nap. That should be enough to enjoy the fashion show tonight and hit another party afterward.

Coffee in hand, Diane headed out of the Starbucks. Just as she passed the tables outside, she heard someone speaking to her.

"You must be real smart. Your bag look heavy as fuck wit yo fine ass."

Not wanting to be bothered because she was tired and most locals, she learned, didn't receive no very well. She turned around and smirked at the skinny chocolate drop, smiling up at her.

"Why is it that lil skinny niggas gotta challenge the big girl?"

She lifted her right eyebrow. He chuckled.

"Yeah, I may be skinny but ain't shit about me little. It ain't about no challenge either. You fine as fuck and I'm trying to dig your guts out. Where yo country sounding ass from anyway?"

Diane's tired as hell, but this little nigga talked mad shit. Her Yoni screamed

"Fuck him, bitch!"

"Does it matter?"

"Not really. So what you bout to do?"

"I'm about to drink my coffee and then get fucked by you."

"Is that right?" Diane eyed him up and down. Maybe he'd fuck shit up. The regret of lying to Jared would be dealt with later. Shit, it was homecoming and technically she's single. She hoped this skinny nigga didn't gas her up for a poor performance. Nodding her head toward the Towers, the chocolate drop got up and started walking with her. Diane observed him checking out his surroundings as they entered the courtyard at the front of the building.

It's crowded because of the time of year, there are a lot of celebrations around campus. People visiting, walking in buildings to get a glimpse into Howard's culture to see if it lived up to the hype. Chocolate Drop remained quiet until they got on the elevator.

"Yall some high flaunting niggas in here. I ain't mad at it, though. Everybody got a hustle, some just legal in the eyes of the law."

Diane sipped on her coffee and allowed him to process his emotions. She learned that when people are in unfamiliar situations, they had to build up the mental confidence to justify why they belonged.

"I feel you. They're a lot of crooks in the government, but they never get caught since they have the power to write the laws to make it legal. Weed became profitable without killing a bunch of white folks. They started smoking that shit heavy, liked it, and looked at what happened. That shit is legal in almost every state."

He grabbed Diane by the neck and pulled her to him. He licked her bottom lip and then bit it hard enough to sting.

"Yeah momma, I'm digging them guts out real good."

He stepped off the elevator when it opened and waited. Diane walked to her door. When she walked past him she looked him up and down again.

"Yeah Big. Dick. Energy."

Diane sat her coffee and crossbody on the desk while asking Chocolate Drop if he wanted something to drink. He came up behind her and wrapped his hand around her waist, cupping her stomach.

"Yeah, I'll take something to drink."

He got down to his knees, bringing her leggings and panties with him. Diane fell over when he pushed on her back. She reached for the seat of the futon as Chocolate Drop buried his face in her from behind.

"Ah fuck nigga!"

He parted her lips with his thumbs and pushed his face in deeper.

"Shit."

Diane pushed back and moaned as his tongue worked her over. He slapped and jiggled her thighs as he shook his face from side to side. Diane's knees buckled as she came.

"Shit! Nigga!"

Her pussy and clit throbbed as he continued to slap her thighs, which heighten the sensations rolling through her body. Chocolate Drop lifted her right leg, then left. He placed her thigh on his shoulder as he scooted closer to her entrance. Diane was down for whatever the hell this nigga did to her. Once settled on his shoulder, he kept a firm grip on the back of her thighs and dove back in. He sucked on her clit from behind as his nose buried itself in her canal. After a few minutes, another orgasm rose and her juices drenched his face. Chocolate Drop licked from her clit to her ass and back. After the third swipe. Diane grind on his face, urging her another orgasm to come, but he had other plans. Chocolate Drop stuck his tongue in her ass.

"Lawd, this nigga nasty."

He tongue fucked her hole, which felt amazing. She's shocked that ass play caused her clit to jump. Afraid to fall, she maintained her hold on the futon instead of stimulating her clit. He eventually moved back to her pearl, latched on, and she exploded.

Raising his head from between her legs. He licked his lips.

"Damn girl, that pussy is slushy, sticky sweet, and gushy."

He gently placed her on her feet as he got up. Diane tried to gain her composure because she intended to give him the best head he ever had, but before she had a chance to move, the head of his condom-covered dick tapped her entrance.

"Hold tight momma, Imma give you this dick. I just need to wet this condom up."

As he moved his dick up and down using her juices. His thumbs and parted her lips.

"Damn your lips, thick as shit. A nigga like me? Girl, I'd suck them mutha fuckers all day."

Chocolate Drop opened her up and slid in. He's not as thick as Jared, but his long dick knocked against her walls as he stroke in a circular motion.

"Fuuuuck!" Diane screamed as she squirted for the first time. "Holy shit, what the fuck!"

"You welcome." He said as he power drove in and out as an orgasm followed the squirting session she just had.

Exhaustion hit her body after Chocolate Drop released his load in the condom. She laid on the futon, watched him discard the condom, pull up his pants, and walked out of her room. She reached for her phone, set the alarm and closed her eyes.

Refreshed from her nap, a shower and the sex session with Chocolate Drop, Diane threw on a pair of jeans and a blue Howard sweatshirt with her Atoms. She made it just in time for class. On her way, she sent Kim a text about foregoing the fashion show and attending a kickback instead. Between studying for exams, writing papers, classes, and partying, she hadn't had a full eight hours of sleep since the start of homecoming. Diane figured she could catch up on sleep during Thanksgiving break.

Resto loved this time of year. It's both crazy and exciting for professors and students alike. The students tried to enjoy homecoming as they prepared for midterms. Professors tried to ensure the students remained on schedule by accepting some late papers and eased up the scoring on exams so they'd be able to return for the next semester. Resto saw Diane in the classroom.

"She looked fucking fantastic!"

She had sides of her hair freshly shaven, and the top colored a deep red. Her face seemed different. It had a glow to her like she'd been pausing, he tilted his head, then noticed it. The anger surfaced as he wondered who she'd fucked! He huffed a breath and pinched the bridge of his nose. He walked in and began writing on the board.

Diane suffered painfully in silence in poetry class. It seemed as if half her classmates had the same affliction. The other half didn't bother to show up.

"Sleep after a soak in the tub would be so clutch right now."

She hadn't realized she moaned while stretching until the class started laughing.

"Rough night Ms. Diane?" Professor Resto said, looking at her in the weird way he did.

"My apologies. I haven't been getting much sleep. Writing papers and studying for midterms. You know."

"You sure that's all it is?" Resto asked as one of the students coughed out.

"Got that back blown out." The entire class, including Diane, erupted in laughter.

"Just playing Diane. It's all love."

She shrugged at the guy Keith, she believed. "It's all good."

"Okay, can we get back to what we are in here to actually do? Learn."

Resto spoke to the class, but his eyes stayed on Diane, which is where they stayed the remainder of class.

The door slammed so hard he thought he'd taken it off the hinges. He didn't care. Pissed by the comment and that smile she gave that guy, told him and the entire class that his statement was fact.

"Who. Is. She. Fucking!"

He grabbed three beers out of the fridge, opened all three and guzzled them one after the other. His shakes were out of control and he needed to take his anger out on someone, and doing so in his dreams wasn't enough.

Resto picked up his phone. He sent a text, grabbed another beer, popped the top, and headed to the shower. Extreme anger called for extreme play.

Freshly showered and calmer, Resto walked to the door opening it as the bell rang.

"Your name is Diane."

She walked in and nodded in understanding. Happy to see she'd follow his instructions and even had her long mane in a makeshift mohawk, just like her. Her skin color is a few shades darker. She's slightly smaller than Diane, but a great substitution. Smiling, he traced the back of his hand down her cheek, grabbed her by the throat and placed a gentle kiss on her lips. He played with the kinky coils, then gripped tightly as he yanked "Diane" by her hair and pulled her toward the bedroom. She yelped slightly and hurried her steps. Resto threw her toward the bed. She bounced slightly as he watched and imagine Diane with that guy. He paced to calm the oncoming shakes.

"The guy I saw you with on the yard?"

"Diane" seemed confused. "I don't know what you mean?"

"Don't. Lie. To. Me."

He removed the jeans and the Howard sweatshirt off her gorgeous ass body. She had on a lace bra and panty set in the same color as her sweatshirt. Blue.

He kneeled on the bed, tied her hands together above her head. Resto saw the woman wanted to smile. Her arousal invaded his senses. She loved it but stayed in character. He flipped her over taking off his belt and waited.

"Did. You. Fuck. Him?"

"No."

Resto came down on her buttocks. Whack! Whack! Whack! The welts bloom on her ass. Satisfied, he used a pair of scissors and cut up the sides of her panties and bra. Resto leaned forward and licked between the crevice of her ass.

"Please stop. I did nothing. I only want you."

Smack! He slapped her ass hard as he continued to lick in between them. She didn't move a muscle. In fact, she relaxed into the sheets. He parted her cheeks and continued his assault on her ass as he noted her glistening pussy.

"Naughty girl. You're fucking soaked."

Diane turned to him. "I swear I haven't been with anyone."

Excitement bubbled in his gut as she uttered those words. He lightly slapped across her back to buttocks.

"Liar."

Smack! Smack! Smack! Even though she didn't have that toffee color skin as Diane her face did not disappoint, she was fucking gorgeous.

"What's the matter 'Diane'? You're not afraid to get fucked after you let that guy fucked you, are you? What's his name?"

He pursued her body and couldn't resist pushing his index finger in her ass to the knuckle. She moaned.

"Ah yes, Christopher, fuck you so hard you barely kept it together in class today. Is that why he asked to sit in? Some kind of foreplay for you two? Huh?"

She took too long, and he came down on her face again.

"Answer me." Satisfied with the fear and tears in her eyes, Resto's dick hardened.

"Yes." She whimpered. Gently, he flipped her on her back. She closed her eyes tight as he pinched and caressed her nipples.

"You like that? You fucking slut?"

He squeezed harder to get her attention.

"Ahhh. Yes."

He took a deep inhale. That's what he wanted. The fear needed to be greater than the arousal. The more her fear increased, the more his arousal increased.

Resto leaned down, took her nipple in his mouth, and suckled. He tugged on the other. Every time she moaned, he pinched hard until she cried out in pain. Punishment for fucking Christopher.

"You're hurting me."

"You hurt me first." Resto rotated, suckling each nipple like receiving milk from her breast until his dick got hard as a brick, almost bursting. He saw both his mother and Diane using their names interchangeably.

"Mama," he said as he licked down her stomach to her pelvis. "I called you. Mama? You hear me?"

"Yes. I hear you Hijo."

"I want to suck your pussy. Can I suck your pussy, mama?

"Si Hijo."

"Will you tell me if I'm doing it right?"

The tears were streaming down her face. Perfect. Fear in her eyes and the wetness between her legs. Amazing. "Spread them." She spread her legs, but not enough. Whack! His came down on her leg and she spread them farther.

"Is this how you spread them for Christopher?"

She nodded. Whack! "Use your words, Diane."

She whimpered "Yes." Fingers glided down her center. He parted her folds and licked, suck, and fuck her with his tongue.

He didn't know how long he ate her out, but "Diane" had at least three orgasms. He was ravenous for her, only stopping because he wanted to be inside her. Resto couldn't wait any longer.

"Diane, you taste so good. Are you okay?" He rose and laid on top of her.

"Oh Diane, I've wanted this since the first moment I laid eyes on you. Did you enjoy it, my love?"

"Yes."

Resto kissed her softly on the lips as he inserted his tongue. "Fuck mama, you taste so fucking good. You ready to give your Hijo that pussy?"

"Si me Nino." Moving her up the bed so her head and shoulders resting on the headboard, Resto got on his knees, tracing her lips with his fingers.

"Open." She did. "Mama, you ready?"

"Si Nino."

Sliding his dick in, he fucked her mouth. Diane pumped back and forth on his dick as he increased the pace.

"Fuck Mama, you feel so good. Can you suck harder?"

He said in a childlike voice as she complied.

"Fuck. Bueno Mama."

He pumped in and out her mouth. She gripped him like a lollipop. Clasping his hand behind her head with her hands still tied above her, he pumped harder and grind into her to the back of her throat. "Mama" gagged on his dick, but he didn't stop. She continued to gag, and the tears flowed more freely.

"Ah, Mama can't handle this dick?"

Even though she couldn't speak, he expected an answer.

When she didn't respond, he pulled out and got up. Resto walked into the bathroom, grabbed a warm cloth and cleaned her mouth and his dick. He placed her into the prone position. It had to be uncomfortable, hands tied above her, being moved around and used, but he didn't care. She deserved it for leaving him.

"Mama, I want to feel where I came from."

She looked up at him confused.

"I need to be back in your warm cocoon."

She played along. She needed to get paid and Resto paid well. Resto's proclivities are weird as hell, but so were a lot of her clients. He got a hold of her ankle and slowly pushed them up to her waist. Just below her lush stomach, her protruding pussy shined up at him. He gave her a condom earlier. He surged his condom covered dick forward, entering her pussy with ease.

"Oh my god, Mama. You feel so good, just like I thought you would. Why did you leave me before you let me have you?"

Not looking for a response, she didn't give one. He had his eyes closed and he fuck "Mama" reveling in the softness of her folds.

His dick was warm and cocooned in her pussy as he forced himself not to cum. He reminisced about all the times since he was fifteen years old. He couldn't have this in real life, but role play was fine. The Oedipus complex was her fault. The deeper he sank, the angrier he became. Resto grabbed her neck.

"Keep your legs up."

She quickly raised her legs. “That’s the least you could after leaving me. Why did you leave me “Mama”? I was a good boy and always did what Abuela told me.” Pound. Pound. Pound.

“Fuck Mama, I’ve dreamed of this pussy since I was fifteen and now you give so willingly. Why wasn’t I good enough back then?”

He pushed deeper pausing in her as his grip tightened around her neck. She tried to remain calm as she forced out shallow breaths, and he continued his assault.

“Ah fuck. “Mama” you feeling so fucking good.” Pound. Pound. Pound “I’m going to cum in you Mama, is that okay?”

“Si.’ After he realized she had difficulty breathing, he eased up on her neck but continued to push into her. Resto’s orgasm crawled up his spine, he grabbed her legs again, and pushed one last time. He released in the condom.

On his knees, he smiled down at her.

“I’ll pay you an extra $500 to lie with me for thirty more minutes.”

Nodding, he removed the tie from her hands and flopped down on top of her, exhausted. He rubbed up and down “Diane’s” arm, he wondered how he could find Christopher.

Chapter 10

Christopher has been throwing parties at Howard since freshman year. He and his roommates needed a way to make extra money. They invited a few people provided drinks and music, it just popped off from there. Howard is going to be missed, but it's almost time to move on. He had few regrets but the most recent one he wanted to rectify before the end of the week. Diane is fine as fuck and confident with who she is as a larger woman. He wanted to get with her a few more times before the end of the semester. Christopher was high as fuck and missed his chance to enjoy her like he'd wanted. He hoped she would want to chill with him to make up for passing out in her pussy. They were both fucked up. He didn't have her number to call her, but he did remember she live in the Towers. Christopher decided to walk home from the iLab to combat all the drinking and smoking he'd been doing. A light jacket was enough to have him straight. Daylight savings didn't matter at this hour, it's dark as fuck but not too cold. Turning right at the corner, he had another two blocks before he made it home. It was around midnight and the streets were deserted.

Laughing to himself, he figured everybody was hungover or locked away studying and writing papers. Tired and hungry, he was going to eat, get a shower, and a nap before pulling another all-nighter. It was fucked up how midterms fell during homecoming every fucking year. It's as if the school wanted you to become a fifth-year senior for the extra coins.

"Fuck, I can't wait for midterms to be over."

Stepping past the alley, Chris felt eyes on him. He shook it off, assuming it was sleep deprivation that had him paranoid. DC is gentrified now, and he was cool with the locals in the area so he knew he'd be good.

As he passed the alley, he made it to the last block. He saw his place in front of him. But before he could take the first step, "Whack" a hard object crashed over his head. Turning to fight and find out what happened, Chris got another hard hit on the left side of his face. His cheek split and what he assumed was blood ran down his neck. His attacker was covered in a mask and hoodie so he couldn't see who the fuck it was, but he was determined to fuck the nigga up as much as possible. He focused on drilling his attacker with body blows instead of trying to reveal his identity but he was no match for the mini Louisville Slugger that was putting in work over his head, neck and back.

The attacker was strong, fast, and manic with the way he swung the bat repeatedly. Christopher's body jerked as he got rocked. Whack. Jerk. Whack. Jerk. Whack. He continued his assault until Christopher slumped over in a heap a few steps away from his house. The attacker looked around to make sure he wasn't seen and then continued to hit Christopher on his back and head. He didn't want to kill him but teach a fucking lesson he'd never forget. He continued to hit Christopher repeatedly, harder and harder with "Diane." Yes, he named his weapon of choice after his obsession. Why? She causes him pain, she's going to cause everyone pain. "Diane" had a wrist attachment and swung loosely from the assailant's wrist. He swung it as if I weighed nothing when in actuality it weighed about four or five pounds.

He'd drill a hole in the base and fill it with a mixture of steel pellets and cement in the middle to give a heavier weight to it. Just like Diane.

Snapped out of his thoughts, he realized he'd been there too long and Chris was no longer resisting. He checked his pulse to make sure he was still breathing. He turned and ran deeper into the alley.

Back in the safety of his car, he removed the hoodie and mask, closing his eyes and reveling in the memory of that first crack. It got his adrenaline pumping. *"Diane" slammed across the side of Christopher's face. He watched the motion of the blood squirt and traveled down his neck. The assailant took a deep breath. He inhaled the metallic smell of blood.* Christopher is kind of a big dude, so it took a few more blows to handle him, but that nigga got handled.

He never wanted to resort to this, but she was it for him and he would have her. He had one last thought before starting his car and pulling away from the street.

"Diane and my mother are alike in a lot of ways, but unlike my mother, Diane is staying in my life. Until the rims hit the road."

Chapter 11

The door opened to a beaming Jared with a big ass bag that had the aroma of greasy goodness inside. It was noon, Diane had a midterm exam, a paper to finish, and an hour study session. She and Kim got in late. Even though she didn't overdo it last night, Diane was hella hungry and appreciated Jared thinking of her. They decided to forego the fashion show but went to the afterparty. Jared texted her nonstop this morning ruining the few hours of sleep she tried to fit in. Kim and her held it the fuck down last night. Diane smiled at the thought.

Kim and Diane had developed a close friendship over the few months they'd been roommates. They looked out for each other, listened, cried, and studied together. Even discussed getting an apartment together after college since they both wanted to stay in the area after graduation. They had a lot in common and bonded over those commonalities.

Kim is a relationship kind of girl and didn't want to get "it" out of her system before finding "the one." She'd been kicking it hard with Jared's line brother. Diane hadn't remembered his name, but she referred to him as "Ginger." He had fiery reddish hair with freckles all over his body, according to Kim, and his skin was light bright, damn near white. Ginger loved saying he was Blackity Black Black, but somewhere down the line she and Kim decided some leprechauns lurked behind the bushes of his family tree.

Jared placed the bag on the kitchen counter and opened the fridge with one hand while responding to a text with the other.

"What you drinking? Juice, coffee, or water?"

"Coffee. I hope you brought enough for Kim? She'll probably be hungry."

"Yeah, that's who I just texting. My boy in her room. This nigga said he had to end his night with his face buried in her neck." Diane laughed.

"They need to keep that lovey dovey shit ovea there."

Jared's smile faltered, but he shook it off as Kim's door opened and she and Ginger walked out, looking well fucked, and turned out. Diane smiled. Even though she didn't want a relationship now, she's happy her girl was getting what she wanted.

"Morning. Jared got us breakfast."

All of them gathered in Diane's room, since it was the largest. They ate in silence enjoying the wings and fries with mambo sauce. Halfway through the meal Ginger and Jared started this weird communication thing with their eyes. They looked from Diane to each other and back again.

"Okay, what the fuck y'all looking at my girl like that for? Please don't let me have to go fuck somebody up."

Kim said in a frustrated tone that made Diane proud. She leaned over and touched Kim's forearm.

"Oh friend, that's so sweet. I would kill a nigga behind you, too."

With eyebrows raised both looked from Jared to Ginger, waiting for one of them to respond.

"That's your girl, nigga, you tell her."

Ginger said as he shrugged at Jared. Jared frowned at Kenny then focused on his phone. Diane was two seconds from going off when Jared turned to her. Taking the phone Diane saw it was his Kappa's group chat.

There had been a posted about a student that was attacked last night in front of his home. Diane didn't react until Jared told her the name of the student.

"Christopher, that dude who had the party at the beginning of the week."

He nervously looked at Ginger then back at Diane.

"The one who let you lie down when you got dizzy. In the basement."

Jared cringed at the thought of how he found her but recovered quickly. Diane looked at him with her mouth agape, tears brimming in her eyes. She rose and fast walked to the bathroom before anyone stopped her.

Once in the bathroom, Diane tried to calm her stomach from rolling. Tears streamed down her face as she lifted the toilet seat regurgitating everything she'd just eaten. It continued even when her stomach was empty. The dry heaves wreak havoc on her body but she didn't know how to stop it.

"Beauty? Christopher? Who would do something like this to him?"

Diane didn't know him well, but he seemed like a decent guy. Closing the lid to the toilet and rinsing her mouth she sat on the floor and cried.

Diane owed Kim big time. She got Ginger and Jared to leave before she exited the bathroom. It allowed her the time she needed to process what she'd heard. It was more difficult than she imagined. She pulled it together and made it to class on time. Diane and Beauty only fucked, however, the thought of someone she experienced intimately being beaten to within an inch of their life. It was hard to come to terms with. In the bathroom, she decided not to go anywhere tonight. She couldn't. Diane grabbed her bag and headed to class.

Resto would have to address what happened the other day. It was all over social media and the news. Even though the attack took place off campus, the school sent out a memo requesting that each Professor stress the importance of walking in pairs, being aware of your surroundings, and keeping your cell fully charged for emergencies. These kids kept their phones charged just enough to plug them in at their next destination. He didn't feel bad for Christopher. Resto felt vindicated. He was too close to her, slept with her. Their body language told him that much and justice had been served.

Students rushed out of class, probably heading back to their rooms to get some rest before the next party. It was poetry night, the excitement showed in class today. The students were full of questions. It reminded him why he chose this profession while pursuing his passion. Resto looked up as Diane passed his desk.

"Diane, can you meet me in my office before you head to your next class?"

Resto tried to gauge her emotional state. "I don't have a class after this one so I'm good."

She half smiled. His dick jerked at the thought of having some uninterrupted time with her.

She waited, and they walked out together to his office. Resto strode over and took a seat at his table. He asked her to close the door. Resto knew he was taking a risk, but it was a risk he wanted to take if it meant getting closer to her.

"Hi Professor Resto. Did I miss an assignment or did I do that badly on my midterm?"

She smirked, knowing she was one of the top students in his class.

"No, you're doing really well in my class. I just wanted to ask you how you were doing with the news of your friend. I'm assuming you two knew each other pretty well?"

He probably knows what you taste like. Resto thought, as he felt his anger rising. He remembered his competition, if you want to call it that, is lying at Howard University Hospital (HUH) near death or recuperating. Resto didn't care which, as long as he wasn't an obstacle anymore.

He shook out of his thoughts and focused on Diane as she spoke.

"Yeah, it's sad what happened to him. I met him at a party and we hung out a bit. He was, is, a really nice guy."

She quickly corrected. "I'm going to see if I can see him later. If he can have visitors. I don't know why or if I should care. We weren't really friends. Fuck buddies, but not friends. I mean, we hooked up like twice, well, kinda twice. I don't know. I guess I'm doing okay. Sorry, I'm rambling."

Resto watched and listened as Diane spoke more to herself than him. The range of emotions she was going through told him she was still processing. He didn't like that she'd admitted she'd fucked him. He wanted to take her to his house and punish her for it, but he had to remember his long-term plan, to have her forever. She smiled down at him and his anger dissipated, just like that.

"Sorry again for rambling. I don't know how I should feel. I know him physically and the little I know mentally was okay, but not enough to act like the grieving girlfriend. You know?"

Resto wanted to comfort her at that moment, but he had to remain the concerned Professor. "Just know you are allowed to feel what you need to process this. I just want you know if you need extra time because of it, you can come to me. Maybe a classmate. If you're more comfortable with that?"

She looked so vulnerable with minimal makeup, worry lines on her forehead, and that mouth. That pouty fucking dick-swallowing mouth.

"Professor being an adult in college, it's difficult trying to convey your emotions to kids who have had no lived experiences."

She sat at the table across from him. With her head held down, she asked.

"Would it be okay to chat with you via our poetry Facebook group? Just us? Sometimes I feel like no one gets who or how I am. Probably not, though. You'd probably think I was psycho or something."

Resto reached out and lifted her head by the chin with his index and thumb. He gently stroked her cheek where a tear had fallen. He felt pre-cum gather at the tip of his dick in his pants as sensations by his touch control his body. Their eyes met, and he wanted so badly to bury himself in her mouth. Her time was coming and he could only imagine how wonderful it would be to have her. Resto removed his hand.

"I think it'd be okay for you to message me if you need someone to talk to."

Diane thanked him as she rose. "Well, I've taken up enough of your time. Thank you again. This meant a lot."

Diane said as she walked to the door, opened it, and walked out.

Resto squeezed and released the need in his dick until it went down so he could make it to his next class.

Down the steps of COAS, Diane headed to HUH before going to her room and settling in. As she walked down the hill, she thought of Professor Resto and how kind it was that he was worried about her. She couldn't lie to herself; he was a very attractive man. If given the opportunity, she would pop her pussy for the Professor's fine ass.

Diane also thought about Jared and how sweet he had been to her the past few months, even knowing she was not ready to commit. It confused her with how much of himself he'd been giving so selflessly knowing she was with other men. Maybe it was hard for Diane to commit because she didn't know what it was like to feel supported and cared for by anyone. How could she give something to someone that she herself never received? With Beauty in the hospital and the Professor being so concerned, Diane felt out of sorts. A smoke session later is exactly what she needed after the day she had.

The closer she got to the hospital, the more on edge she became. What little she knew of Beauty she liked, but if she was being honest with herself, he was nothing more than an amazing fuck. Maybe a part of her felt guilty about that because deep down he was a means to an orgasmic end.

Diane rushed to the elevator after she'd lied to the register nurse to get Christopher's room number. Stepping of the elevator on the fourth floor, she opened the door slightly. Diane released a breath as Beauty turned toward her and smiled. Well, smiled as much as he could through all the swelling. She smiled and walk toward the bed, leaned down, and kissed his forehead. That seemed to be the only place with little to no damage. Head bandaged, face swollen, Christopher's eyes were bright and alive. Both arms were in casts and his ribs wrapped as if he was being mummified.

"Hey, Beauty. How you feeling?"

He whispered, "I can't talk very loud, but I'm doing okay, considering. I'm glad you came to see me. A nigga missing you for real."

Diane's chest ached from relief. He sounded happy and like the Beauty she knew. Well, what she knew of him.

"Do they know who did this to you?"

"No, I couldn't tell the police much. The mutha fucker had a mask on and a hoodie pulled over his head. He snuck up behind me and beat my Black ass like I kicked his dog."

His eyes shine a little with wetness. "I didn't have a beef with anyone. I'm not that type of dude. I'm just as confused as my friends and family. The shit was just random as fuck."

Diane felt horrible for him. She did a bit of asking around when this happened and everyone confirmed what Chris had said. He wasn't the type of guy to cause trouble, or did anything that would jeopardize the trajectory for his life. They were more alike than she cared to admit because if this could happen to him, who's to say she or someone else wouldn't be next?

"The police seem to think it's a local that just doesn't like the college kids living in the area. I'm thinking that could be it. You know how these locals are."

Diane smiled and responded "Yeah." Out of sorts and not liking it she wanted to change the mood, and she knew it'd be a boost to Beauty's spirit.

"Hey, you leaving?" Christopher whispered yell as Diane walked to the door.

"No."

She said, turning the lock. The confused look on Christopher's face caused her to giggle. She could sense his uneasiness. This attack had rightfully rattled him. In an attempt to calm his fear, she walked back to the bed, pulled the sheet that was at his waist down.

"Baby, I'm going to help you escape."

She was grateful he didn't have on any underwear and that the beating did not affect his lower regions.

"Baby, try not to do any additional damage by moving." Chris realized what Diane was about to do and his dick jumped. "After this, you're going to start calling me Hoover."

Diane pressed her lips to the tip of his dick and opened her mouth slowly as she slid down, giving the "bussing the pussy open" effect on his dick.

"Fuuuck. Got damn girl."

Beauty whispered. He attempted to lift his hips and failed because of the apparent pain it caused. She swallowed all the way to the base, nearly gagging, he deserved it so she didn't stop and let the tears flowed as she closed her lips tighter when he reached the back of her throat. Diane sucked like she had a firecracker popsicle in her mouth.

She bobbed up and down like a jack hammered on his dick. Diane's eyes watered, her neck hurt and she thought she'd throw up and ruin the moment. She bobbed up and down for about five minutes, her jaws flamed. Chris was about to blow. Diane jacked the rest of him with her hands. She took one long, tight suck to the tip of his dick.

"Oh, my muthafucking gawd girl. You trying to finish what the nig-ggg..."

He couldn't complete the sentence as came down her throat.. Moving down further on his dick, she swallowed it all like a good girl.

Diane kept Christopher company for about two and a half hours and in that time she learned so much about him. Not only was her nickname for him fit his appearance, but it also matched his personality. Too bad she wouldn't enjoy more of him. He explained his parents wanted him to return to California to heal and finish his degree at UC Berkeley.

Homecoming

Diane and Kim sat on the futon in her room, lighting a J. Kim had on her Onesie, and Diane remained wrapped in a towel after a long, hot shower. She'd given Kim the run down before getting ready for poetry night being held in the Student Center in one of the many ballrooms. Both of them are on the fence about going.

After a couple of puffs of the J, Diane loosened up and told Kim about her Professor reaching out and how she wanted low-key shoot her shot. Kim heard of Professor Resto and fully supported Diane's pursuit of him. Her rationale was the same as Diane's. She was an adult, and he was fine as fuck. There's a mutual attraction, but do it after the semester ended. She didn't want to be accused of fucking for grades. By the time they were on their second joint and split an edible, Kim chatted up Professor Resto on Facebook chat while Diane dictated what to say.

The messages were flirty, funny and not too serious. As long as he engages they continued to converse. At the end he asked for Diane's phone number, which Kim happily supplied. They decided on similar outfits for the event. Sweaters that came mid-thigh with leggings. Kim opted for booties with three-inch heels. Diane decided on a pair of thigh-high boots with a two-inch heel. She was already high and didn't want to embarrass herself trying to be cute.

"You think Jared is going to be there?"

"I'm not sure. I haven't spoken to him since this morning. What about Ginger?"

"Same, but I'm sure he'll come over after."

"Yeah Sis. Keep that love shit in the room next door. I don't want that kind of energy right now. And before you say anything, yes, I care for Jared. Yes, I really like him, and yes, I would love to entertain a relationship with him. Just not right now. Now thank me for being honest with a nigga instead of leading him on and bringing a bunch of drama into the process."

Kim nodded "Thank you."

"You welcome. Now let's go."

The shuttle was in front of the Towers when the ladies walked onto the courtyard. It was a beautiful night on the yard but chilly. Walking in the Ballroom they spotted Alyssa and Jennifer. Two chairs were available, so they sat together. Jennifer passed around a ziplock that had gummies and they each ate a half of one. California edibles hit differently than the East Coast stuff. They wanted to chase a high not an ER visit.

"Please try to remember to send me your location cause Bitch I don't know if I will remember to send you mine."

Kim looked at Diane and they both burst out into laughter which caused Alyssa and Jennifer to do the same while not having a clue why they were laughing.

Jennifer was rocking a sweater, dress, and leggings. Alyssa had on a long-sleeved bodysuit. They were getting attention from both sexes and seemed totally oblivious, as if it was a natural occurrence. Kim and Diane weren't insecure women, but no one would check for them with those two close by.

The ladies had to have known they were gorgeous but were the most down-to-earth people Diane had met. The competition and cattiness could be toxic as fuck, at an HBCU, but with these two, and Kim, Diane, never picked up on that type of energy. All the ladies sat near the rear as a backup in case the event was too long or boring and settled in for the show.

A lot of English and music majors performed at events like these, hoping to showcase their talent for the scouts in the audience. Howard was notorious for having industry people at these events, hoping to discover the next big thing. As they should. The school's motto was "Excellence Without Excuse." It was not only the crème de la crème of wealth but also talent, regardless of economic status. Shortly after the lights lowered, Diane and the others got drowsy. Weed was, of course, weed. Standing she offered to go to the concession and bring back waters with hopefully a little pick me up in the form of Molly or Addie.

The group had an extra bounce when the first half of show ended, thanks to the Adderall. It wasn't hard to find drugs during midterms or finals. Everyone from the "Nerds" to the "Slackers" used them during intense all-night study sessions when paying attention to detail was a pass or fail. Diane didn't know if it was the drugs or her lack of interest in the current performer, but her thoughts were on Beauty and the possibility of never seeing him again. She'd heard stories of the locals in the area but never paid any attention to it, assuming it was just Uppity College Negroes being Uppity College Negroes. What she didn't get is why would a local attack Beauty?

Deep in thought she didn't notice the guy until Kim nudged her and looked up. She saw a tall, thin loc'd man standing next to her.

"Why do all men with locs and a lighter pigment look like one of Bob Marley's kids or grandkids?"

He wasn't her type physically, and she really wasn't in the mood but thinking she needed someone, anyone, to make her forget, he'd do.

"Hi, how you ladies doing this evening?"

In unison they all said, "Fine." He looked at her and extended his hand. "I'm..."

Cutting him off before he could finish "Dred. Nice to meet you."

Chuckling and shaking his head, he continued. "What you getting into after this?"

Biting her bottom lip. "The better question is who you getting into tonight?"

Alyssa, Jennifer, and Kim giggled. Diane knew it was bold, but what happened to Beauty fucked her up. Her feelings for Jared were strengthening. It was homecoming, and she was high as hell. Her way of coping was to replace uncomfortable feelings with the ones that always made her forget.

He leaned down to Diane's ear and whispered, "If you give me the chance I'd get deep in your bones."

"So your love is like the holy ghost?"

"You've never had such a feeling. Like you've been born again."

Alyssa clasp her throat. "You better sing Bar Kays!"

Kim laughed. "Jared gonna kick your ass."

Diane set her location for Kim as she stood. "He can't kick it over something he isn't aware of."

"Masochist," said Kim. "Masochism in 3, 2, 1..." Both laughed at their foolishness Crossbody in hand, Diane followed Dreds out the ballroom.

They walked back to the Towers since it was nice for fall and wanted to smoke. He was from Jamaica, but moved to the US at such a young age he lost the accent. Majoring in political science, he wanted to one day return to his home country and enter the political arena.

Diane listened to him and realized she was right; he was not her cup of tea. He was a good guy, but she picked up on a few red flags that you found in traditional patriarchal households. The combination of the Addie and weed made her feel as if she were floating mentally and physically. Diane had to pace herself to keep from toppling over. Dreds picked up on her vibe and slowed his stride as well.

"Good, he won't be selfish in bed," she thought as they reached the courtyard.

When they got to the elevator, he pushed the button for the second floor. "You have a single?"

"Yeah, I like my space and am too old to room with someone, especially if I'm unclear of their maturity level and a group of friends."

Stepping off the elevators, Dred reached for Diane's hand, which she took and guided them down to the end of the hall. He turned his head and looked down. After what felt like forever, Diane asked, "What?" Sighing while gently grabbing and massaging the back of her neck, he said, "Now I'm not in love with you, but I'm going to try my damndest to take all that shit away."

She didn't know how to respond, so she didn't.

A single is nothing like the room she and Kim shared. This nigga had a proper kitchen with a living room and a separate bedroom.

"Your room has a very different feeling than mine."

"Not the time for talking."

He said as he walked Diane into the bedroom while rubbing over her body. It felt like he had more than two hands. They were gently sweeping over her like a breeze in summer. Her head fell back on his chest. The constant stroking had Diane closing her eyes. She released a sigh thinking about Beauty, the attack he suffered, regretting not getting to know him better because she was so fucking emotionally detached and didn't know how to form a genuine connection. Then there was Jared. Sweet, honest, real Jared. Sighing again she moan when she felt his gentle caresses become something different. She was sexually aroused and emotionally depleted.

Dreds focused on her breast and stomach. The way men seem to love caressing her stomach made her feel fetishized even though they weren't. They just love big women. He continued to rub while his hands moved down to her waist. He lifted her sweater slightly and slid his hand in her leggings. Thank goodness she didn't wear panties. Dred slid his middle finger directly down and over her clit as he whispered in her ear.

"Feel everything I'm about to make you feel mentally and physically."

Why did he and Jared want her feeling shit? She felt his finger as it found its way past her clit and right to the apex of her opening. Dreds slid his middle finger up and down, rotating between fast and slow. Of its own accord, her body rocked in time to the music he was causing between them. Definitely not a selfish lover.

He stroked and stroked until her body trembled and she came. Dreds continued to learn her body with his hands. The tears were streaming down her face and she didn't know why and right now she didn't care. She just allowed herself to feel. Dreds guided her to the bed and push her back. Diane melt into the covers.

"Wait! What kind of bed do you have? This is not school-issued."

He placed a finger on her lips and Diane complied with the silent command.

Dreds stop and watched Diane as he removed all his clothing. He was on the thinner side of the male spectrum, but the Red Hot between his legs allowed her to breathe a sigh of relief. He wasn't the largest or longest, but that look told her he would be giving her something she could feel. Dreds rubbed her boot-covered feet. His hands seemed like they were skin-on-skin.

"Why don't you lay your head back and stop worrying about what I'm going to do? I'm good at my job."

"Go to work then."

His hands moved up and down from her thighs to her pussy over her leggings. She closed her eyes again and imagined it was the Professor instead of Dred. His hands applied more pressure and her leggings became a soaking mess. He continued up and down harder and harder until she burst from his hands. The constant loop on her drug induced mind was Beauty, Jared, and Professor.

Dreds placed his forehead on the bottom of her stomach and buried his face in her legging-covered pussy as he sucked. Diane lifted but didn't get far, his hands had a firm hold on her stomach. His pussy eating skills had her feeling like she was on a flotation device. Weightless. He sucked and sucked, focusing on her clit as it throbbed so hard she thought it would detach itself from her body. She didn't realize she was screaming until she crested from the orgasm as her tears continued to fall.

Diane lifted her head and smiled down at him.

"I'm going to fuck you nice and slow. Just because I'm moving at one pace, you don't have to match it. Do what you feel you need to or want to do."

Nodding, she closed her eyes and did just that.

Dred slid the shirt up and over her head. Unsnapping the bra and licking the tip of her areola before capturing it in his mouth. He used his other hand to cover her other breast and massage it into its own peak. He took his time as he moved back and forth over each breast. His hands eventually traced down to her leggings. Diane felt a cool breeze at the core of her pussy. Did he just split her legging in the middle? She realized he did exactly that. Dreds grabbed the material from the wet spot at her middle and pulled them apart until they gave, leaving her open from the waistband in the front to the elastic in the back.

The next thing she felt was his tongue working its way into her pussy. He was fucking her with his long thick tongue.

Diane grabbed his head with both hands and pressed it to her core. She faced fucked his mouth, and it was glorious. The third orgasm hit her like a bolt of lightning and she gushed all over him and herself. She laid back and tried to put her legs that she didn't realize she'd raise down, but his muscular forearms kept them in place. He moved his body so his condom-covered dick was at her now creaming pussy. She didn't bother to remember when he put it on and stopped caring as he slowly pushed into her. He forced her legs to bend to her shoulders and came close to her face, staring at her as he began to slow stroked the fuck out of her.

Diane noticed two things that night; vulnerability doesn't have to be seen as a weakness and two, a man can give you what you need sexually and you don't have to be ashamed.

As Dreds looked into her eyes as he stroked her at a languid pace, she cried. Her body was relaxed and tingling all over. Diane believe she cried because her body felt so fucking good. She caressed his cheeks and trembled as her fourth orgasm hit her at her core. This time, it was an ache in her belly as she bit her lip to hold back the soft grunt. Dreds fucked her all night in her boots, torn leggings with only her upper body exposed, into the early morning hours.

Chapter 13

Diane left Dreds' room around 6 a.m. She dressed as best as she could, stretching her sweater to cover her torn leggings. It didn't look too bad, though. The thigh-high boots helped, and she was only going to the sixth floor. She'd texted Kim earlier to confirm where she stayed and Kim was safe. Dreds walked her to the elevator and even offered to ride up, but she turned him down, knowing she'd gotten everything she needed. Diane noticed Kim's door was closed when she walked in, which meant she had company. They never closed their door unless they wanted privacy.

In her room, she turned on her desk lamp and began undressing.

"Man, where the fuck you been?"

Startling her, Jared was sitting on her bed fuming. Jared often crashed in her room when Kenny visited Kim. She didn't ask him over so he had no right questioning her. Diane had been upfront with what they were, he had also been upfront with what he wanted. She never understood self inflicted pain.

"Holy fuck!" She whispered yelled.

"You scared the shit out of me. What are you doing here?"

"Where the fuck have you been?"

Standing up in a non-threatening way with a mixture of hurt, anger, and something else in his eyes. Diane looked down guiltily as Jared observed her hair that was in disarray, her bloodshot eyes, and noticed that, she was wearing bottoms, torn, and hanging over her boots. He shook his head as he walked closer to her.

His nostrils flared as he smelled the combination of weed and sex mingled together on her. Eyes red rimmed, Jared used his finger to lift her chin so he could see her.

"Breathe."

The tears cause those gorgeous brown irises to glisten. He wanted to kiss her, but the stench prevented it.

"Jared, I'm sorry. Ever since what happened with Beauty and my friendship with Kim and you just allowing me to be," she huffed out a breath, "I been feeling feelings I've never felt before and I don't know how to handle it. I do what feels good and unknown feelings are scary as fuck and I just..." She sighed again.

"I fucking care about you so much but I don't know how to feel about how I think you feel about me. How the fuck am I supposed to process that and act on it so I don't fuck it up? I need time. I. Fuck! I don't know."

Jared listened to her rambling and was thankful not that she was distressed, but she was allowing him an opening and he knew he had to stay on track to have her forever. Masking his facial expression, he looked at her for a moment longer, "Did you use protection?"

"Yes."

"Go take a shower and throw everything you got on in the trash. I don't want to see none of that shit again."

He walked over and stretched across her bed. Jared released another breath as watched Diane exit the room.

Resto smiled as he walked over to the Student Services building after his conversation with Diane via chat. She was funny, charismatic, intelligent, and flirtatious. It surprised him when she reached out so soon after their talk. She, for him, was an enigma that had to be solved.

In the ballroom, he spotted her. She had on this beautiful wheat colored turtleneck sweater. Her breasts were sitting high like two ripe cantaloupes.

He loved the way she didn't hide her stomach in those tight ass undergarments. He could tell she didn't wear them by the way it jiggled when she laughed at something the woman next to her said. She had her thick thighs snuggly tucked in a pair of thigh-high boots.

"Good God."

Stepping back into the cocoon of the curtains, Resto squeezed his dick, trying to ease the ache until it calmed down. He sent a quick text before he stepped on stage to start the show.

Halfway through the show, Resto put his focus back on Diane. His expression quickly changed when he noticed some guy standing over her, reaching out his hand.

"She fucking took it!"

She said something to her friend while holding his hand, got up and they walked away. He followed them outside to get a better look at the guy. Resto noticed it was one of his students from last year. A quick roster search should be able to confirm who he was. Watching them pass a joint back and forth. Resto wanted to contact the campus police, but he didn't want to punish her. He calmed himself as much as he could before heading back into the auditorium, salivating at the thought of teaching her a lesson about her behavior. His phone pinged. Confirmation received.

Resto allowed his anger to bubble to the surface on the way home from the event. She owed him nothing this soon and the rational side of him knew that, but that did not mean he couldn't feel how he'd felt about seeing her leave with that guy.

"Was she going to fuck him?! Does she go around fucking random guys just because it's homecoming? Fuck! The other guy was still in the hospital. Was she a whore?! Was. She. A. Fucking. Whore!"

Banging on the steering wheel, he sped up, needing to get to his house as soon as possible.

Done with the shower wet and naked, Resto looked at himself in the mirror. He tried to figure out what everyone saw in him. The softer textured hair, "rooted in racism" the brown skin with the foreign accent, "rooted in self-hatred and a fetishization of a people just as oppressed as they were". They were all superficial things that meant nothing. If they saw the real him, deep down, they would see the ugliness at the core of who he was. He wanted to show Diane the monster because he had a feeling she was a monster, too. He hoped she didn't leave him feeling rejected as she'd done tonight. Brushing his hair back with his hands, taking one last look in the mirror, he entered his bedroom and smiled at "his family." Mama and papi were laying on the bed kissing. He smiled to himself.

"Mama and papi will make it better."

He was upset but receiving the confirmation text that his favorites were available calmed him.

"Are you two afraid to show me how much you love each other?"

With sad eyes, he walked closer to the bed, which was a California King. It was large enough to handle his nightly shakes and proclivities. As if on cue, the pair began touching and playing with each other.

"More. Put your fingers in her pussy. Let me see you fuck her."

"Papi" began sucking "mama's" breast while working his fingers inside her. "Mama" began moaning and moving her body in rhythm with "papi's" fingers.

"That's it keep going." Resto stroked his dick to fullness.

"Mama?" Turning, she looked at Resto.

"Open your legs wider."

She did. "Good girl mama."

"Go deeper papi."

He did. The smell and sound of her wetness permeated the room, and Resto inhaled.

Standing in front of them as "papi" please "mama" Resto continued to stroke his dick. "Papi, you can stop now. I want to taste how wet you made "mama" while you wet my ass. Can I have that?" In unison, they agreed. Resto got on the bed and nestled himself between "mama's" legs.

Not waiting any longer, he first kissed her lips and sucked as he pulled away, pausing as he savored the flavor, allowing it to make them closer. He bent and feasted on her pussy. "Papi" took it as his cue to tongue fuck his ass. This act continued until he felt "mama's" orgasm rising along with his own. Pre-cum was leaking from the tip of his dick as she came on his tongue.

Resto positioned his dick near her pussy. "Papi" covered his dick in a condom. Moving behind him, "papi" waited.

"Mama? Papi? Can we fuck each other? As a family?"

"Mama" lifted her legs at the knees, opening herself wider to him as "papi" massaged his ass cheeks while separating them. Resto ease in "mama's" pussy as deep as he could go, stilling as he waited for "papi" to start. Once fully seated, "papi" came behind him, thumbing the lube in and around his ass as he whispered, "Ready, Mijo?"

Not waiting for an answer, "papi" pushed into Resto's ass and began fucking him in staccato. "Papi's" movement caused his body to surge forward in "mama." Resto closed his eyes and marveled at the closeness of it all.

"Papi" began swerving, his hips going deeper into Resto.

"Fuck "papi." That feels so good."

He allowed himself to be fucked a little longer before leaning down and kissing "mama" on the mouth.

"Mama, you feel how good "papi" is fucking me. I'm going to fuck you just as good but I want you to feel how I'm being fucked first."

He kissed her again. "Is that okay?"

"Yes me amour."

As "papi" continued to deep stroke Resto, his dick dove deeper in "mama" turning her on. Resto allowed the pushes in his ass to move him in "mama." They moved in sync, all guided by the head of the home. He held back as long as he could. The urge to fuck got stronger and stronger the more aroused he became.

"Papi please!"

Resto's grabbed "mama's" hands in his above her head as he deep stroked her. "Papi leaned forward on Resto's back and licked his ear with the tip of his tongue "Papi" gave Resto the command.

"Make papi proud and make mama cum."

Resto began moving in time with "papi as he fucked "mama's" soaked pussy. The sounds of her wet pussy and the push of the dick in his ass sent tingles through his entire body. Sandwiched in between both. This is the love he so desperately craved as a child. Closing his eyes he savored the feel of her walls contracting around his dick as his anal muscles contracted around "papi's" dick. The bed rocked as they fucked each other, banging against the wall as the cries of pleasure, smell of sex and heat increased in the room.

"Hijo, can I cum?" He heard his "mama" say as he felt "papi's" balls slapped his.

"Please mi amor. Por Favor" Resto felt his nut rising at her words and tight walls. "Papi's" balls, grunts and dick pulsing in his ass was almost too much as he screamed.

"Cum mama and papi! Cum!"

They did, together as a family.

Kim, Ginger, Diane, and Jared slept well into the afternoon. It was Friday, and you were a fool or an unlucky bastard to have a class on a Friday. Uber Eats just delivered their pizza and wings, so they started shuffling about to handle hygiene before digging in.

Diane only got to rest because she was exhausted, not because she was comfortable. Jared was wound so tight around her she couldn't tell where he started and she stopped. She wouldn't say anything that would cause him to leave. Emotionally, Diane was a wreck and needed the company. And she'd missed him.

Jared didn't know how to respond after Diane's mini meltdown, confession or whatever you want to call it. He wanted to fight and fuck her at the same time. Even after she showered, he had a hard time sleeping next to her. He wrapped himself so tight around her, hoping the anger would subside. Eventually it did.

"Where you going?" Diane stopped just short of the bedroom door.

"Just getting another showered before we eat. Food's here."

Jared got off the bed. He walked to his overnight bag on the futon and pulled out his toothbrush and deodorant.

"I'm showering with you." It wasn't a question. She needed to see him as the man who wanted her would support and dig in that ass when she got out of pocket.

"Kk."

Brushing his teeth at the sink, Jared watched Diane as she washed and moisturized her face. "What?"

"What do you mean what?"

"Why are you looking at me like that? Creeper"

"I'm not a creeper."

He bumped her with his hip. "Just making sure you okay."

"Yeah, I'm good. You good?" Jared threw both thumbs in the air with a goofy grin.

"Come on, let's shower."

Diane adjusted the temperature and stepped in. Jared following behind her. It took a few seconds for him to realize how hot the water was, but when he did, he hurried to the back of the shower.

"Why do women like there showers so fucking hot? Cool that shit down some."

Rubbing his water bruised arm.

"Big Baby."

Adjusting the heat level, Diane grabbed her African net cloth. She squirted Native body wash on it and began scrubbing her body. He watched her as she took care to focus on her arms and shoulders. Moving to her large breast, they were so heavy she had to lift slightly and his dick responded. How the fuck was a woman lifting her breast to wash was such a fucking turn on? Or was it just Diane?

He wanted to have his mark on her. It wasn't there anymore, not since she'd fucked somebody just last fucking night. He grabbed the net, turning her around.

"What are you doing, creeper?"

She moved closer. Jared said nothing, just started washing her breast again, lifting as she had moments ago. Giggling.

"I can't believe you're jealous of me washing my body."

"Creeper."

"Oh yeah, I'm a creeper, huh?"

Jared continued to wash down her body as her head fell back. "I love your belly."

"Creeper."

"Turn around and bend over."

"You haven't finished the front."

Giving her a death stare, she turned. At the base of her neck, he washed in gentle circles down to her lower spine while pushing his fingers in her pussy, moving in slow circles that matched the motion on her back. Diane pushed back on his hand, rotating her hips. Jared pulled his fingers out. The suds traveled down the crack of her ass after he washed her cheeks. He pushed his fingers back into her pussy, resting his hand on her lower back. He placed his thumb in her ass to the knuckle.

"Fuck Jared."

Diane pushed harder and faster as Jared worked his fingers in and out both holes.

"I'm fucking your ass today."

Pausing, Diane turned.

"I've never had anal and you may not know this, but you're big as fuck, nigga."

She stood upright, but Jared pushed her back, keeping her folded over.

"I'm getting in that ass. You trust me Diane?"

He inserted two fingers. Jared worked in and out in a scissor motion. He felt her anus contracting.

"You may be nervous, but this ass is ready." He knew she was with the way she rocked back and forth on his hands.

"It's just a natural response to help get the shit out, not to get the shit in."

"Ugh, get away from me."

Removing his fingers from her. She shook her ass.

"What, you don't want my contracting ass no more?"

His hand wrapped around the back of her neck. He maintained the tight grip as he put his dick at the entrance of her asshole.

Diane placed her hand on the wall.

"Jared! What the fuck are you about to do?"

Jared pressed the tip in. He moved in and out about an inch.

"You asked me a question. I'm just giving you my answer."

Her sphincter clenched as he pressed in a bit more. It tried to suck him in or push him out. He couldn't tell which.

"Jar-red! Your dick is going to split me. I'll be in depends at thirty! Stop fucking playing!" She whispered-yelled.

Jared snickered while holding his position. He pushed in further, about three inches deep.

"I'm almost in lil momma. Relax."

He continued to push in and out within the three inches. He heard Diane take a breath and relax. Moving his grip from her waist, he placed his hand on her front and massaged her clit between his index and middle fingers. Jared slid both fingers in time with the movement of his dick in and out of her ass. Diane's body relaxed so much she almost went limp.

"Holy fuck nigga, don't stop! Don't fucking stop!"

She was close. Her legs buckled a little, she started pushing back faster. He squeezed her neck tighter to signal her to slow down. Jared realized she stopped thinking and started chasing her nut. She still ignored him and seemed to push harder as his fingers held her clit like a hot dog bun.

"Oh. MY. Fucking. GOOOOOOD!"

She shot off like a rocket and Jared surged his dick forward, burying it to the hilt in her ass.

He started stroking her ass at the pace she was pushing back to chase the climax. Jared maintained the motion on her clit and by the time she came down he had a rhythm as he swerved and grind in her ass. Diane's ass took his dick like a champ. It sucked him in and pulsed around his dick. Jared grabbed her waist and pounded in her like a madman.

"Fuck lil momma, your ass is so fucking tight. Got damn. This is my ass. Don't let nobody fuck you here. You hear me?"

When she didn't respond, he slapped her right cheek. "Answer me. Who is the only one getting this ass?"

"You. Oh, fuck, I'm bout to cum again!"

She screamed as her pussy gushed all over their thighs.

"Fuuuuck!"

Jared screamed as he came in her ass. He leaned on her back to catch his breath and spoke in her ear as he grind harder.

"Baby, it's gon' burn a bit. I'm sorry I couldn't pull out."

He wasn't sure if she heard him or not since she was still trembling from the orgasm. Jared pulled out slowly as he gently turned her around, still bent, hoping the water would ease the burn that was going to come.

"Can I stand now?"

"Hold on. I'm going to rinse you a bit."

Diane wrinkled her forehead, confused, and then she felt it. A slight burning sensation. Stepping from foot to foot.

"What the fuck is that Jared?"

"Sometimes anal causes tearing and when semen makes contact with the open wound... You know the saying adding salt to the wound? That's anal the first time if you're not gentle or don't pull out before ejaculating."

Diane was bent over with, "Mr. Pre-Med" at her ass just now explaining that he literally set her asshole on fire.

"Jared, I'm gonna fuck you up. Why didn't you say shit before?"

"Look, calm down. Do you trust me?"

"No!"

Laughing, he told her to hang on. He got out of the shower and looked under the sink. He found a store brand nasal flushing system.

"Jared. What the fuck are you doing? This shit hurts like a bitch!"

Diane pushed her ass further under the shower.

"This shit isn't fucking funny."

Jared stepped back in the shower laughing with the nasal system in hand.

"Nigga. You using my nasal flusher thing! You flushing out my ass!" J

ared filled the bottle with water and gave Diane a homemade enema. Both were unable to control their laughter.

Chapter 14

Kim and Diane missed the concert on the yard due to fatigue. Both agreed to chilled for tonight since midterms were over and they'd been partying pretty hard all week. Diane and Jared were still avoiding a much-needed conversation after her meltdown. He must have recognized she needed more time and didn't push. She was thankful to him for allowing her the space she needed to process everything that'd happened recently.

She also found out Beauty's parents were in town to pack up his place. He was heading home in a week. She didn't want to intrude. They didn't really owe each other anything, so they said their goodbyes over the phone. Her parents hadn't reached out since she arrived. She didn't expect them to and was okay with that.

Professor Resto hadn't reached out, but it'd only been a couple of days, so she'd wait until he contacted her in case he was having regrets. She'd done well on all her papers and finals. She also received a few more scholarships, which would be deposited soon.

Kim was such an understanding friend. Diane poured her heart out. She listened to her, advised her, cried with her, and laughed at the ass flushing incident. Kim didn't have as much going on, but she and her mom kinda fell out. Finances were still a struggle, but classes and Ginger were good things. Diane Zelle'd her some coins since she had more than enough money to last until the end of the year. They got wine drunk and slept in the same bed since they were sad about their parents. Diane laid next to Kim while she snored, thankful she finally had a person. She sunk deeper under the covers. Diane held Kim's hand.

"I'm glad to have your sistership."

Jared and his line brothers had been rehearsing for the step show for weeks and today was the last practice. He couldn't wait for homecoming to be over and done with. It's been nothing but stressful. His obligations with his fraternity, classes, not being able to get home. He was so glad Kenny started dating Diane's roommate so he would have an excuse to see her.

He smiled, remembering how she gave his boy the nickname Ginger. That was one of things he'd grown to love about her. The quirks, goofiness, her honesty, and that sexy ass body. He wanted to hit her sweet spot yesterday, but he couldn't get the smell of that nigga out of his head. Jared definitely didn't want to take her anally without preparing her more, but she was so vulnerable the night before and he wanted to give her some kind of comfort.

Thanksgiving was around the corner and he wanted to ask Diane to come home with him to meet his family. Knowing her past, Jared wasn't sure she would accept, so he was on the fence about bringing it up. He understood she wanted to figure out her feelings, but he had no doubts about what he wanted. Jared wanted Diane, and he was tiring of waiting. Sighing, he grabbed his bag and headed to class.

Sore and satisfied, Resto nestled further into his overnight guest's embrace. They were too tired to leave after the multiple sex session and he didn't want to lose the feeling of family. Last night brought back so many memories of the stories his Abuela would tell him about his mama and papi before the drugs. He remembers sitting on the floor playing with his toy cars and she'd be listening to her favorite singer Celia Cruz while knitting on the sofa. A bit of nostalgia prodded his thoughts.

"Your mama was beautiful. Her skin was beautiful. When she was a little girl, I used to call her my little Tamarindos. Hair soft like cotton. It was so fluffy. She loved wearing it like Thelma from Good Times. Your mama had stars in her eyes. She wanted to be famous like Celia Cruz, but she couldn't sing. Ah Carmen. I named her after the actress you know?"

"Yeah, I know the funny lady on the old shows you listen to."

Laughing. "Oh Mijo. You are correct. I name her after the funny lady on the radio."

Her eyes were sad. She smiled and continued.

"In high school, Carmen was the smartest, most popular girl, which was a good thing. And bad. Carmen, I'd say, you can't know everything. Sometimes you have to listen. Learning is worse than listening. I don't know how she did it, Mijo. The school, the working part time and partying. How I worried. She kept going and going. For a little while, I thought she was okay, just full of energy. Then I became proud, proud that she could handle it all. Until I saw she couldn't."

"You've got your mama's creativity and smarts, but your Papi's common sense. Your Papi was completely opposite of you mama. Not better, just different. He loved your mama so much. Would do anything for her?" Her eyes went sad again, then the look of resolve. I could see he was good for her. I thought Jorge would help her calm down. And she did for a little while..."

Feeling the bed move, Resto snapped out of his daydream. She was walking out of the bathroom wrapped in a towel. He was stepping in. Falling back on the pillow, he'd wait until they left before starting his day. Maybe he would send Diane a text.

Kim was off to work study for a few hours to make up for missing so much of work this past week. Diane cleaned the bathroom, kitchen, and foyer before deep cleaning her room. In the past, it helped her think when she needed to come up with solutions to a problem. Lately, she needed a lot of answers. A commitment to Jared was at the top of that list. Was Diane ready to make that jump? The decision would be made after Thanksgiving break. Hardly no one would be on campus. She could walk the grounds and think. That was the closest to a solution she'd gotten so far.

After washing and deep conditioning her hair, Diane two-strand twisted her fro hawk for the step show tonight. Her phone indicated she had an incoming text. She picked up her phone and smiled at the text.

Unknown: Hi! This is Professor Resto. I was wondering if you're feeling any better?

Her: A man who can text in full sentences. I think I'm in love. I'm doing much better. How are you?

Naughty Professor: Good to hear. My day has been very productive. I'm working on a new book.

Her: Oh? Another poetry book?

Naughty Professor: No, a graphic novel. I need a break and thought of you so...

Her: How sweet of you. I really appreciate it. I would love to know what it's about?

Naughty Professor: It's in the early stages. Maybe when I have more pages. Speaking of, I need to get back at it. Again, I'm glad you're feeling better. I hope to talk to you soon?

Her: Definitely! Have a creative productive Saturday!

"Aye!"

Diane fell back on her futon. Professor Resto made her feel so good without trying. How could she commit to one man while feeling something for another? She knew more about Jared. He made her feel cared for, was patient and non-judging. But Professor Resto was mature, knowledgeable, and sexy as fuck. Maybe she was just letting her newfound freedom make her lose sight of what was important. That's why the decision she was making during Thanksgiving break was going to be crucial. Once made, there was no going back.

Resto scoops the last bit of eggs as he re-reads the conversation between him and Diane. Even though it was brief, he noticed her flirtatious sense of humor, and he loved it. She reminded him so much of the stories his Abuela used to tell him about his mama. How funny and smart she was. Her bright eyes, beautiful brown skin, and luscious lips caused his dick to tighten in his pants. He stroked the head of his dick as he watched the pre-cum leak from the tip. He grazed his thumb over the tip; smearing himself as he continued to stroke. Gripping tighter, stroking harder, he imagined her lips on him and that was all it took. Streams of cum shot on the table, landing on his finished Huevos.

Instead of driving, Diane and Kim took the train to the Stadium Armory for the step show. Traffic wouldn't be bad, but parking would be ridiculous. Both ladies went for comfortable, but cute. Kim was wearing a white long sleeve mock turtleneck with the Howard logo on the chest and red bands around the sleeve. Jeans and combat boots complete her look. Diane opted for a red cropped Howard t-shirt with the school's name in white across the chest and a retro Howard bomber jacket. She was also in jeans with her favorite pair of Atoms.

The stadium was thumping with excitement. It was loud. Diane noticed the crowds were just as segregated as campus.

The Divine Nine sat with their various fraternities or sororities, the acting students, music students, etc. Friends were grouped with each other and the locals mingled throughout. Almost as if they wanted a glimpse into what made "this college thing" so special. Diane wouldn't see Jared since his frat was competing, but she dressed up for him just in case.

Diane and Kim were buzzing after the step show. They were high from all the weed and alcohol being passed around by locals and students. Everyone was partying like it was a club instead of a step show. The music had various couples bumping and grinding in between the performances. There were a few of the locals Diane would love to take back to the dorm. A rough fuck had no emotions. It was what it was. A release. That kind of thinking confirmed she needed time to sort her shit out.

By the time the step show ended, Diane just wanted to go home and lay down. But it was homecoming, and she didn't want to disappoint Kim.

"So where we heading tonight? It's your world. I'm just a squirrel."

Diane chuckled as she wrapped her arm around Kim's.

"I don't know. We have been doing a lot of partying, and I am tired. Besides, I don't want to go to a club. They always jack up the prices around homecoming. I'm still trying to figure out tuition for next year. My mind isn't on it."

"Yeah, I get that, but you know I got you tonight if you need it."

"No, I'm good. You've been holding us down with food and stuff for the room."

"I don't mind if you really want to go out."

"Awe my Sis looking out. I'm good. I'm going to drown my sorrows. What about you? Don't let my mood stop you."

Diane put four twenties in Kim's jacket pocket. She'd find it later. "I think I'm going to walk around campus and clear my head a bit."

Jared was feeling good after placing second in the step show and he was ready for the frat's afterparty, which was always wild. He wanted to spend time with Diane, but understood he needed to give her time, he would surround himself with his frat family until she became his. Jared wanted to have a definitive status between him and Diane before he entered med school. It was going to take a lot of his time and he wanted to invest and grow their relationship beforehand. She was it for him. Now he just had to convince her of the same.

The ladies split up at the courtyard of the dorms. Diane walked up the hill at a languid pace, deep in thought. Once she made it to the top of the hill, she wasn't as winded as she was at the beginning of the year so instead of stopping to catch her breath; she took in the University and how the light cast shadows on the buildings. It was about 10 p.m., but she wasn't afraid since she was on campus and could take the shuttle back. Diane strode past the Caribbean tree. She sat in the grass the middle of the yard.

"You know you shouldn't be out here by yourself."

Diane looked up and saw Eli from her production class. "So what are you doing out here, then?"

"Heading over to the production room to finish an assignment I missed. Come, hang out with me? That way I won't be worried about somebody snatching you up?"

Shrugging her shoulders, Eli helped her up. "Sure, why not?"

Eli and Diane made small talk as they headed to SOC. Eli swiped his badge, and they entered the halls of SOC. The lights remained on all hours since the radio station was in the building. They took the stairs to the third floor. Eli pulled out the key for the production room RTC3.

"Where'd you get the key from?" Eli looked down at the key.

"Oh, my boy works in the media room and gave it to me since the sign-in sheet was full today."

"Friends in high places. My nigga."

“Come on so I can get this project finished.”

Once in the booth, Eli pulled out a half bottle of some concoction. Diane sipped and vibed to the beat he was mixing. Eli pulled out a baggie.

“Is that Molly?” Diane leaned forward.

“No. Ecstasy.”

He placed a green pill with an Alien on the tip of her tongue. She let the pill slowly dissolve in her mouth. Eli took Diane, pulling her to him as he started unbuttoning her jeans while he kissed her. She just smiled and went with it. Turning Diane and he bent her over the audio mixer. He pulled her jeans to her knees.

“I want to get you on my project.”

This is the feeling she needed. So she chased it.
Eli released his dick from his jeans. Diane gasp at how large it was and attempted to move. He held a firm hand on her back.

“It’s kinda big but my dick never goes all the way in. But don’t worry I won’t hurt you.”

Diane sobered up a bit almost regretting her decision. He palmed her pussy gently playing with.

"Got damn your pussy fat as fuck. I know my dick is going to be happy."

Eli moved his dick up and down until Diane lips parted. When he entered her. She grabbed the production board harder.

"Holy fucking shit! My pussy is having mixed feelings."

Once fully seated in her, Eli grabbed Diane's neck. He deep stroked her nice and slow. Diane closed her eyes and tried not to cry out. He was huge, but it felt fucking fantastic. As he sped up, she couldn't hold back or control the deep moan coming from her. The banging against the board got increasingly louder. Eli's grip tightened on her neck. Diane couldn't figure out if it was the hard fucking, the alcohol, or the X but she was feeling good and without thinking she blurted.

"I like the way that fuckin' boy abuse me. He gotta a big dick and knows how to use it"

Jared would've missed Diane's call if he didn't have his handi capable feature on. Stepping outside so he could hear above the loud music,

"Hey baby, is it boring where you at?"

After a few beats he realized that she'd butt-dialed him, and he could hear her moans and the sound of wet pussy getting fucked.

"Diane! Di! Fucking! Ane!" Throwing his phone across the street, Jared screamed.

"Ahhhhhhhh!"

Chapter 15

It's been a month since homecoming and things were back to normal. Kim and Diane were closer than ever. And after a three-week break, Jared started coming back around. She would've been more concerned about Jared if the Professor was filling those lonely evenings. She and Professor Resto formed a cute little friendship over text. It was all surface level, but it comforted her while Jared was catching up with school, frat commitments and family. At least, that's what she surmised.

Thanksgiving was in a couple of weeks and professors were in group project mode, it seemed, for all her classes. Diane hated group projects because there was always one person who did none of the work and got the grade everyone else worked hard to earn. Bag on her shoulder, she headed back to the dorm from the iLab. She and Kim spent time together before she left for Thanksgiving. She and Ginger had gotten so tight, he invited her to his parents for Turkey Day. Diane was grateful to have the place to herself during that time to make all the final decisions that needed to be made regarding her personal life.

Finn was walking back to his dorm from "Ho Chi." They had the best wings and fries in the city, especially if you got it with mumbo sauce. He'd been in his room all afternoon finishing up his portion of the political science project before Thanksgiving break. Smiling, he remembered the chick who kept calling him Dreds wishing he'd gotten her name and hoping he'd see her again before the break. She was mad, cool, and he wouldn't mind being better acquainted with her. Finn knew she was on the sixth floor but didn't want to be a creep. He got off the elevator and walked down the hall to his room. He was ready to dig into his food.

The assailant was ready as soon as he heard the key. He got into a stance with his hand raised and his grip tight around the mini slugger, "Diane." Once the door closed, he swung.

"Crack!"

The bat came crashing down on Finn's face so hard he dropped. The assailant continued his assault, not caring that he was out cold. He bashed his back legs and arms and continued to beat him until he was tired. He wanted to leave a reminder of tonight, so he'd never think to bother her again. With the pair of scissors from his pocket, he cut all his locs until nothing but a mini afro remained. He wiped the bat on the back of Finn's shirt, tucked it in his pants, and walked out.

Jared had been thinking about Diane for the last few days. Things were hectic. School was ending soon for Thanksgiving break so everyone had their heads down playing catch up trying to finish strong before going home. He'd given her the space she needed to focus on herself and school. She'd seemed happy when he finally came back around. Jared didn't mean to ghost Diane, but that phone call took something out of him and he thought this time he was going to leave her alone. His heart wouldn't allow it. It'd been a month since they'd been intimate with each other and he was ready to take back what was his.

Diane opened it immediately when she heard the knock. Jared sent her a text stating he was on his way.

"Hey."

She said, wrapping her arms around him.

"Hey. You missed me, huh?"

She grabbed his hand and walked to her room. They just stood and stared. Jared wanted to convey so much, but knew he had to wait.

"Let's just get undressed and lie down. I just want to be close to you."

Diane was fragile, and if he was being honest with himself, he was as well. Thinking about how he gave her the space to be with other people, hoping to find her way back to him, made him feel weak. He was angry and hurt, but not at her, with himself.

"No sex. I just want to hold you. I want you to feel what I'm feeling, and I think the best way to convey those things is in stillness."

Head held down, she turned her back to Jared. Diane paused as the tears fell. She nodded her head and began unbuttoning her shirt.

Resting comfortably for about ten minutes, Dianne realized Jared was not playing about cuddling and just feeling what he wanted to say through touch. It wasn't sexual, just gentle strokes down her arm, across her back and neck. He wrapped his arm around her waist. Cupping and squeezing, becoming softer and slower as he fell into a deep sleep.

Diane couldn't sleep. She had a plan; she would not think about anything until Thanksgiving break and Jared threw a wrench into that with this cuddling and feeling shit. Diane lowly spoke.

"It'd only been last month when I discovered I had feelings. The home I grew up in, I learned to push down any emotion that bubbled to the surface for fear of it being neglected, ignored, or dismissed like an inconsequential thing. I didn't know how to hug until my first sexual experience. Mom, forget it and daddy would do the one arm pat on the back. How can Jared expect me to correlate emotions with touch, commitment, or relationships.? How could he? Even my boyfriends, if you'd call them, that made me feel good physically

and it gave me what I needed in the place of having to expose those feelings or emotions that healthy people felt and shared with each other."

Parents gave provider feelings; boys gave you sexual ones. And those were the only ones she knew.

Diane had to love who she was unapologetically, even if no one else got it. She realized an important thing about being with the guys she was with in high school. There was nothing wrong with loving sex, loving the feelings it brought, the pleasure and pain. Diane learned not to be ashamed of it and the more accepting she became, the more immersed she was in seeking that pleasure. Did she use it sometimes to fill the emotional void? Of course, however, she knew when she was doing it seventy-five percent of the time for pleasure not to fill a void.

Friends, Diane didn't have any to know what the fuck they gave. Girls tried to befriend her, but she made no genuine connections. She didn't click with the nerdier girls because she wasn't a nerd. Yes, she studied hard and a lot but only to leave. Singularly focused on getting out of that house, town and away from the people that procreated and formed her life. Diane practically lived in the library. She never had the opportunity to meet anyone else to connect with.

Then there was Professor Resto. They've been maintaining a student/Professor relationship in the class, but over text and chat they were, she couldn't name it. It was something different. They talked a bit about her past, his grandmama, or Abuela, as he called her. He spoke little about his parents. His dad was around most of his life and his mom passed when he was a toddler. He had a great sense of humor and just allowed her to say whatever she wanted, no expectations. No judgment.

Diane checked her phone and saw it was 3 a.m. Sleep still eluded her. She was bored, horny, and wanted to avoid thinking. Moving her hand behind her, she closed it around Jared's flaccid dick.

Loosely stroking it up and down. His dick hardened. Jared's eyelids fluttered open and whispered in her ear. "You missed this dick huh?" He squeezed her stomach.

"When was the last time you had some dick?"

He hated how insecure he sounded, but he needed to see if she was going to lie.

"What? It's been a minute."

"How long is a minute?"

Hands on her stomach, he gently dragged his fingers even harder. He squeezed. Diane flinched when he applied pressure on her tummy, answering honestly.

"The last day of homecoming."

Remember how they sounded while the dude was pounding into Diane cause something in Jared to snap.

Jared knew he shouldn't have been as angry as he was because she had no idea he'd heard what he'd heard. It was wrong of him to blame her, but it is what it is. He hated that even in his anger she still affected his body the way she did. It hurt knowing she fucked somebody on the night his frat performed. Diane should have been there for him. Fuck! Moving her hand away from him. He slid his hand from her stomach to that sweet pussy. By passing her clit, Jared stuck his middle finger in. Diane stayed ready for him, and who else? His rage took over as he fingered her harder. It was like macaroni in a pot and he was ready to eat. Jared moved between her legs and pushed them up and wide.

"Grab your legs."

Once she had her legs in her hands, he put both hands on her stomach and pushed while burying his face in her dripping pussy.

He gathered she was close because she dropped her legs and started backing away. Clutching down on her clit, Jared followed her up the bed, hands still pressed on her stomach until she couldn't go any further while keeping a tight suction. Diane's legs started shaking, and she almost catapulted off the bed as she came into his mouth. Moving his head in a circular motion, he continued to suck until she crested. Jared crawled up her body, taking her legs with him as he went. The smell of her pussy on his mouth Jared pressed them to her lips and asked her.

"Did he eat your pussy?" She shook her head and smiled as if remembering something he did that was better.

He put his hand around her throat and squeezed. Her smile disappeared and fear mixed with lust gathered in her eyes. Jared clasped tighter with his left hand. He raised her left leg with his and surged forward. Jared banged into her so hard, he tried to make her experience the pain that lingered in his chest. His heart fucking ached! He blinked back the tears as he fucked her harder. The grip around her neck got tighter.

A part of him didn't care about her comfort level. He was uncomfortable as fuck every time he thought about someone else having what's supposed to be his. It'd been a month since he'd been in her and shit and he missed it. Jared finally gained enough control to pull back and out of her. He eased his grip.

"You okay?"

"Why you stop!?"

Jared moved to his back. He told her to take the dick if she want it. Diane climbed on top, planted both feet flat on the bed, and slid down his dick. Eyes rolling to the back of his head, Jared almost blacked out at that feeling. He nutted and his dick was still on bricks. Yes Diane's pussy is just that good. She rode him nice and slow, rocking back and forth on each downward stroke. Jared's hand was on her titties, pulling and pinching her nipples. Each pinch earned more wetness from her. He forced her face down to look at him. She intertwined their hands together as she maintained her balance. Her lifts got higher and her speed increased. She kissed him softly and slowly, with nips along his lip. He grabbed her throat again and wrapped an arm around her waist. His hold was tight as he pounded upward in rapid succession but he was too caught up in the moment. Diane's eyes rolled to the back of her head and Jared kept fucking. He could feel her juices on his pelvis and thighs. The harder she creamed, the faster he pounded. When he felt my second nut rise, he released his hold slightly. She seated herself on his pelvis and rocked him through his orgasm.

Waking up in Jared's arms felt amazing. Diane didn't realize how much she'd missed it until she hadn't had it for a few weeks. She definitely missed the dick. Jared pounded her like he was tenderizing meat and she enjoyed every minute. He squeezed her from behind and asked if she wanted to spend Thanksgiving with him and his family. Flattered, Diane would have agreed to go, but she had already had her Thanksgiving plans made. They included being alone with her thoughts and no outside distractions to confuse her later about the decisions she'd have to make regarding monogamy and Jared.

"I really want you to come and meet my grandpa and dad, but I understand you want to be alone to decide about where we're going and if this is going to be a commitment. I really hope you decide to give us a real chance. It won't be perfect, but we can learn and grow together. At least that's what I want."

Cupping his face, Diane leaned in and gently kissed his lips. He closed his eyes and let out a breath as if she was breathing life into him. She was.

"Jared, I've been hearing everything you've said and I really appreciate how patient you've been. I promise I am really, really trying so we can move forward."

A few days before Thanksgiving, Diane had to drop off the notes on her final project. Kim had left with Ginger aka Kenny last night and Jared headed back to the Gold Coast this morning.

She needs to add housing to her list from December 19th through January 1st when the school would be closed for winter break. Even if she and Jared became a couple, she wasn't sure if she'd want to meet his family. Diane was looking forward to a long soak in the tub once she got back to the dorm, smoking a J, forgetting for tonight.

The door was ajar, and she saw Professor Resto with his head buried in a book.

"Hi Professor. I'm just stopping by to drop off our notes from the project. I hope I'm not interrupting?"

Resto tried to smile. "Come in. You know you guys should have the notes turned in with the assignment."

"Yeah, I know, but you know how it's always one that doesn't pull their weight and the others have to jump in or jump that bitch!" She quickly turned serious when she saw his facial expression change.

Shocked but loving the way Diane said what she felt, he stood, walked over, and closed his office door. On his way back he stopped behind her so close his breaths caused goose bumps on her neck. He waited until Diane became uncomfortable.

"I love they speak your mind. Do you always speak so frankly in every situation?"

Slowly walking away, grazing her backside with his body before taking his seat. Diane released the breath she was holding while squeezing her legs for fear the wetness would ruin her leggings. Waiting for her to answer, Resto leaned back in his chair with his elbow on the arms with his hands clasped together.

"Every situation." She turned to leave and once in the hall, she said loud enough for him to hear, "Especially when I'm feeling good." The door closed. Quickly grabbed his phone.

Naughty Professor: We should do something one day since you'll be in town this week.

Her: You don't celebrate?

Naughty Professor: There is nothing celebratory about genocide.

Her: Touché. Sure, we can hang out.

Diane figured she might as well have one last hurrah, since it was highly likely that she and Jared would make things official when he got back.

Resto couldn't stop thinking about Diane last night into this morning. It was amazing to have his mama approve of her replacement. His mama made an appearance last night in his dreams but this time she watched as he and Diane made love. She even masturbated before disappearing. He had papers to finish grading and a few changes to make to his book before sending it to the editor. He'd ask Diane to meet up with him tomorrow. Hopefully she'd want to make a day and night of it.

Bath and Body Works candles burned throughout the room as Diane meditated this morning, completing thirty minutes of Yoga. Now freshly showered. She sat on the floor with her door and window open. She wrote out the Pro's and Con's on the benefits of being in a committed relationship with Jared. She decided not to base it on feelings alone since they were new to her.

Her phone interrupted her with a text message from Resto.

Naughty Professor: Good morning. How'd you sleep last night all alone in the dorm?

Her: I sleep like a newborn babe. How was your night? Uneventful I hope?

Naughty Professor: Uneventful? It depends on what you'd consider an event.

Her: Cryptic

Naughty Professor: Very. I'm texting because I wanted to know if you'd meet me at the theater in Maryland for an independent film?

Her: Depends...

Biting his bottom lip, Resto's dick twitched at her flirting.

Naughty Professor: On what?

Her: The name of the film and what we're eating after.

Naughty Professor: A 1972 film, Black Girl and whatever you want to eat as long as I get enjoyment from eating it as well.

A burst of laughter escaped Diane as her thumbs hovered. She was feeling frisky, so she texted.

Her: Well, if you don't like it, I'll bring something you'd enjoy as a second option.

The third time, Resto read her message as he stroked his dick a bit before he responded.

Naughty Professor: See you tomorrow at 11. Meet me at AFI theater. And Diane, you may not handle the way I eat my meals. I'm very methodical. Enjoy the rest of your day.

Fanning herself. Diane put the phone down and got back to figuring out her life. Resto didn't make her heart ache like Jared, but her pussy was on full throttle.

The Holidays

Resto went to the store and picked up a few items in case Diane spent the night. Hell, if she came over. He stocked up on alcohol, juice, coffee, and bottled water. He had every intention of working her over all night if she allowed it. Being a little concerned with how she would perceive his proclivities, he would gauged her responses to certain things to know if she was ready. He may be worried for no reason; she may not even come over. He still wanted to be prepared in case she did.

Diane spent the rest of the afternoon in a contemplative mood. She decided on what she was going to do with her and Jared and housing during Christmas break. Everything else in her life was simply a work in progress. Diane accessed the new feelings and old, allowed them to be present and deal them head on without pushing them down like she used to in the past.

Jared made it home in no time and spent most last night catching up with his grandfather. He was getting older and Jared wanted to treasure the moments he had left. He'd spend time with his dad later today, he needed readiness of mind and emotions. His father was firm in his beliefs and it didn't allow room for any other opinion, no matter how valid. He wanted to figure out how to tell his dad about Diane and his decision to go to medical school here at Howard instead of John Hopkins in Baltimore, MD. He'd mentioned that he wouldn't cover the cost of his medical degree if he went anywhere other than John Hopkins.

Jared was grateful that his grandfather set up a trust in his name for his education. It allowed Jared to be prepared for the argument that he knew he and his dad would engage in. It wouldn't be a visit home if it didn't happen. He believed his dad loved him and knew that he only wanted what he thought was best for Jared, but he wouldn't bend or compromise on any decision, regardless of what it was or who it affected. He knew it was the biggest factor in his mother leaving not just his dad but him.

Jared's dad and mom were never happy based on his observations from the age of around five until his mom left him at age nine. His mom walked around the home in an exasperated state. Nothing she suggested held any weight. Decisions regarding the home, business and Jared, his dad made the final call. Gerald and Cheryl met at Johns Hopkins University and fell in love. Majoring in biochemistry, his mom met his dad in the lab one day while she was working on a final project. He said he took one look at her and that was it for him.

"You look flustered. Anything I can assist you with?"

Gerald spoke as he noticed the crinkles in her forehead and upturned top lip. She looked as if she was working out why the experiment hadn't given her the result she was expecting.

"I am. I need to finish this," she said, pointing at the experiment on the lab table "and turn it in by the end of the day, but it is not cooperating." Exasperated, she threw up her hands in defeat, stomped over to Gerald and asked, "Can you look?"

"Sure."

"I'm Cheryl, and thank you for helping." Cheryl allowed the help not only because she thought he was gorgeous but he was also the TA for her Bio Chem class.

"You're completing an enzyme study, right?"

"Right! By immobilizing glucose in high fructose corn syrup."

"You're trying to save the diabetic world?"

"If I can. My mom had diabetes, but she attempted too late to combat it. She was a big believer in taking a pill and not changing her diet until her

amputation. Our community has such a long history with 'sugar' but doesn't grasp the concept of diet change. Instead, most rely on a pill and continue the same unhealthful habits." Embarrassed for her mother, Cheryl wanted to walk away.

Not looking away from the experiment, Gerald responded, "Yeah, I get it. The Black community is so untrusting of anything new, with valid reason based on the history of this country." He turned, lifting Cheryl's face with his index finger.

"So, how's your mom doing now?"

Cheryl made eye contact with Gerald. "She died."

Gerald was older by Jared's mom by four years. Jared believed he used it to his advantage to override every suggestion she'd made. He looked at it as being the head of the household. Leading and being the role model that Jared and Cheryl need, but in reality, he was a fucking tyrant. Plain and simple. Jared's dad loved his mom, and it gutted him when she left and never looked back. A pillar of strength. He never called or looked for her and forbade Jared from doing the same.

He didn't see his mom again until he was about thirteen years old and his school took a class trip to Philadelphia. His American history class was studying US Constitution, Liberty Bell, and Independence Hall. *He was with his friends running the steps at the Philadelphia Museum of Art, recreating the scene from Rocky. Jared got to the top step and ran right into her.*

"Mom?" He jumped into her arms.

"Mom, it you! It's really you! Oh my God, mom I missed you so much!"

Startled at first, Cheryl realized who it was and held on for dear life.

"Jared! What are you doing here? Look at you!"

She hugged and kissed his face as tears streamed down her cheeks. Jared explained his class trip. She introduced herself to his teacher, and she allowed Jared's mom to join them for lunch. It was one of the best days of his life. Jared didn't realize how much he needed a woman in his life until that day. He never questioned why she left. He was going to take what he could and hopefully he'd be able to spend more time with her since he'd found her again. His mother had other plans.

"Jared, I know you must have a lot of questions and you may not understand or accept my answer. However, it's the truth." Jared became uncomfortable with the topic but he wanted to hear her side.

"I was suffocating to death. Literally. My fire had died down to embers and if I didn't leave when I did, I would've killed myself. It wasn't a reason not to take you with me, but honey, if I had, your father would've given me the fight of my life. He had friends, resources and I didn't stand a chance."

Jared saw the sadness and regret. But, he was sad also and wanted to hold her accountable for the pain she'd caused him.

"I understand putting you first, but what about me? I was nine and needed you and dad. He was so mean. Well, not mean just hard. He was always so hard on me and I needed you."

Jared didn't want to cry, but he couldn't help it. His mom was on his soft landing whenever dad got to be too much.

"Jared, I know and I'm sorry. There was no excuse or explanation why I didn't come and explain things. To tell you goodbye. So if you hate me, please hate me for that, but try to understand why I left, even if how I went about it was wrong."

She pulled him in a tight hug and he reciprocated. It didn't matter what she'd done. She was his, and he loved her. "I know you don't understand and it makes little sense right now, but it will when you're older. I'm truly sorry that me and dad's issues caused you pain. There is no excuse for how I did it. All I can do is apologize."

Jared released her and smiled. He didn't understand everything, but it was enough. She was right. His dad was a wonderful dad, just overbearing, but he never lacked the love he needed because of his granddad. For that, he was grateful.

He hadn't spoken to his mom since that day, but he followed her career at Jefferson Health-Thomas Jefferson University Hospital, and it was a successful one. That day, he decided he would be just like her.

Diane had on a cute sweater dress with some combat boots and a jean jacket. It was cold in DC, but she was going to be spending most of her time in the car or in an establishment. She wasn't nervous or scared to meet Professor Resto and assumed it was because of the friendship they'd developed over the text. It was almost as if she was going to meet Kim for the movies and food, but not like meeting Jared. Jared was different. She'd realized and resolved that he was a special person in her life. Professor Resto was a person who had similar emotions or lack thereof, so they connected on a level of feeling non feelings. He was a snarky smart ass, but went dark and when he did, she happily followed along. Diane hustled to her car, placed her "ho bag" in the trunk and a heavier coat in the backseat. She was being presumptuous but did not care.

"Measure twice, cut once. Right?" Typing in the address to AFI on GPS. Diane pulled out of the parking lot.

Diane spotted Professor Resto right away, seated in the middle of the theater. He was looking as luscious and milky as he always did. He seemed fully immersed in the movie that had started ten minutes ago. As quietly as she could, Diane sat next to him and handed him a small bag of popcorn. Every time she saw him, he was snacking on something. She assumed it was the effects related to the shakes. He'd alluded to it in their text conversations they'd had over the last couple of weeks. Knowing what it was like to have a toxic parent you loved, she didn't push. If he wanted her to know more, he would reveal it in time. Trust had to be developed in order to be that vulnerable. She knew from experience.

"Hey Professor, how are they hanging?"

She snickered. He looked at her with a raised eyebrow and laughed. "You're late. And they're hanging and swinging."

They stared at each other and burst into giggles as they each reached for popcorn.

Resto understood the intricacies of race in the Puerto Rican, especially the Nuyorican community. He prided himself on being Puerto Rican and Black through the slave trade to Puerto Rico through his grandmother's side of the family. Diane had little knowledge of Puerto Rican culture, so she was happy to listen and soak in as much as the Professor wanted to reveal. They made their way through the popcorn while sharing a soda. She and Resto sipped from the same cup as if normal thing they'd done countless times before. They definitely bonded over emotional childhood trauma.

Together they walked to a Lebtav, a Lebanese restaurant close to the theater and shared an amazing family style meal. Both feasted on the popular favorites of falafel, Baba ghanoush, Chicken Shawarma and a drink between them. They visited a downtown market on Fenton street with various vendors selling homemade food and handmade products. At an apple cider booth, they shared a cup of hot cider. It was close 7 p.m., both unaware they'd spent the entire day together.

In the parking lot, Professor Resto nestled Diane between himself and her car. "So, do you have to leave, or would you like to spend more time with me at my place?"

She leaned in and placed a soft, deep, wet kiss to his lips. "I'd loved that."

It took everything in Resto not to put his hand under her dress and finger fuck her senseless. In due time, he reminded himself. He wanted to go slow and savor the moment before devouring her like a ravished animal. He leaned further into her mouth, tasting hummus and falafel. She reciprocated. A slow dance of tongues and lips, soft, slow, languid kisses continued. Moaning in his mouth, Diane reached further down and grabbed his jean covered dick.

The drive back to Professor Resto's seemed to take forever. Diane was on fire and she needed him to quench the flames before she exploded. She didn't know what made her kiss him in public like that. They weren't close to the University however anyone could have seen them. The day was turning out to be the perfect first date, and she just wanted to express to him how good she'd felt. The massive weight he was hiding with his "swinging balls" was all the confirmation she needed that he wouldn't disappoint.

Diane noticed the beautiful Craftsman's style house as they slowed. She parked beside Professor Resto in his driveway. He got out before she did, open her door and he assisted her out of the car.

"Wait, I have to get my overnight bag."

Pausing mid-stride as he reached Diane's car, Resto doubled back and helped her with her bag.

"You were being a little presumptuous, weren't you?"

"I was all the way presumptuous, sir." Holding his hand for her bag, he pecked her lips.

"Come on."

As Diane entered Resto's house, she nodded in approval at the decor. There was a beautifully designed desk near a large window. One wall housed a bookcase that was filled to capacity. Most of the space had African and Hispanic art and sculptures.

"You know I'm going to want a history lesson on all the artwork and sculptures in here. They are amazing! Really! You do practice what you preach with Black and Brown history. I'm impressed, Professor."

Diane continued to peruse the living room, taking it all in. She was giddy with all the books he had in his collection. The classics; not white classics, but Black, Indigenous and Puerto Rican classics. Everything from the Harlem Renaissance to the early nineties. Everyone from Jessie Fauset and Claude McKay to Nikki Giovanni and Sonia Sanchez. Resto returned after putting Diane's overnight bag in his room. She looked back at him and said, "I would sell my soul for this collection of books."

Laughing, he walked up and down the rows of books. He stopped in the far corner of the room searching among the sea of authors. Resto picked up a book and brought it over to Diane. It was a manuscript for *Out of Orde*r *or The Masses Are Asses* by Pedro Pietri. Pedro Pietri was a famous Nuyorican poet and actually co-founded the Nuyorican Poets Cafe in New York. She felt his breath on the back of her ear.

"You won't have to sell your soul, but after tonight, you'll give it willingly."

He licked the outline of her ear as Diane eased back further into Resto. Careful not to damage the book, she placed it on a nearby end table.

He continued to lick and kiss her ear. Resto reached around and grabbed Diane's breast through her dress and squeezed. She was being receptive. He continued pinching her nipples through the fabric.

"Fuck yes."

She said as she pressed her breast closer to his hands.

"Diane, if we go there is no going back."

"I know."

"I have certain proclivities in the bedroom that you may not agree with," he said, as he continued to pinch and squeeze while seeking permission to move forward. "Even though I'm no longer your Professor after Christmas break, it's still..."

"I don't see you as my professor, Resto. I see you as a person with whom I'm developing a budding friendship with. We talk about things that I never talk about with anyone else. I'm sure you do the same. I feel we both have this twisted way of seeing things in order to cope. There's no doubt for me. But you?"

Questioning his doubt was like giving him the green light, and that was exactly what he wanted.

On his knees, Resto unzipped her boots and removed her socks. She wiggled her toes in relief. Sliding his hands up her dress to her thighs closing his eyes. His eyes flew open when he heard her whisper.

"Yes, Papi."

Inhaling a deep breath, Resto marveled at how perfect she was. Moving further up her thigh to her pussy, he slid his pointer finger in her honey pot.

"Yes, Papi, just like that. Fuck!"

"Papi, you're so good to me. Fuck yes, so good."

He removed her panties and applied pressure as he moved back and forth on her pussy. Diane opened her legs and looked down as he looked up. He slapped her thigh.

"Did I ask mama to move?"

"No papi"

"Then don't do it again."

"Yes, papi"

"Face forward. Close your eyes for me, mama."

Diane complied as Resto started the gentle slide between her legs again. It took everything in Diane not to rock, but she didn't want him to stop, so she remained still as her orgasm build.

"Fuck Papi, it's so fucking good. Please, can I move?"

"No mama this is a punishment for making me wait so long to have you here in the flesh."

Sensing she was on the edge, he stroked his finger in hitting her g spot continuing the sliding motion on her pussy lips.

"Mama going to be a good mama and cum on my hands?"

"Yes, Papi"

She moaned. She stopped and looked down at him as if it finally clicked. He didn't look up, just waited.

"Call me Mijo."

Resto warred with himself, but it's what he needed her to see.

"Yes Mijo."

Diane moaned. Resto released the breath he held and worked Diane's pussy until she shook, nearly collapsing as she came.

Diane didn't know why calling him son turned her on, but she liked it. He had mommy issues but didn't understand fully how deep they ran. She was about to find out. Standing, Resto took her hand and led her to the bathroom. He stripped all his clothes off. Diane shivered a bit at Resto's dick. It was long and thick, not as thick as Jared but with the nine inches he had and the girth; she was in for a world of hurt.

"Mama, you okay?"

Resto asked with a mischievous smile. Not answering, she took her jacket off and pulled her dress over her head. Unclasping her bra, she stepped into the back of the shower and waited.

"Does Mijo want mama to give him a bath?"

Resto's dick instantly stood.

"Yes, Mama."

He could not believe she accepted this. He couldn't contain his excitement. Resto turned on the shower, adjusted the temperature, and stood under the spray. Diane grabbed the Native Cucumber and Mint shower gel and squirted a bit on the sponge. Diane closed the distance between her and Resto.

"Mijo, just know this is new to mama so tell me when I'm doing something wrong. Your pleasure is my pleasure. Can you do that, Mijo?"

Hoping he would understand her meaning. She needed Resto to tell her what he wanted from his role-playing session so they would both enjoy the experience.

"Ay Dios Mio Mama." He whispered.

"Si, I'll let you know."

Diane ran the sponge under the water and methodically washed Resto from top to bottom. She noticed he was an average size man, five eight, medium build with the warmest brown skin tone. He was unblemished and beautiful. Once she finished with his feet, Diane stood, removed the shower head from the base and rinsed him from head to toe. On her way up, she stopped at his glorious dick.

"Mijo?" Resto looked down in tears.

"Si, mama?"

"Will you hold the shower head and focus on me while I focus on you?" She looked up to see if he understood.

Not acknowledging the tears that fell to her face. He took the nozzle and held it like a rainfall over Diane.

Resto gasped as Diane licked her lips and covered the head of his penis with her mouth. Closing his eyes, he focused on breathing while she went further and further down with each motion, back and forth. She sucked his dick so softly he thought he was going to cum at any moment. She kept a firm grip on the base to tamper it down. Diane sucked Resto with a firm, slow grip as she held the base of his penis with her right hand while massaging under his balls with the other. Lost in her own world, Diane sucked harder and faster, releasing the base of his penis and grabbing his butt cheek. She grabbed his other cheek and separated them. Diane gave a final downward slide on his dick and face planted at the base. She didn't move but continued to suck while pushing and pulling his checks. She stuck her middle finger in his ass and pumped in and out.

Resto was on the brink of lunacy as Diane sucked him with the suction of a vacuum. He was barely holding on and couldn't speak. The words weren't forming into a cohesive thought. Resto kept the water flowing over her. He didn't care if she could breathe as long as she didn't stop what the fuck she was doing. Grunting, moaning, and wet sucking were the only sounds bouncing off the shower walls as Diane worked him. When her finger eased in his ass, he nutted down her throat, dropping the shower head and grabbing the top of hers. He pushed her further into him while he continued to pump his release.

Chapter 17

Still wet and naked, Diane and Resto fell into bed after three rounds in the shower. Resto couldn't believe what he'd experience. Diane was not weird about what he wanted; she even took it further. He knew it was a sign from his mama that she was it for him. He laid back on the bed and Diane nestled comfortably in his arms.

He close his eyes as she shared stories of her childhood. He tried to merge her story and his mama's together, but realized they had totally separate experiences. Neither was more nor less tragic, just different. Diane didn't have an awful childhood as far as physical abuse, but abuse was abuse regardless of if it was physical or mental. Sometimes mental scars were worse.

It's funny how they both had fathers who were there more than their mothers, yet they yearned for their mother's love more than they cared for their father's. He shook out of his thoughts when he heard his name being called. "What was that?"

"Tell me about her."

"Mi mama?"

"Yeah." She stroked his chest. Resto recalled the story from a few weeks ago and picked up from there.

My abuela continued knitting, but by this time I lost interest in my cars and sat next to her on the sofa.

"Carmen and Jorge were so excited when they found out you were coming into the world. I didn't know about the drugs then and I knew you would settle her a little. It was important to me she remained who she was, just a calmer version. Ah Hijo, I wished I'd known, but I didn't know until you were born. The crying and shaking, I knew something wasn't right. Carmen said you had energy, but no baby had so much energy they'd shake the way you constantly shook. You all were living with me, so I could help Carmen and Jorge with you."

"She and Jorge spent more and more time away from the house since I was always home. Then things would go missing and I wouldn't see them for days at a time. I worried about your mama and papi, but you were my primary focus. took you to Doctor's appointment to figure out how to keep you calm so the shaking would stop, but the only thing that helped with that was patience and time."

Tu Mama and Papi continued their behavior until you were about three years old and Jorge came home frantically yelling.

"She's gone! She's gone!"

"Ay Dios Mio, that was a pain I wish no one would feel. It's nothing like losing your child."

Wiping her eyes, she then took her hand and wiped my tears as well. "Your Papi straighten himself out enough to become a real Papi to you, but it didn't last long."

His abuela smiled and caught Resto's nose between her index and middle finger, "Now I've you the smartest, beautiful, kind nieto anyone could ask for. Now let's get you something to eat. Yeah?"

It shocked Resto when he looked down at Diane and saw tears. She was crying while looking ahead as if she were imaging him and his Abuela on the sofa all those years ago. It did something to him. An ache formed in his chest. He crawled on top of her, spread her legs with his legs and entered her.

As Diane listened to Resto tell his story and felt her own sadness bubble up to the surface for herself and him. Overwhelmed she had to release it and the only option was her tears. When Resto noticed her crying, he gave her such a look of love. Of course it wasn't. Diane wasn't delusional, but him being concerned moved her. When he climbed on top of her, she was ready to do anything to get over this sadness. As she looked up at Resto, she noticed he also had tears in his eyes as he entered her. They both just stared at each other as he stroked away the sadness.

They "made love" most of the night, taking naps in between. It wasn't until the next morning Diane realized they'd had sex without protection.

She wasn't worried about the pregnancy, just Jared. He'd been adamant he didn't want to come behind anyone else if she'd fucked them raw. It wasn't planned, she just forgot. They were so caught up in the moment of a shared experience. "Ugh," she whispered as she rolled over and face planted into the pillow. Diane feared Jared wouldn't want her after this and all after all the time she spent agonizing over her decision.

"Fuck. Fuck. Fuck."

Resto was in the kitchen preparing eggs, fruit, and toasting bagels. Last night was the first time he had sex with a woman and didn't think of his mama. He didn't know if it was because Diane so closely resembled her or if it was because he purged the pain as she purged her own. He would not analyze it too much. "Que Sera Sera." Plating the food and placing it on the counter, he went to the ridge for the orange juice and then the coffee maker to retrieve the cups for coffee he'd prepared. Diane came walking out in nothing but a t-shirt of his. It was tight on her and stopped at the apex of her pussy. She was sexy as fuck.

"Morning." she said as she stretched, causing Resto's eyes to go to the rise of the shirt. Not being able to resist, he walked over to her. He kept walking, forcing her to walk backward.

"What are you doing? What's wrong? Are you okay?"

Resto said nothing until Diane out of the kitchen to the living room where she bumped into the couch. He forcefully spun her around and bent her over the back of it. Face planting in the seat with only her toes touching the floor. She asked again in a slightly raised voice.

"Resto? What's wrong? Are you okay?"

Through gritted teeth he responded with a whack to her ass and said, "Fine."

He got on his knees and pushed his face to her pussy. "Ah!" Diane cried out as Resto sucked. "Fuck Papi, that shit feels so fucking good. Oh fuck!"

Resto slapped her ass as he moved his face from side to side, slurping and sucking as he did. "I'm about to fucking cum!" He put his thumb in her ass, pushing in and out as he sucked harder. Diane couldn't move as her orgasm came with the force of a sledgehammer.

Resto didn't care Diane had passed out. He pulled his dick out of his pajama bottoms and entered her. Sinking as deep as he could and settled. Wiggling his hips from side to side, Diane stirred, so he slowly started pumping in and out of her. He reached up and grabbed her neck with both hands. Resto pumped harder and harder as she matched his thrust with the same force.

"Shit Diane, you feel so fucking good. Got dammit! I'm about to cum!"

"Please don't stop." Resto continued his slow, hard pump until Diane's second orgasm caused her pussy to squeezed his dick.

Resto shot his load as his grip tightened around her neck. He stayed seated in her after he was done and wiggled his hips for good measure before pulling out and helping her from the couch.

After showering again, Diane walked back into the kitchen and sat in front of a warmed plate on the counter. Resto watched thinking.

"Diane is fucking me."

Later that morning, Resto was sitting at his desk working on the revisions for his book while Diane laid on the couch and read. Most of the day they'd have mini conversations between his breaks, just casual, nothing too serious. The same as their text interactions had gone over the last month.

"What the fuck?" Resto whispered.

"What wrong? What happened?" Diane raised up to the sitting position.

"One of my students. Finn."

"As in Huck Finn?"

Diane laughed until she saw the expression on Resto's face didn't change. "Sorry, the door was open, and I walked in before reading the room."

"One of my students from last year. He took my creative writing class. The kid is an amazing writer. Someone attacked in his dorm room last night. The school sent a memo."

Diane worried. This was the second attack, and this one took place on campus. It couldn't have been a local. "I'm sorry they hurt your student. Did they say if he was going to be okay?"

"No, just that he's in the hospital recuperating from his injuries."

"Damn, that's fucked up. First my friend and now your student." Resto looked at her a little annoyed.

"Don't you mean both of your friends?"

"No." Diane said sarcastically, moving her neck and hands. "I don't know anyone named Finn."

"So you going off with people you don't know? Or are you lying? You don't need to lie."

"Lying? What are you talking about? I didn't go off with anyone." Diane stood up as she raised her voice to Resto.

Disbelief settled on Resto's face as he realized Diane had a one-night stand and didn't bother to ask his name.

"The guy you left with at the poetry event? You didn't know his name?"

Realization dawned on her as she fell back on the couch with a worried look on her face as she bit her bottom lip. “His name was Finn?” She said, more to herself than Resto.

“I just fucked him, dressed, and told him I didn’t need to know his name. We were just fucking that night. Shit. Shit. Shit.”

Diane stood and paced the length of the room. He wasn’t my type, but he was sweet in a hippy dippy sort of way. Damn, they attacked him?” Resto held an expression she couldn’t read.

“I hope you used protection?”

“Yeah, I did. I always do. Well, except for you and Jared. And I told you about him so...” She was right.

“The only guy who she considered committing to.” Her words.

“Resto?!” Snapping back to the present, “Yeah.”

“This is the second person I know that’s been attacked. What if I’m next? What about Kim? Who would want to harm people I know?”

Stopping her before she had gone too far, Resto got up and pulled her on the sofa with him.

"Hey. Hey. Don't worry, you're going to be fine. These attacks can't be related. You didn't even know Finn's name. Besides, you haven't been at Howard long enough to develop enemies. Relax."

"Maybe, but I don't know. Admit it, this shit is kinda creepy." Resto didn't like the frown Diane had all over her face. He got up and walked over to his desk and pulled a knife out of the drawer.

"Here." Sitting down, placing a small pocketknife with a pearl handle in her hand.

"What's this?"

"It's a pocketknife. Don't let the small size fool you. Go deep and once you're in, move it around to cut any vital organs that are within striking distance. It was my dad's, and he gave it to me when I was being picked on for my shakes."

Diane twirled it around in her hands. She opened and closed it as if getting a feel for it. "You ever used it?"

"I grew up in the Bronx. What do you think?"

Chuckling, "That's not an answer Resto"

"It's the only one you're going to get. Now do you know how to use it or you want me to show you?"

"No, I think I've got it. Thanks." Flipping it around, she noticed the name.

"Who's Carmen?"

"My mama."

They spent the day taking naps, reading, and feeding each other. Diane agreed to spend another night with him since they were having such a good time. Resto became annoyed when she kept asking if he really meant it or was it was because he felt sorry for her. She relented after he pinned her down and started tickling her.

Diane rested in his bedroom as Resto prepared dinner comprising Pernil con frijoles y arroz con ensalada. He said it was his Abuela's recipe. The smells woke her but it was too early for dinner to be ready, so she snooped a bit. She opened the drawer of his nightstand. Surprised and excited by what she found, she kept snooping.

The pork roast in the oven would take some time to cook, so Resto relaxed on the couch. He slept no more than ten minutes when he felt Diane standing over him. One eye opened, he saw she went on a scavenger hunt and found his vibrator. Looking down, he shook his head. The only thing she had on was a pair of boy shorts and his strap attached to her hips, shaking it side to side.

"Why didn't you open your freak drawer last night?"

"Because the moment didn't call for it. Besides, last night I wanted to be the one fucking not getting fucked."

The burst of laughter that escaped her relaxed him. It did not freak her out, knowing he enjoyed being pegged. "I've never used one. I wonder if I'd be any good at it? Will you let me know? I mean? I mean, will you teach me?"

Resto loved the way she rapid fired questions when she was nervous.

"Are you serious? You don't mind that I enjoy getting fucked?"

"No, why should I? Get it how you get it? So, does this mean you're bisexual or just like being pegged?"

"Both."

"Oh." Resto had to ask. "Is that a problem for you?"

He had plans for him and Diane. If she didn't agree with his life choices, he didn't know what he'd do.

"No, I don't have a problem with it. I mean, if we were in a relationship, I'd expect monogamy just as if you were hetero. Have you been using protection with your partners? I mean, since we barebacked it last night and all."

Fully upright, he observed her standing there big beautiful breasts with their natural hang, her stomach so fucking juicy looking and her pelvis with a strap-on hiding all of that pussy from him. God, he fucking loved her body.

"I never not used protection even with my girlfriends since my twenties, that is until last night. I don't intend to not protect myself unless it is with you. You okay with that?"

"Yeah, I'm okay with that and just so you know Jared and now you are the only guys ever I've gone bare back with. Are you cool with that?"

He reached for her hand and she accepted.

"Cool with you fucking someone else? No. Fucking Jared bareback? No. I can't tell you what to do since we aren't official or anything yet. I don't want you to fuck him. Condom or not."

Standing, he reached for the vibrator. She handed it to him. Resto clicked the button. The vibrator buzzed. He placed it under the strap-on in her pussy.

"For the record, when I'm in a relationship, I'm always monogamous.

"Fuck" Diane moan as she closed her eyes and rocked on the vibrator Resto moved up and down in her.

"Resto?"

"Yeah?"

He said, his lips on her lips, "Can I fuck you?" More pressure was applied as he wrapped his arm around her waist and Diane came.

"Yes."

Kissing Diane through her orgasm, Resto led her to the bedroom. Her lips made a pop as he freed them while he fondled her breast. Resto told her to imagine how she wants a man to make her feel while penetrating her. What she would and wouldn't like, telling her it's the same for men just at a different entrance. Nodding in understanding. Diane kissed him inserting tongue, she nibbled his lips.

"What about your penis?" Smiling, she continued to kiss and lick his lips.

"You would jerk it if you could keep the rhythm, if not, I can."

Diane wrapped her tongue around his and sucked as he pinched her nipples. She squeezed his dick.

Laying sideways facing each other on the bed, Diane stroked Resto while he sucked her titties.

"Fuck, Resto, that feels so good. Don't stop, it's making me wet."

Resto compiled while taking the vibrator switching it back on. He pulled the boxer briefs from her thighs and inserted it in her.

"Oh shit. Fuck yeah."

He smiled as he watched Diane's eyes closed.

"Remember," he said, "Your goal is my pleasure, my goal is yours. You ready to please me?"

Instead of answering she slid down while the vibrator continued to work on her now soaked pussy, taking Resto's penis in her mouth. She sucked up and down in time with the vibrator.

"Holy fuck yes, fuck."

Diane bobbed up and down as the vibrator cause trembling throughout her body. She pushed her lips to the base of his dick and sucked through him and her through their orgasm. With a huge smile on her face as she removed the vibrator, lifted and slapped his thigh.

"Turn over. I want to taste your ass."

Resto couldn't stop the smile that appeared on his face as he complied with her command, his forearms and knees resting on the bed. He felt Diane kissing and licking his cheeks as she ran a finger down his ass crack applying pressure to his perineum. His dick bricked immediately, which shocked him after just cumming.

Diane buried her face between his cheeks and licked from the bottom to the top while massaging his dick.

"Fuck. That feels good." Diane lifted.

"I'm enjoying this. It's liberating as hell."

She took both hands, one on each cheek, she open him and buried her face in his ass, licking and tongue fucking him as he rocked into her. Diane swirled her tongue as Resto moaned and cursed. She gently slapped his left cheek and loved the way it sounded. She sucked her middle finger and slid it in his ass slowly at first and as he loosened up, she went faster and deeper.

Resto grabbed his dick and began squeezing it to prevent himself from nutting again. He couldn't believe she was here and willing to allow his proclivities to play out. It was mind blowing.

"Mama you feel so fucking good."

"Do I Mijo?" Falling right into the role. Resto squeezed his dick harder.

"Si mama."

"Mijo I'm going to open you up more so you can take my dick. So be a good boy for mama, okay?"

He felt pre-cum on his fingers as he nodded his head. His words were lodged in his throat. Diane added her index and ring finger, fingering in and out while twisting in his ass. Standing, she continued to work his ass as she reached for the lube she left on the bed when she found his sex stash. Resto groaned, when she removed her finger and popped him on the ass.

"Me Mijo not being a good boy for mama?"

"Fuck. Lo siento mama"

"It's okay Mijo, I know you're excited. Mama is going to make it good for you." Resto nodded as he continued to squeeze his dick.

She inserted the buzzing vibrator back in her pussy.

"Fuck yeah."

Diane popped open the lube and squirted a bit in her hand. Her face was back in his ass and licking a bit while massaging the strap with the lube. She positioned herself behind him. Diane slapped his hand away from his dick and wrapped her right hand around it while holding on to his waist with her left. She aimed the penis at his opening and pumped little pumps at his asshole. After a few minutes, her strokes synced with the pumps to his opening. She went deeper, pulling back, deeper, pulling back. She pushed in his ass until she bottomed out as she jerked his dick.

Resto couldn't believe how good she felt. He wanted to nut and wait as long as possible at the same time.

"Mijo, mama needs your help. Can you help mama?" It took the strength of God for him to answer.

"Yes, mama"

"I want to go deep but I don't want to give you more than you can take, so help me by pushing back as I push forward. Can you do that for me?"

Unable to answer, Resto pushed back as Diane pushed forward, she continued to stroke his dick. It was sensory overload, and he was about to lose it.

The vibrator was working with Diane's pussy and the closer she came to cumming, the harder she fucked and stroked Resto. "Oh God Mijo! Mama is going to cum! You going to cum with mama?"

"Si! mama Si!" Resto yelled.

"Okay baby. Grabbed your dick and stroke it while mama takes you to another level."

Doing as she said when Diane released him, he grabbed his dick and started stroking, urging his nut to come. She continued to hold his waist with one hand as she pounded into him and used her free hand to press his perineum in a circular motion.

"Fuck! Take this dick, nigga! Who's ass is this? Who. The. Fuck. Ass. Is. This?!"

Diane asked, and she pounded harder and harder as the vibrator had her chasing her own orgasm.

Resto's body seized as he shot his load while Diane pounded him from the back with pressure on his balls. The warmth of his seed on his chin was the last thing he remembered before blacking out. Diane moved so that both hands were on his waist as she tried to pound her pelvis into him.

"AHHHHH! Shit!" she screamed as she came.

Collapsing forward on the bed, Diane followed Resto, easing the strap out as she did. On her back, she lifted her hips, removed the strap and vibrator out of her sore pussy. Resto turned his head to face Diane, who was now lying on her side facing him.

"I don't give a fuck what you or Jared say. You're fucking mine."

Too tired to argue, Diane closed her eyes and fell asleep.

Chapter 18

Waking up early the day after Thanksgiving, Diane left Resto's after breakfast. As she drove home, she replayed the conversation they'd had, or rather what Resto expected from their situation ship from now on. She'd agreed since she felt the same way.

"I want you to take the time you need to resolve whatever you need to with this other guy."

"You know his name. Why are you being like that?"

"Yeah, I know his name, but it's irrelevant or will be in a few months. As I was saying, take whatever time you need to resolve your feelings for him and we can continue seeing each other as friends who sleep together unless you changed your mind. I'm hoping if you want sex, you'd come to me before messing with any other guys at school. It's bad enough I'm agreeing to share you as is. I know I can't say anything to convince you we should be in a relationship. Just know you are mine."

"No public displays of affection at school. Did I miss anything or leave something out?"

Looking pensively at Resto. "Just to be clear, I'm going to start a getting to know you phase with Jared. I owe him that after being pursued by him for the last few months, and I really want to make sure I make the right decision and have my feelings sorted through thoroughly."

Diane realized Resto didn't understand how much Jared meant to her. she was going to have to let him go and soon.

He helped her off the stool and walked her to the back of the sofa. "I love that you like wearing dresses and skirts."

Resto pulled up her pleated skirt and moved her panties to the side, he stuck his fingers in her pussy. "I fucking love this pussy."

Diane bit her bottom lip and held onto the back of the couch as her head fell back while Resto finger fucked her with three fingers. He removed his fingers. Sliding his rock-hard dick in and not stopping until they were pelvis to pelvis. He grabbed her waist and start jack hammering in Diane as she placed her legs on each side of the back of the sofa.

"This pussy weeping for me."

Slowing his pace and capturing her clit in his index and middle fingers, he squeezed as he continued to fuck Diane. She definitely enjoyed this, but it had to end.

Once parked she text Resto, she'd made it home. Diane had her overnight bag secured as she made it safely in the building and in her room. Checking for any other text that may have come in, she noticed Kim sent her a Happy Turkey Day text, but nothing from Jared. True to his word, he was giving her this weekend.

The first week of December Diane and Jared agreed to getting to know each other with the intent on becoming a couple. They also agreed to monogamy. Diane was going to hold herself accountable as long as she could, but deep down knew she would be in Resto's bed if he called. She'd figured this one lie wouldn't affect anything. As long as he didn't find out.

She was meeting Jared at Starbucks, so they could go back and study before the weekend. As she reached the doors, someone grab her around the waist. Spinning to curse a nigga out, she noticed it was Chocolate Drop.

"Hey." She spoke, looking back for Jared.

"Hey lil momma, how my pussy doing?"

"Your pussy? Naw, that was a one time thing. I have to focus on school."

"The opportunity has presented itself. Let me make that thang thang squirt again."

Diane pushed out of his arms. "I'm talking to someone now, so it won't be happening with us again." He seemed unbothered.

"That nigga ain't got shit on me lil momma, but I'll let you have it. Women go to college to find a husband. No, correction, a college educated husband."

"I didn't say..." but before she finished, Jared came out the door. "Hey Jared. I was on my way in when I bumped into my friend."

"Your friend huh?"

Jared grunted as the two sized each other up. "It's cool college boy. She let me know what's up? Lil' momma, keep the squirting game reserved for me."

Before he could part his lips to laugh, Jared knocked him square in the jaw. "You need to watch yo mouth disrespectful ass nigga. I was gon' let you have it. Fuck round and find out. I'm local, just like you, and I can get you that work."

Snatching Diane by the hand, Jared took his time walking to the corner with her. Wishing that the nigga was feeling froggy. "Jared, I promise you

I wasn't entertain..." Cutting her off, "Man, shut the fuck up. I'm trying to calm the fuck down and you bout to make it worse."

They crossed the street and headed to the Towers. Never seeing Jared act this way before, Diane was a little nervous going back to the dorm with him, however remained quiet, giving him the opportunity to calm down as he requested.

Fast walking to keep up with Jared, Diane knew for a fact he hadn't calmed down by the time they'd reached the elevators. Once she got on the elevator and caught her breath, she looked up at Jared, who was looking straight ahead at the doors. Biting her bottom lip, Diane could understand him being upset, but she was with that guy when they had still been friends. The elevator doors opened and Diane rushed to open the door. Kim and Ginger were in the kitchen cooking something and kissing. Jared looked at Ginger and he immediately whispered in Kim's ear, asking her to give him a second. He and Jared walked into the bathroom and closed the door.

Kim and Diane looked at each other. Kim waited for Diane to give her an explanation. Huffing, she jerked her head toward her room.

"Okay, girl, what the fuck did you do already? Y'all just started this "talking to each other stage."

Using air quotes and plopping down on the futon. Diane sat on the bed and kicked off her shoes.

"Some local I fucked homecoming week. He stopped me, started being touchy feeling and Jared saw. Of course, they had a dick slinging contest and Jared knocks that nigga on his ass and now he's pissed."

Shaking her head, Kim laughed. "You know what is it? He spent all this time patiently waiting for you to, "Get your shit together."

Now that he has you, he's going to hold you accountable for everything you did that he knows about when y'all weren't together."

Diane looked up at Kim. "I told you, never tell a nigga that ain't your man shit."

"I was trying to be honest, so he'd know I was trying to fuck him around."

"Yeah, I get it, but if he wasn't your man, you shouldn't have been treating him like he was."

Shrugging, Kim looked at her like it was something she should know. Crossing her legs, she sat further back on the bed. Diane felt like it should've been something she knew, but she'd never been in a relationship. She was an honest person and didn't believe lying benefited anyone.

"Yeah, you're right. I know now. He went bananas." She and Kim were laughing when Ginger and Jared walked to the door.

Kim got up and gave Diane a half hug and whispered, "Stop telling that nigga shit." Giggling, Diane hugged her back.

"Thank you girl, I will." Jared stepped further in the room, leaning on the desk, allowing Kim to walk out.

Closing the door, Ginger gave Diane a shrug smile then looked at Jared. "You think this shit a joke, huh?"

Diane stood. "Jared no, I don't think this is a joke. I fucked him before we switched this," moving her finger between them, "up. What you need to realize is I have hidden nothing from you and if you'd asked for a rundown, you would've gotten it. I'm not apologizing for enjoying sex and as long as it was safe, you can cancel that anger shit!"

Jared made his way to her, slid his hands down her arm in order to release some of the tension he was holding in his shoulders. Diane asked, "Do you want to know the run down before we go any further?"

Hoping he'd say no, he looked at her as if to say well. "Fuck it. Fine!"

Putting some space between them, she looked at him again and saw the anger bubbling to the surface. She wasn't a bitch, but Jared was a man and a hurt man could do anything.

"What you backing up for? I don't hit women. Stop playing with me Diane, like I'm an abuser or something."

"I'm not saying you are, but you are not you right now. You sure you want to know?"

Closing his eyes, he blew out a breath chuckling. "Why you look scared?"

"Because I am. You sure?"

Blowing another breath Jared watched as Diane took another step back, clearing her throat she said, "There was Brenda, Latisha, Linda, Felicia. Dawn, LeShaun, Ines and Alicia."

Laughter erupted in the space as Jared pulled her in a hug. "You DMX now? You wild as shit. I'm about to fuck all that shit outta you, though. Cause these niggas stop today."

Raising her chin for confirmation. She nodded.

Jared ran his hands down between her breasts. It's going to be rough, and he didn't care how she felt about it. The need to consume Diane was strong. Even if he doubt he ever could. Jared grabbed her neck and squeezed while pulling her closer to him. He stroked her tongue with his, biting her lips, devouring her. Water gathered in her eyes and he didn't know if it was from the pressure or fear. She stood still, looking at him in confusion and unknowing. He wanted her to feel uncomfortable, so she'd never forget what it felt like if she ever tried to be with another guy.

Diane had on her Howard sweatshirt and leggings. Her hair was it a twisted out mohawk, and her feet were bare.

"Take off your clothes and don't rush."

Jared watched as Diane removed her sweatshirt, then her bra. Her breast swung slightly from being restricted and they were fucking gorgeous. It reminded him of grapefruits.

"Stop."

He said when she hooked her hands in her leggings to remove them. That fear and confusion in her eyes was what he wanted. Diane looked down.

"Don't. Look at me. I want to see you. Vulnerable you."

Tears pooled in the corners of her eyes as Jared continued to stare. Her stomach looked so fucking soft. Jared loved the lower half, that hang made his mouth water. He got on his knees and pulled her leggings down just below her stomach.

Gliding his fingers along her stomach, squeezed the lower half. He leaned in and licked from her navel down to her pelvis and back up. Jared gave attention to every part of her stomach. Diane grabbed his head for balance and he pushed her back onto the bed. Hooking his hand on the side of her leggings and underwear, he pulled them down to her ankles. Holding on the middle of her leggings and the strap of material she called underwear. He raised her legs up and pushed them forward above her head.

Her knees bent outward, opening her wide. He could smell her arousal and see her glistening pussy as her ankles stopped at her shoulders.

"Take both hands and grab the middle of the leggings."

He ordered. She did. Jared watch Diane in the position. Her breast were delectable and her pussy opened wide with her asshole puckered. He had a perfect view of everything.

Watching him watch her, Diane felt exposed and aroused at the same time she was slightly crying. Jared had her fully opened vulnerable. She didn't know how to feel about it. Jared slid his middle finger from her clit through the wetness that gathered in and around her pussy, pushing his finger in her ass. Startling Diane, she almost released her leggings. Jared paused and looked at her.

"You okay?"

"Um yeah."

Jared repeated the motion, middle finger from clit through pussy in her asshole. He repeated it until Diane's pussy and puckered hole pulsed in and out, wanting to be filled.

"Holy fuck Jared!" Diane's entire body convulsed.

"Shit lil momma, that pussy and ass wet for me. Which one should I take first?"

His finger entered her ass again, and he circled it inside her.

"Oh, my fucking God! Jared!"

Jared didn't look up at Diane. It enthralled him with the way her body reacted to him. This was punishment, so he was going to take his time. He pushed his thumb in Diane's pussy with four fingers on her clit. He fucked her with his thumb while applying pressure. Jared lined his dick to her ass and looked at Diane.

"I'm not going to go easy."

Head still lifted, Diane couldn't speak. she tried to move her lower half to chase the feeling of her pussy and clit being worked. Head back on the pillow.

"Shit I'm so fucking close. Fuck!"

Jared slowed his movement to a languid pace as he pushed in her still pulsing ass. It sucked him in.

"This ass missed me."

He pumped in and out for her ass as his thumb and finger worked her pussy and clit.

"You gave my ass to anybody?"

Diane was so overwhelmed she didn't answer. The only noise was the wet sounds from her pussy and the slap of Jared's dick. Burying his dick deeper in her ass, he buried his thumb as far as it would go in her pussy and swept upward.

"Ahhh fuck!" She screamed.

"Answer me! Anybody been in my ass?"

"Fuck no." she cried. He wreaked havoc on her body. She was shaking and convulsing at the pleasure he extracted. Jared pounded in her ass, he grabbed her lower abdomen. It always pushed his nut forward.

Every time Jared stroked up, the entire side of the bed banged on the wall. Diane's legs trembled as she repeated she was close. When she looked like she was about to come, he pulled out, moved his hand, and stepped away. Grabbing his dick, he tried to stop from cumming. Diane paused and before she could open her mouth to say a word, Jared latched onto her entire pussy and clit and sucked. He sucked and sucked as he squeezed and released her stomach. On the fifth suck, Diane exploded and Jared continued his assault. Once she crested, Diane attempted to move. Jared stopped her from getting up.

"What are you doing? We not done."

He pressed his hand on her thighs as he stuck his leaky dick in her ass and pounded into her like he was tenderizing meat. His nut came so hard, Jared saw dots behind his eyelids. Burying himself as far as he could go, he leaned all the way on Diane and pressed her thighs even farther. Diane's eyes glazed over.

"I'm ruining your whole muthafucking life. I hope you're ready."

After showering, Diane rode Jared to another orgasm before they called it a night. Lying in bed with Jared half asleep.

"There was only one more you don't know about. Eli. He's in my production class and it happened after I left the step show."

Resting her head on his chest, she let out a breath. Squeezing her tighter, Jared didn't tell her he heard that night, but was glad she told him. "Thank you. Now get some rest." Nodding, Diane closed her eyes as she thought about Resto.

Chapter 19

Resto and Diane continued learned more about each other over the next couple of weeks. He was happy that she seemed just as enthusiastic and excited about their budding friendship. She mentioned the incident with Jared at Starbucks and he told her that maybe she should take her friend's advice and not mention her past. He felt like Diane was more mature compared to Jared and she should adjust herself around him. Airing on the side of caution, she also told him about Eli stating she didn't want any secrets between them.

Mi Amor: How are you feeling about all of this?

Naughty Professor: All of what?

Mi Amor: You know me and Jared, the production sex with Eli, all of it?

Naughty Professor: I'm fine with you doing what you need to as long as it leads to me.

Mi Amor: Make me wet. LOL.

Naughty Professor: Get your mind out of the gutter. When am I going to get some of your time?

Mi Amor: Well, the last day of classes, finals and grades are due this next week and a half, so the week before Christmas? There won't be any classes and I'll just be bored.

Naughty Professor: Are you saying I get the entire week? You? Here with me?

Mi Amor: LOL yes! I mean if that's what you want? Is it?

Naughty Professor: Having you in my space to read, talk and have sex with each other? That would be a hell yeah!

Diane enjoyed Resto the more she conversed with him. It wasn't this way with Jared. Not fully. She realized his insecurities determined how he operated around her. Diane enjoyed spending time with him when it was just them. He was at ease, relaxed, just Jared, but when they spent time out with Ginger and Kim, he gave off stalker vibes. Too close, too possessive, just different. She hung in there because she wanted to make sure that it wasn't just her issues. She didn't want to make the wrong final decision.

Resto was more mature, of course. He was older and had lived. Diane felt like they could relate to each other more due to their childhood trauma. They laughed, talked about life, dreams, and the past. He wasn't afraid to open up once he realized he could trust her. That was the one thing missing from her and Jared's relationship. He didn't trust her and knew part of it had to do with his mother's absence. He never discussed his mom and would shut her down every time she asked. It was becoming too much work, and she was exhausted.

The holidays were around the corner. Jared asked Diane to spend Christmas with him and she agreed. A part of her wasn't sure if she agreed because it was a place to stay or to get closer to him. Maybe it was a little of both. Classes were empty and professors didn't seem to mind. The professor for her production classes never showed. Diane walked with Eli both excited about the holiday break. It wasn't awkward at all. Actually, Eli was just as cool as he was in class. Some guys act weird when you hook up like you want to be with them be with them.

Once they got to Georgia Ave., they hugged and went their separate ways. Heading to her room, Diane didn't notice Jared until she almost ran into him.

"Hey! Jared." Hugging him as his attention went elsewhere.

"Where you heading? Do you have time to hang out?"

Diane noticed Jared looking a bit distressed. "Hey are you okay? What's going on?"

Finally giving her his attention "Who was that? That guy is a classmate or something."

Focusing in on the direction he was, Diane saw Eli's back. "Yeah, that's Eli. He's in my production class. The Professor never showed, so we bounced."

"Huh."

Shaking her head, Diane took his hand. "Come on. I want to be horizontal with you so we can cuddle, talk, and sex each other up."

She ignored what she knew he was thinking. If he was going to trust her, she would have to act like Eli was no big deal. It was yet another strike against him.

Jared noticed Diane's change in demeanor when they got to her dorm room. He didn't understand how she didn't see that shit as disrespectful. Jared entered the space. He spoke to Kim and Ginger, who really was his LB Kenny. As soon as he entered Diane's room, the energy felt different. She was standing in the middle of the room, bracing. For what he didn't know, but he had the act right for whatever it was.

"What the entire fuck is wrong with you, Jared? The fuck happened to you that made you so fucking insecure? What was it? Cause the shit you've been on lately is fucking sad."

Diane was looking at him with disgust "What the fuck is wrong with me?! How does your nonemotional ass don't see that the shit you did was fucking disrespectful and fucked up? Huh?

" Getting closer, they were about six inches apart, facing each other. "First of all, this is my pussy! My pussy nigga and before we made things official of "starting" to get to know each other better," she said with air quotes. I could and did give it to whomever the fuck I wanted to. Now your weak ass can't handle that. You want to mean mug every nigga that hit?"

"Diane! Heard you fucking that nigga! I heard that nigga put his dick in you and how you moaned when he did it! I heard how wet your pussy was when that nigga was knocking the box down! So you muthafucking right, I mean mug that nigga!"

Jared fist balled. He tried to get control of his feelings. Kim and Kenny were now standing at the door refereeing in case it got physical. "I should smack you for that shit. How the fuck you butt-dialing me when you getting dick! Huh? Answer that shit! Acting like a mutha fucking hoe!"

Jared smirked in gratification from the expression on Diane's face. She was shocked as she replayed what had happened that night in her head, right in front of him.

"Yeah, now what the fuck you got to say? And on the night my frat placed at the step show. You should've been celebrating with me, Diane. Me! But you were getting your pussy worked by a nigga you don't even fucking know!"

Tears formed in his eyes and his throat tightened, which caused the rage deep in him to bubble to the surface. It did not embarrass him to show his emotions. She didn't get it. "Fuck!"

Lowering her tone "I apologize for what you heard. I didn't know, but I do not apologize for fucking him or anyone I ever fucked since I started fucking. You act like I didn't set the expectations when we first got involved. I'm making concessions for you can't you see how difficult it's been for me and how much that means I care for you."

"Un fucking believable!" He yelled.

"You make it sound like it was an inconvenience to give us, not me, us, a chance at something amazing. Yeah, your parents really fucked you up. You sure you weren't sexually abuse you as a child cause..." He knew she wasn't, but he wanted to make her feel as bad as he did at that moment.

Diane let the tears she'd been holding fall as she threw her fist as hard as she could at Jared's jaw. Shocked, Jared couldn't believe she'd hit him. Conflicted and happy, she finally showed emotion, but he pissed because she had fucking hands. His jaw was on fire. The swings kept coming, and he attempted to grab her wrist to stop her.

Kim must have thought he was going to hit her back and suddenly he felt blows from behind. They were coming so quick and fast he didn't know whose punch was whose. His LB knew he would never hurt a woman and was thankful when he pulled Kim from behind, wrapping his arms around her and sitting them both on the bed. Gaining control of Diane's wrist, he pulled her to him and encased her arms and body in a hug.

"Man, I'm sorry. That shit was outta pocket. I'm sorry," he said. Diane shook as the tears turned into cries and he noticed movement to his right. Kim was trying to get loose, to get her lick for making her girl cry. "Man, you're shorty got hands. Don't piss her off."

Jared smirked at Kenny, trying to defuse the situation and let his boy know he was calm. Laughing, Kenny asked with his eyes and Jared responded, "Yeah I'm good, thanks bro."

Kissing Kim on the neck, she stopped struggling and looked at Kenny. "Come on, let's go lay down."

Kissing her again. He helped her up, and they went to Kim's room.

"I'm sorry, baby. I overreact with you, but I don't know what to do about it or how to control it. It'll get better. I'll be better just please give us a chance. A real chance."

Diane looked at Jared. "Why won't you tell me about your mom? I feel like I would understand you better if you would open up to me about certain things. You may not be closed off emotionally like I am, but you hold shit so tight to your chest. I'm surprised your sternum ain't cracked."

Jared released her and looked down into her eyes. With a tight jaw, he didn't respond.

Eli was smoking and relaxing on his bed. He hated the Meridian dorms. They were so far away from campus and next year he was getting something closer or a room in a shared house. Feeling sleepy, he was thankful when he heard the Door Dash driver at his door. He didn't get called downstairs this time. The lazy RA probably wasn't at the desk.

The assailant was playing it close, walking into Meridian. Anyone from campus could've recognized him. He was pretty popular even though he didn't associate with many people. He would leave via the stairs if anyone came down the hall. It was pretty dead since the holidays were around the corner. Tucked in his sleeve, Jared made sure Diane could easily slip out. He took a breath as the door opened.

Pushing Eli's chest with the palm of his left hand, he lifted his right and as he came down, Diane slid out into his palm perfectly. Crack! The first hit stunned him. He kept pummeling him in the head as he walked further in the room, kicking the door closed behind him. It took Eli a minute before he realized what was going on. Thinking he was being robbed by the DoorDash guy, he cried out as he attempted to block the hits.

"My wallet and laptop are on the desk, take it!" Stumbling back on the floor, the assailant began stomping him in the stomach and chest. One last crack and Eli blacked out.

The assailant smirked at his handy work. He wrapped Diane in a t-shirt, stuffing it back in his sleeve. He calmed himself and walked out of the dorm room, hoping no one would see or ask why he was in Meridian.

Resto text Diane to make sure they were all still a go for this week. School was closed, and he was ready to get to know her a bit better. Since sleeping with Diane, his mother didn't visit his dreams anymore, and the shakes weren't as frequent.

Naughty Professor: I can't wait to have you the next three days

Mi Amor: I can't wait to be in your arms. You comfort me. I didn't know I need or missed.

Naughty Professor: Mismo. I'm going to cook for us. What do you feel like?

Mi Amor: You

Naughty Professor: Tomorrow

Diane was hoping Jared didn't come by before she left to go to Resto's. He may want sex and she couldn't sleep with him and Resto back-to-back. It was bad enough she was lying to Jared, but she wanted to explore whatever she and Resto shared a bit more.

As she packed her bag, she thought of the time they spent conversing with each other about everything and nothing at all. She didn't feel butterflies; she felt a connectedness she couldn't explain and didn't want to try. Her phone beeped. Kim and Kenny made it safely to his hometown for the long break. As she zipped up her bag, she heard the door to the space opening up. "Did I forget to lock the door?" Jared came in and locked it behind him.

"So we just leaving doors open?"

"So we just walking in unlocked doors? I must've forgotten to lock it when Kim left."

"That was five hours ago."

"I know I got distracted." She said as she placed her overnight bag under her desk, hoping he didn't notice.

"I thought you had fraternity business to handle before break."

"I do and am handling the intake of the soon to be Neo's but I wanted to stop by and show you some love."

Jared pull out a chair and sat at the desk. "Come here."

He pulled Diane by the arm over to him. She sat her hips on the desk. He pushed up her nightgown and pushed her knees apart. "Jared, what are you doing?"

"What I'm doing? I'm about to taste my pussy. Stop asking questions, lean back and hold on." Hooking her knees in the crook of his arm, Jared pulled Diane forward and buried his face in her pussy.

Diane's head hit the wall as she held on to the edge of the desk as Jared ate her pussy like it was his lifeline. He sucked on her clit as his fingers worked her g spot over and over. "Fuuuuck! Jared, what the..."

The scream died on her lips as she shook. She could feel the pool of wetness on the crack of her ass and wondered what had gotten into him.

Why he hungered for Diane so much, he had no clue, but he couldn't stop tasting her. He ate her pussy until his dick got hard. He felt his nut rising to the tip. Abruptly standing, he unbuttoned and unzipped his jeans. Diane's glazed over eyes focused on his face as if on a heroin high. She smiled at him with the sweetest look of love. The tip of his dick was at her entrance. He leaned to her left ear. "I would do anything in this world for you. You get that, right?" Nodding as her head fell to the side, he slid in to the base of her cervix. He slowed his stroke in the hopes she understood what it meant. Grabbing her by the neck, he squeezed to get her attention. Once she focused on him, tears welled in his eyes. Through gritted teeth, "I would murder a muthafucka behind you. You hear me?" Squeezing tighter, her eyes rolled to the back of her head and she trembled through her orgasm, with Jared following close behind.

Diane was a little worried about Jared and wanted to make sure he was okay, but he left as quickly as he came. Literally. Something was up with him, but she assumed it was the upcoming holidays and the argument they recently had. She'd talk to him over the holidays to make sure he was okay. Diane felt deep down she and Jared would be okay once they got over this hump.

Maintaining just a friendship with no sex is the only option with Professor Resto. Once she'd fully commit to Jared. Diane and the Professor got along so well because of the shared family trauma of neglect. It's good because it was familiar, but that didn't make it good for you. Maybe Resto was Diane's way of slowly letting go of the old to embrace the rightness of the new. She blew out a breath as she closed her eyes.

Texting Resto, she was on her way. Diane threw her bag in the trunk and hopped into the car. She'd told Jared she wanted to take a few days to herself, so she booked a room for a mini spa vacation. It was the best she could come up with, since Kim was her only friend and she would never return to Radford.

Diane's heart decided this morning as she allowed her emotions to do what they do. This was definitely the last fling before fully committing to Jared. She set her phone on Do Not Disturb, turned on the GPS and pulled out of the parking lot.

Chapter 20

The door opened. Resto pulled Diane into a tight embrace and kissed her lips. She returned the kiss, deepening it. "Hey, let me get your bag. Make yourself at home."

At the door, she removed her coat and shoes. She wiggled her toes and looked around at his space, as if she was committing it to memory. She wouldn't be back. Diane sat on the sofa and noticed the book she was reading still on the coffee table. Stretched out on the sofa, she grabbed the book and flipped to where she left off.

Resto stood at the entrance to the living room and marveled at how much Diane resembled his mama. The way she spread out is how he imagined his mama lounged at his Abuela's as a teen.

"Why don't you go shower and get into more comfortable clothes while I finish dinner?" Sitting up she asked. "Oooo another Puerto Rican dish?"

"Pollo Guisado con arroz or as Black folks call it, Stew Chicken and rice."

"Nope, not if it has Sofrito in it."

"Touché. Now go shower."

With a towel wrapped around her body, Diane stepped out of the shower. She reached in her bag for her body oil and began moisturizing from head to toe. She threw on a Fruit-of-the-Loom tank top, a pair of red boy shorts with matching ankle socks. In the kitchen, she walked to the fridge and grabbed a bottled water for her and a beer for Resto. They watched each other drink.

"Go relax while I make a salad to go with the meal."

Resto bit his lip as he watched her ass in those tight boys' shorts with her lower cheeks peeking out. She had on a t-shirt and no bra, which had her palm size aureoles on display. He squeezed his dick, hoping it'd give some relief. Sex was a no no for now. He wanted them to do what regular couples did around dinnertime after work. He wanted to give Diane a peek into what life would be like with him, living, eating, sleeping in the same home. That was his end game.

Seated, Resto called Diane over. The counter filled with plated platters of rice and chicken with salad. They ate in silence while making eyes at each other. Diane got up and grabbed two beers each for her and Resto. Diane grabbed a bit of rice and sauce with her fingers, placing them in front of his mouth. He opened, and she pressed the food on his tongue. Resto closed his mouth while he sucked her fingers before pulling away as he chewed his food. Both fed each other the remainder of the meal.

Diane took a nap as Resto entered the last grades of the semester. An email notification from the school appeared. Another attack had taken place at the Meridian dorms off campus. The student was beaten so badly he was in a drug-induced coma. Resto kept reading until he saw the name Diane had mentioned the last time she visited. Decision made, he shrugged his shoulders. Nothing was going to ruin this time with Diane, so he deleted the email, turned off his laptop, all the lights, and walked into the bedroom to cuddle with her.

Resto stood at the bedroom door and watched as Diane slept. Her hair was in flat twist with no scarf. Remembering her words, *"I don't need one, my sides are shaved."*

One arm was stretched out under her head and the other thrown behind her back. Her grapefruit shaped breasts were resting nicely in her shirt and her thighs slightly spread in the scissor position. The covers were folded across the foot of the bed. Resto made sure his home stayed at a toasty eighty degrees in winter. He discarded his pajama bottoms and crawled in the bed behind Diane.

Boy shorts down to her knees, ass cheeks apart spread, Resto buried his face in Diane's puckered hole, working his tongue in and out of her. He continued licking her up and down the crack of her ass, hoping to have her wet enough so by the time she woke, he'd be dick deep in her. His window was small, but her soft snores told him he had time. He used his hands to push her right cheek, turned her slightly face down, to give him better access. When she lifted her head, he moved fast and flipped her completely on her stomach, hand placed on her back. He moved his body between her legs, while his face stayed buried in her ass.

Diane woke up to moisture on her ass and thought she'd had an accident. Fully awake, she lifted to get up when suddenly she was face down and Resto's body was between her legs with his face in her ass. Moaning when she realized what he was doing, Diane raised her ass which allowed him to continue as she moved her hand to her clit, rubbing in gentle circles. Shrugging she moaned, "Might as well."

Resto smiled when he realized Diane was playing with herself while he was at her back entrance. He got on his haunches as he watched. Her head turned to the right, hand between her leg was a sight he committed to memory. He reached forward with two fingers and fucked her pussy as she continued to strum her clit.

"Oh, fuck Resto," she whispered. He could hold back any longer. His dick was at her entrance. He placed both hands on either side of her hips, raising them as he entered her wet walls. He pushed and withdrew all the way out with Diane's wetness coating his dick. She remained up in the air. He grabbed her cheeks, separating them as he entered her ass, pushing until he bottomed out. Resto groaned.

"Somebody's ass has been fucked before. Who else is enjoying this tight hole, Mama?"

He withdrew to the tip then surged forward until he bottomed out again. He repeated this motion as he waited for an answer.

Moaning and pushing back, hoping to get Resto to increase his speed, Diane whispered breathlessly, "Jared was the first and only until you."

He grunted out a moan as he paused, buried to the hilt. Resto wanted to punish her for allowing someone in her ass, he knew it was irrational to be upset. He wasn't hers and she was a sexual person. How could he be mad at her for experimenting sexually? She pushed back harder as he began with long hard strokes. "Uh fuck Diane, this ass feels so good baby fuck! I'm about to cum."

Before she could respond, he grunted and pressed even harder, shooting everything he had in her. After a few minutes, Resto slid out of Diane, got a washcloth to clean her, then himself. Back in bed, they faced each other.

He kissed her softly. "What's on your mind?"

"I told him I wouldn't allow anyone else back there."

Resto kissed her again and again. He continued to kiss her until he was on top of her with his dick pressed in her. "I don't care what you told him. I'm not committed to him and didn't promise him anything. Now close this."

Pressing her lips together. "And these."

He grazed his fingers over her eyes. Resto slipped in her wet pussy and fucked her at a calming pace.

"It's for Papi only right now."

Saturday and Sunday were just as Diane expected: morning sex, meals, conversation, and naps. Not sure how Resto was going to react, she waited until her last day with him to end the benefits but offered to keep the friendship. Diane realized it was going to look as if she used him and a small part of her did. Both of them mentally used each other to figure out the past and make steps toward healing.

Diane was sitting on the sofa with her feet stretched out while Resto worked at his desk. With her head in a book, "Papi?"

He turned in her direction, "Si, mama?"

"Do you think you've healed from all of your abandonment issues with your mom and dad? I mean, I get you're working through them in your own way, but what about the dreams you have about your mom? Not judging. Just curious."

Attention back at her book, she wanted to give him the space he needed. Resto stood from his desk and joined her on the sofa. He lifted her legs and sat. "The wet dreams, you mean?"

Resto decided full transparency would be the only way they would move forward. Or backward. "I haven't had any since I started spending time with you. You look so much like her. If you weren't around, maybe the dreams would come back, but for now, they're gone. The role play? I do that for two reasons."

Diane's focus was solely on Resto now. "It started as my own twisted way to feel the comfort and love I didn't get from my parents and, two, I enjoy threesomes. I cope in weird ways and before you say it, yes, therapy is healthier, but this is the only thing I have of my parents that's just for me. I don't want to share that with anyone."

"Except me?"

"Like I said, you are so much like my mama. It's as if I'm talking to her. I think you are her to me, but the day we fucked, it became different. It wasn't her but you." He rubbed her feet comforting himself.

"What are you thinking?"

"Just maybe we are using each other so we won't have to address our trauma head on. We find comfort in each other. Make sense?"

"Yeah it does."

They woke up on the sofa in the position they fell asleep. After they handled their hygiene naked and wet, both got into bed. It was a melancholy mood. Sleep eluded them as they fondled each other. An attempt to memorize what they were about to lose. Diane got on top of Resto, aimed his dick at her entrance, sank down and they both moaned. She rode him slow as he held onto her breast, squeezing and pinching her nipples. They understood this was purge sex, nothing healthy, mentally or emotionally, would come from a relationship together. They couldn't continue to see each other.

"Mama you've left me again."

He whispered as he closed the door.

Chapter 21

Jared couldn't hold back his excitement as he confirmed with his granddad and dad that he and Diane would arrive for Christmas break.

Jared FaceTimed with his Dad and granddad. "I'll have the staff prepare the guest room for your lady friend."

Jared paused. "Dad, you can't be serious. Why separate rooms? She's the one."

With the definitiveness of his son's tone and the nod from Pops, his dad relented.

"Okay, son, just be respectful while you two are here." Jared understood what his father meant, but he is crazy if he thought he had not planned to blow Diane's back out while there visited.

"I will and thank you, dad."

"I can't wait to see you, Jared."

"Me too grandad. You're going to love her. She is everything. Everything."

Jared ended the call, grabbed his bags, and did a quick walkthrough his room. Ensuring he hadn't missed anything, he left to get Diane.

Diane was glad she had a few days in the dorm by herself. The time spent with Resto was intense but needed. She was going to miss him, but long term, it would not work. The relationship with Resto, helped her to solidify the things for her and Jared. It was time to express those feelings mentally and emotionally with him.

Diane's anxiety increased at the idea of being introduced to Jared's dad, but she's cognizant Jared would protect her as much as she could. Diane was used to parents who checked out in every way, so being around parents who were involved would be an experience. She'd just treat it like an extensive job interview.

Yelling it's opened when Jared knocked, Diane put her carry-on upright on the floor so he could roll it out. She gathered her crossbody, keys, and phone.

"Hey lil momma. You ready?"

"Ready for anything with you."

Washington, DC, away from Howard's campus, was like entering another world. Tree-lined streets with miles and miles of sidewalk. No dirt in sight, only grass on the yards of the row houses. Traffic was light until they reached 16th and Missouri Ave NW, which was one way to get to the Rockville, Silver Spring and Bethesda areas of Maryland. In the opposite direction, you'd be toward downtown DC in areas like Georgetown, Dupont Circle, and the museums. Diane looked out the window and relaxed into the newness of her current place in Jared's life.

Jared worried how Diane would view him when she found out his mom left, how he found her again, and how she didn't love him enough to stay. He reached over and grabbed the back of her neck, tugged to get her attention. She turned and said, "Hey you."

"Hey you. You doing okay? You look nervous, but I got you. I won't let anything happen, okay?"

"I know," she said, focusing back out the window.

It only took about twenty minutes to get to 16th street, Gold Coast. Jared was thankful traffic was light and glad to be home before all the cars lined their neighborhood to view the Christmas decorations that his father, along with his neighbors, paid to have professionally installed. In the driveway, Jared and Diane exited the car to retrieve their bags. Before Diane could walk toward the house, Jared grabbed her by the back of the neck and kissed her.

"Just promise me you're in this with me. Promise me you won't hold anything against me. Promise me you are in this until the rims hit the road." Bursting into giggles, Diane shook her head.

"Not until the wheels fall off? The rims hit the road?" He stood and waited.

She looked up at him. "I'm in."

The house was vast, but not large enough that it seemed sterile.

"Do you all have full-time staff?"

Diane recognized Jared came from money, but she never questioned him about it. Honestly, it didn't matter. It's the man, not the money for her.

"No. My grandfather has a nurse that comes in twice a week and we have a cleaning crew and a chef that comes in once a week. My dad's kind of a health nut, but grandad is all about soul food."

The entrance was warm, with thick area rugs that lead to a reading area to the left and a kitchen area to the right. The stairs were dark mahogany and gorgeous, leading to what she assumed were the bedrooms.

"Come on, let's put the bags in my room and then go find my grandad."

Jared's room was a huge master bedroom had the same dark mahogany of the stairs. The color was limited to the built-in bookshelf, bed, and windowsills. His bed had a beautiful cream-colored duvet that matched the color of the walls. The windows brighten the space with the sheer curtains and it gave the room an airy feel. He had a chaise near the corner of the room between a window and the bookshelf. Diane imagined being seated with a blanket to cover her legs, deeply engrossed in a thick book. There was a master bath the size of both her and Kim's room together. She couldn't wait to get a better view of everything it had, hoping for a sunken tub in order to take a long soak. Wistfully sighing, she felt Jared touch her hand.

"Penny for your thoughts?"

"Sunken tub filled with bubbles."

Laughing, Jared informed Diane that in fact there was a sunken tub and he could provide bubbles and entertainment. He led them down the stairs and into the room that Diane realized was a reading/living area. Diane spotted a handsome medium brown man with graying hair with a bright smile sitting on the sofa. He looked up from his book and stood with the help of a cane.

"Jared!" He said excitedly as Jared rushed to give him a hand and a hug.

"Granddad, it's so good to see you."

"We act like we didn't just see each other a month ago at Thanksgiving."

Chuckling in a deep baritone voice, he turned toward Diane, "And who is this beautiful young lady?"

Diane blushed and stepped forward and extended her hand. "Hi Sir. I'm Diane. Nice to meet you."

"Nice to meet you also, young lady. Come on, sit. Let's convene together." Diane took a seat on the sofa next to his grandfather. She looked over at Jared, who sat in a chair in front of them. He smiled at her, which didn't calm her at all.

"So tell me about yourself, Diane."

"Well Sir," Cutting her off he said. "No Sir, call me Daddy Grace."

"Okay Daddy Grace. There isn't much to tell. I'm twenty-seven from Radford, VA, a Radio, TV, and Film major and that's about it."

"What about your family? Are they still with us?" Diane's face became distressed, Jared's grandad realized he shouldn't push. "So how'd you and my grandson meet?"

"Well, he helped me move into my dorm room."

"Ah ha. So you two are just friends, or are you a special lady in his life?" Wiping her palm on her jeans, she was about to answer, but Jared cut her off.

"She's my forever. This is the one grandad." Daddy Grace looked from Jared to Diane.

"Well?" Diane couldn't predict if she and Jared would have forever, but she knew they would work toward a healthy long-lasting relationship.

"Absolutely," she said, winking at a cheesing Jared.

The longer they sat and talked, the more relaxed Diane became. Jared opened up a bit when his grandad mentioned his mom. She was hoping to gain insight even if it wasn't much. It would be more than what Jared has told her. His grandad left to take a nap and Jared took that moment to show Diane around the house. Afterward they headed to his room to relax before his dad got home and had dinner. Curled up in the bed with Dane in his arms felt right and Jared felt like everything he'd done for her was worth it.

Gerald entered quiet a quiet home. He figured Jared and his friend would have been spending time with his dad. He expected his dad to entertain them until he got home. It wasn't often he got company. Upstairs, he entered his bedroom and changed into a pair of jeans and a Polo shirt. He was thankful he closed the office for the holidays. The staff deserved a much-needed break. Gerald had been thinking of retiring for the last few years, but he wanted Jared to get on his feet before doing so. He didn't know what would he do as a retiree and until he figured it out, he would continue on as chief of staff at the office.

Stepping out of his room, he checked Jared's room before texting. He didn't want to be overbearing, but he wanted to make sure his son arrived safe and sound. Slowly opening the door, Gerald saw Jared nestled behind a beautiful young lady with his hands resting on her midsection. Even though he'd gotten the information secondhand through his dad, he was happy to see his son had found someone special. He'd left them to rest and check on his father when he paused. The position of Jared's hand he'd noticed was protective over her stomach. Was she pregnant? Is that why he wanted the family to meet her? After a deep breath, he decided he'd speak with his father first and then question Jared. He did not want his son ending his promising career before it got started.

He found his dad at the kitchen counter sampling the hors d'oeuvres as the staff he'd hired for the holidays hustle about preparing dinner. Daddy Grace patted his son on the shoulder and picked up a grape. Gerald asked if he'd meet Jared's lady friend. His father was being tight-lipped, but stated he had. He'd talk to his son about her separately. Gerald sat next to his dad. They snacked in silence, lost in their individual thoughts. Gerald considered if his son's friend was expecting, that'd give him a reason to retire and have a purpose. He'd have to convince the young lady to get on board with quitting school and living in the family home full time while Jared continued to pursue medicine. If she was with child, the decision was made and she'd have to accept it.

Jared didn't realize how tired he was until his head hit the pillow. This past semester had been a lot to deal with academically and socially. He didn't want to wake a snoring Diane, so he eased out of bed to go find his dad. He had to be home by now. Jared eased out of bed and made his way downstairs. In the kitchen, plates were being placed and doors were being opened and shut. Jared moved further in, hugged his dad, and kissed the top of his grandad's head. He popped a cherry tomato in his mouth.

"How long have you been home?"

"Long enough to peek in on you and your lady friend. She's beautiful son."

"Thanks dad. She is also smart, determined and has a great sense of humor. I can't wait for you to meet her."

All the things Jared said were true, however, he was also attempting to plant a seed in his dad's judgmental mind that Diane was amazing.

"Son, can we speak in private before dinner and afterward I'd like to meet..."

"Diane, her name's Diane."

His grandad patted his shoulder as he strolled by like going he was to the firing squad. Stepping into his dad's office, Jared closed his eyes and inhaled deeply. He loved the smell of wood and leather in his office since he was a young boy. It seemed to be the calm before the storm. Jared loved his dad. He stayed. He just didn't like his methods of getting things done, almost cold and calculating. Jared tried to understand his dad's pain at mom leaving, the regret knowing his firm hand had a lot to do with it. Never being the one to admit failure, he reassessed, recalibrated, and carried on.

Gerald came out swinging asking about school, the Kappas, if John Hopkins is still on his list of medical schools, etc. Once he was comfortable with most of his answers, he moved to Diane.

"So tell me about Diane."

Jared explained where and how they met and where they are now. Jared assumed he satisfied his dad until he asked, "Are you safe?"

"Yeah, she's on the pill."

His dad must have sensed his hesitation. "So you aren't using condoms? What about diseases and also pills aren't 100% effective?"

"I know that dad and she's not being reckless and neither am I. Trust me."

Jared made that statement with more confidence than he felt. He knew Diane slept with other people and trusted she was being safe. He wanted them both tested since they were now committed completely to one another. His dad didn't need to know that.

"Son, I know it feels good to feel skin to skin. You don't want to risk your future for a few minutes of pleasure. It's eighteen plus years of responsibilities you or she may not be ready for."

"I know, dad and believe me, she doesn't want kids right now and neither do I. We are focusing on our careers first before anything else."

From behind his desk, Gerald motioned for Jared to follow suit by pointing to the chair in front. "Son, I'm going to ask you a question, and I don't want to upset you or start a fight. I am only asking out of love and I'll support you, both of you, if need be."

"Dad, I promise you she is not pregnant. Where is this coming from?"

"Your hand was draped over her like you were protecting her stomach."

Jared didn't mean to, but he let out a loud laugh. He stood and walked to his dad, leaned over, and hugged him. "She's not pregnant. I just like holding her stomach. It's soothing for me."

Gerald nodded. "Okay. I was contemplating retiring to help so you could finish school." That gave Jared pause, "Really?"

"Yes, you're my son and I want you to have your dream of being a doctor." At that moment, Jared decided he wouldn't be as hard on his dad as he usually was.

"Thank you for that dad, but if you think the only reason, I'm caressing my lady is because she's pregnant, you've been outta the game too long. I think it's time you found someone that soothes you like Diane does me. It's beyond time."

With that, Jared sat back down and came clean about his Mom. From the day he saw her on that school field trip twelve years ago and his plan to take Diane to meet her. His dad went through a myriad of emotions at the revelations. Things became a little tense, but eventually he understood. He told Jared to be prepared for his mom to not wanting a visit or a relationship with him. Jared blew out a breath and nodded.

They turned to the door when they heard a light knock.

Diane stood at the entrance to the office. "Daddy Grace said it was okay for me to come in? If it's not, I apologize. I'll just go back and wait."

Jared jumped up before she the door closed. He loved the way she rapid fired when she was nervous or scared. "Naw, come in. I want you to meet my dad," Jared said as he pulled her to him and kissed her lips. Diane released a breath as Jared released her.

Gerald spoke with his hand held out, "Hi, it's nice to finally meet you. I'm Gerald."

"Nice to meet you also, Sir."

Jared was nervous introducing Diane to his dad, but after meeting, they seemed to like each other. Dinner was uneventful, and they all gathered in the living room looking through photos of Jared as a baby through college. The pictures of his mom were long gone, but the ache in his chest the remained. Diane saw his pain. She caressed his cheek and mouthed, "Sorry." Jared nodded with a small smile.

Jared's dad had been pleased with his choice in forever, especially when Diane unknowingly sided with him, stating she would choose John Hopkins over any medical school in the country listing everything from the history and advances they've made in medicine. By the end of the night, his father's mood changed to jovial as he gave Jared his approval.

"Son. She is amazing, bright and truthful. She didn't act as if she was putting on airs to please me or dad. Diane might be the one for you."

By the end of the night, the napped they took earlier seemed to never take place. Both were beyond ready to shower and sleep as they climbed the stairs. Jared allowed Diane to shower first. He wanted to give her some space to digest everything that took place tonight.

Moisturized, she walked into the bedroom where Jared laid on top of the covers. "You okay?" She said as she grabbed her pajamas.

"Don't. Get in naked." Crawling on the bed, Diane laid in Jared's arm.

"So are you good? I mean, your dad got a little abrupt but loosened up as the night progressed."

"Yeah, I think you had a lot to do with that. He liked you."

"He liked me, huh?"

"Yeah, but not as much as I like you."

Moving his hand between her legs he fondled her pussy. Diane knew she was going to regret not twisting her mohawk. She reached for a band and gathered her hair in a ponytail.

"Yeah, because when I'm finished, that shit gonna shrink into an afro."

The staff kept busy as they prepared an amazing brunch for Gerald's colleagues and a few of Daddy Grace's politician friends. The food, amazing, and the alcohol flowed. Diane stuck close to Jared since she'd never been around so many important people. Important people with wealth and influence. She needed to make the right connections in order to secure a future, and this is the perfect place to do that. So many businesspeople and politicians gave her and Jared their cards for internships and summer jobs. Jared wanted to take his summer to relax before entering med school. Diane wondered if she should get Kim to apply. Maybe they could work together. Brunch didn't end until 3 p.m., so Diane and Jared took a nap since Jared's dad stated dinner would be at 8:30 p.m.

"How you doing lil momma?"

"Ummm, as loose as a noodle." She leaned over and kissed his lips.

Jared took that as his cue. "So what you laying down for? Come on and sit on this face so I can put you to sleep."

"Baby, I'm so relaxed."

"Get your ass over here."

Jared grabbed Diane and flipped her on top of him, sliding down to her core. With his knees bent and hanging off the bed, he wrapped his hands around her as he pushed her on his face. Diane braced herself on her forearms on the bed as Jared sucked on her lower labia, working his way up to her pussy. Diane moved back and forth as Jared flatten his tongue, allowing her to take her fill. Her arms began to shake and Jared saw she was close. His mouth was soaked. He latched on her clit and inserted a finger curving and hitting her G spot. Diane came hard. "Jared, we're supposed to be sleeping." Diane said as she tried to lay back down.

Crawling on top of her, Jared positioned his dick. “Give me five minutes.”

They fucked for what for hours and slept just as long. They came downstairs looking refreshed and well fucked. Diane sat at the table with Jared’s father and grandfather. Her eyes remained down to hide her embarrassment. The smirks on his dad’s face confirmed they heard her and Jared upstairs.

“So I take it you enjoyed brunch this morning?”

“Yes, I did. I am grateful you allowed me to be in attendance. Thank you again for inviting me into your home.”

“I’m sure Jared experienced how grateful you are.” His dad said with a smirk. Chuckling, Jared looked over at an embarrassed Diane, placing a hand on her thigh.

“My apologies, sir. I didn’t mean to disrespect you or your home.”

“No disrespect. I just ask that you two are safe. We don’t want any pauses in our careers because of an unexpected little one.”

“Dad!” Jared tried to interject, but Gerald held up his hands. “Do you understand, young lady?”

"Yes, I understand and trust me. No one at this table will have to worry about that ever. Children aren't in my life's plan." Jared snapped his head to Diane, "What if I want kids?"

"I mean later, maybe, but definitely not now. You'd want kids?"

"Yes," he said without hesitation.

Diane cupped his cheek. She looked him in the eyes. "If we were together, and you really wanted a child? Yes, I'd have kids, but I'd only want two max?"

Closing his eyes in agreement, she kissed his lips.

"You're nervous because of how you were raised but I don't have any doubts that you would be a loving, caring, invested mom." Gently wiping a lone tear from her face, Jared smiled at his ride or die.

After dinner, Jared's grandad suggested they sit on the enclosed heated porch after dinner with hot beverages wrapped in blankets and watch the people enjoying the Christmas lights.

It was the start of a perfect holiday.

Is This The End?

Resto sat on his couch with his regulars resting comfortably in his bedroom. The unanswered texts he'd sent to Diane had him spiraling. It was time to let her go, even though a part of him didn't want to. She'd literally removed the ache of his mama and replaced it with a new one for her. If he'd known Diane had the power to heal and destroy him, he would've never pursued her. Just like his mama, she left. He thought to himself.

"Time to pick up the pieces find peace, if only to have her one more time."

By mid-December, Jared and Diane got closer every day. She fell in love with his grandad and even his father grew on her once you understood his logic. His father was a little intense, but she preferred that to no emotion at all like her parents. He watched her like he wanted to solve a puzzle. Diane hoped she didn't have to curse his ass out or maybe that's how a normal parent did things.

They all did their very best to make her a part of the family. Jared and Diane spend most of the holiday doing the tourist thing by visiting the African American Museum, MLK Jr. monument, Museum of African Art, and the Anacostia Community Museum in SE DC. They also toured the various farmers' markets, and the Christmas tree downtown.

Jared snuck behind Diane while she was in the kitchen and wrapped his arms around her. "You smell so good."

"Oh, yeah?"

"Yeah. What you up to?"

"What I'm about to get up is in this pussy as soon as I bend you over."

"Your family is here!" She whispered yelled.

"Grandad taking a nap and dad is in his office where he always is. Bend over. You got on underwear?"

"What? I uh." Not waiting for an answer, Jared pinned her to the kitchen island and lifted her pajama gown.

"No panties on this fat pussy. Just how I like it." He slipped his fingers in her. With a gentle glide back and forth, Jared milked the cum from her.

"Oh, fuck Jared. Shit. We're going to get caught. Uhhh, your dad is going to think I'm a..."

The words died on her lips as Jared pinched her clit with his thumb and index finger. Legs shaking, Diane braced on the island as she came over Jared's hand.

"Fuck lil momma. That pussy been missing me, huh?"

Jared pulled his dick out of his PJs, he pushed into Diane from behind. She was so wet it sucked him in halfway. "Fuck Lil momma, my pussy feels so good."

He upward stroked, causing her front to bang onto the island. Diane tried to brace herself and gave as good as she got, but Jared had such a tight hold on her waist she barely move.

"Fuck Diane," he growled, "I will kill a nigga behind this pussy and this." grabbing just below left breast holding her heart.

Jared placed both hands on her stomach. He pounded into her hard and fast. He wished she wasn't on the pill. He wanted to put a baby in her tonight. Jared heard his dad's footsteps in the distance, so he pumped faster and faster. Hopefully, he'd to finish before he rounded the corner.

Diane heard someone walking down the hall and became scared. Jared's dad would kick her out of the house if they got caught.

"Jared, please."

She begged. Did she want him to stop or keep going? The dick had her crazed, but his dad catching them freaked her out. The footsteps sounded like they were getting closer and closer, along with her orgasm.

Being squeezed by Diane's contracting walls, Jared's nut was on the brink. The tingling up his spine said it was ready to explode. "I'm about to nut lil' momma. You're ready?" He slide his hand down and pinched her button. She shot off like a rocket and the screamed that escaped her that sounded like she was being catapulted out of a cannon. He gritted out, "Fuck Diane! I will fucking kill a nigga behind you."

Calming down, still connected. "You're loud ass as fuck. Your dad gonna to come in here and fuck us up."

He pushed into her harder for good measure. "My dad is in the hallway waiting for us to finish."

"Jared." Diane whispered as she looked back at him.

"I've never brought a girl home before so he may be giving me space to knock some shit down cause he's proud." Slow stroking in her again, Diane's head fell back as another orgasm hit.

Gerald walked into the kitchen and cleared his throat. He paused at the kitchen entrance. "Are you two decent? Jared, I hope you're not on any furniture in there."

"We good dad."

Jared called out. Gerald noticed Diane was flushed and looked well fucked. His son gripped his dick in his pajama pants with a face full of lust. He smirked as he lifted an eyebrow.

"Y'all finished fucking in my kitchen? What if grandad came in here? And the way you had her in here screaming, don't be surprised if the neighbors have called the police."

Diane covered her face with her hands. "I'm so embarrassed."

"Don't be embarrassed now. You didn't think about me when my son snatched your soul." He chuckled and he patted Jared on the back.

"Isn't that what y'all say nowadays?"

"Oh my God."

Diane said as she leaned her face on Jared's chest. "Come on dad. We got a little carried away, but you don't have to embarrass Diane."

"I'm not embarrassing her. I'm just making an observation."

He looked at Jared as he rubbed Diane's back. Gerald remembered a time in his life when he had done that for Cheryl. Rubbing the ache in his chest.

"It's late son. Why don't you and Diane go get some rest? Are you traveling to Philly tomorrow?"

"Yes, come on lil momma."

"Sorry again for disrespecting your home." Diane said finally finding some confidence. "It's okay Diane, I was young once, so I get it."

They departed the kitchen they headed upstairs. "By the way, thank you for not messing up the countertops."

Diane tripped and Jared laughed as he caught her shaking his head.

They arrived in Philly and planned to stay for about a week. Both agreed it was a good idea to do the tourist thing like they did in DC. Everything and everybody was more festive since it was the holidays. They took the train from Union Station in DC to 30th Street Station in Philadelphia. The hotel they booked was in the middle of the city. Immediately after checking in they went from attraction to attraction, got cheesesteaks then headed back to the hotel. After a shower, both cuddle on the plush area rug and pigged out on cheesesteak, fries, and soda.

While Diane rested, Jared did some internet searches and found out his mom had retired from the hospital just last year. She lived in West Philly, which had gained popularity in recent years. Jared called the number he found for her. "Mom? Hi it's me Jared?"

The silence on the other end was so long that Jared thought the line disconnected. "Jared?"

"Yes, mom, it's me. I'm in town for a few days and want to come see you?"

"Jared? I haven't spoken to you in years. You're in town? Where? Where are you now?"

"I'm downtown. I want to come see you. I mean, if that's okay and you aren't busy? I shouldn't have popped up on you, but I was just thinking..." Jared was so nervous he sounded like Diane with the rapid fire. Jared took a breath and waited for his mom to say something.

"Yeah. Sure, it'd be good to see you. Are you available tomorrow?" Jared breathed a sigh of relief.

"Yes, I can come tomorrow. We can come. Whatever time you want."

They scheduled to have him come over at noon, and she would have brunch prepared for them. It didn't escape his mom that he'd said we. Cheryl was nervous about Jared's visit with his father. Is she ready to see Gerald again? That is. If Gerald is the person he was referring to.

A ball of nerves, Jared ended the call with his mom. Diane only had one way to get him out of his head. Thankful for the plush carpet. Diane crawled over to Jared. She cupped his face to smooth out the worry lines.

"You okay, baby?"

"Yeah, I'm good. My mom said we can come over at noon for brunch. I'm scared. Scared and nervous."

"Those feelings are to be expected, babe. You haven't seen your mom since you were thirteen years old. You've grown a lot and so has she."

"Yeah, you're right, but that does nothing to stop the nerves."

Diane kissed his lips, neck, chest and continued down to his boxers. She freed his dick from the middle opening. When her mouth met the base of his pelvis, she slowly pulled up. Jared release a sigh he didn't realize he held. He grabbed the back of her head with both hands and guided her movements. Diane followed his lead and increased the pace. This was about her but giving him what he needed. With a firm grip, she suctioned her mouth around Jared's pulsing dick. Diane massaged and tugged his balls as Jared's hips pumped in her mouth. Jared came so hard his eyes hurt from the pressure. Diane tried to swallow as much as possible as some of Jared dribbled out the corner of her mouth. Jared laid limp on the floor as Diane crawled beside him and closed her eyes.

Uber dropped them off in the West Philly neighborhood of Cobbs Creek. Diane tried to comfort Jared as much as possible before meeting with his estranged mom. On edge, like he would blow at any minute. She tried to adjust as quickly, but it was impossible. Jared's mood swings were a combination if distance, sadness and anger all of which he took out on her body. Coochie sore from this morning's session. It surprised her she's able to sit on the not so comfortable seat of the Uber.

Jared explained to Diane that his mom decided a condo fit her lifestyle since she didn't have children and didn't want the responsibility of caring for a home with her busy career. The annoyance on his face seeped out of his pours. It bothered Jared that she spoke as if she was a single woman with no children and no ex-husband. Diane made sure she constantly touch Jared. The touch a reassurance that he had someone. They arrived at Jared's mom a few minutes past noon and Jared clasp Diane's hand like a life source. She wondered if they had braces available for her hand because he had a death grip on it.

Diane's nerves frayed a bit. Immediately intimidated by the pristine building, she wondered how she'd react to his mother. After exiting the elevators, Jared walked to apartment 4B and rang the bell. It took a few minutes, but Diane heard the heels as Cheryl made her way to the door.

She bit her lip as she looked over at Jared, who still had her hand grasped in his. He offered an unsure smile, and she kissed his lips.

Cheryl opened the door, calm but apprehensive, not knowing how she would be received by her son and his dad. She and Gerald hadn't spoken since the day she left. He sent her that letter from his lawyer, advising her to stay away from Jared. Not that she needed that letter, she had no intentions of returning. A family had never been on her long list of accomplishments. Neither was falling in love with Gerald. He offered her the escape she needed away from her home life.

Cheryl lived with her grandmother after her mom died. It had been difficult adjusting to her ways. Her grandmother believed in women being married, having children, and staying at home while the man provided. So when Cheryl met Gerald, she not only fell in love with him, but he offered her an escape. Only she didn't realize it at the time, she went from one overbearing home to another. She did not expect or really want Jared. It sounded cold, but Cheryl became adamant about not having children and explained this to Gerald while they dated. He agreed and led her to believe that they both should focus on their career but would revisit the idea of a family later. He pushed and pushed, but at after a few months never brought it up again. Her birth control would come up missing and he claimed he didn't have a problem with condoms. She believed he tampered with them months later; they found out she was pregnant with Jared.

It shocked Cheryl to see Jared standing there, not with his father but a beautiful young lady with his hand clasped in hers.

"Jared?"

She questioned. He looked similar to the thirteen-year-old so many years ago but had transformed into a striking young man.

"Well, don't stand in the chilly hall. Come inside, take your coats off and make yourself at home."

Once they all stepped in, Diane noticed the spacious the apartment. The furniture, beautifully crafted. Cream color with warm pillows and a throw haphazardly placed on the chaise. The hardwood floors match the industrial beams, exposed pipes, and brickwork throughout. An open floor concept of the living, dining and kitchen areas all flow into one large space.

Cheryl led Diane and Jared to the dining area that held a feast. "I didn't know what you'd like, so I ordered a little of everything."

Diane gave Jared a little squeeze, hoping to unmute him. "This is great! Everything looks amazing! Thank you, mom."

Cheryl stiffened at the term of endearment which had Diane wanting to drag her ass. How dare she abandon her son and then flinch at him, addressing her even though she is nowhere close to being a mom? She didn't like this woman.

Diane startled out of her thoughts when Jared spoke, "Mom, this is my forever Diane. Diane my mom Cheryl."

She shook her hand a little tighter than normal. Diane remained pleasant but sent a subtle message that she would in fact dog walk her ass if she got out of pocket. Jared's mom or not.

"Hi. Nice to meet you." They both said at the same time. "Sit. I bet you two are hungry?"

After a few minutes of enjoying the food, silence ensued. It was too quiet. Cheryl finally spoke. "So you two met at Howard?"

Jared looked up from his plate and answered, "Yes. She asked to share my cart on move-in day, and we've been kicking it since. She's been the best thing in my college life, besides my frat brothers."

"Oh, you're in a fraternity? Which one?"

"Kappa Alpha Psi, the same as dad."

"Ooh okay, that's great. Diane, are you in a sorority?"

"No, ma'am." Diane wanted to keep her answers light. This is about Jared, who came to develop a bond with his mother. His needs came first, not her.

"So Jared, tell me about yourself now. The last time we chatted, you were thirteen. A lot of time has passed."

Jared and his mom conversed for about twenty minutes as Diane sat, listened, and watched. She suddenly became protective of Jared and his feelings, however Jared seemed to ease into the flow of things, and so did his mother. She occasionally looked over at Diane, smiling and offering her something else from the large sections of brunch items available.

Diane noticed that not once did Jared or Cheryl make physical contact with each other. She knew he yearned for it. Hell, she yearned for it for him, knowing what it's like not to receive love from a parent. It made you question everything, what you did, what you didn't do to not be enough for them to love you.

"Where's your ladies' room? Diane wanted Jared and his mom to have a moment alone. "Down the hall.

Once Diane was out of the room, Jared addressed Cheryl. "Mom? I came here today for a few reasons and one of those reasons is Diane. She is my forever. I wanted you two to meet and possibly get acquainted. Second, now that I'm an adult, I wondered if we can attempt to develop a relationship? If not as mom and son, as friends?"

After a deep breath, Jared wished Diane was there, but this was something he had to do on his own.

"Jared."

She whispered as she reached and closed her hands ever so softly over his wrist. Jared closed his eyes and committed it to memory. He hadn't had his mom's touch since he was a boy. He doubts he'd experience it again.

"You needed a mother figure in your life, and I hoped your grandfather gave you some semblance of that. I understand it's difficult for you and I can tell you are seeking something that honestly son I can't give you. And, I don't know if I ever will."

Jared kept the tears that gathered in his eyes at bay and removed his hand from his mother's grasp.

Diane walked out at that moment and noticed Jared's distress. Rushing to him. She tilted his face in her direction, looking him in the eyes. She wiped the lone tear that escaped.

"Hey, look at me." He did.

"It's okay. Whatever it is, it's okay and you're going to be okay. Do you know why?"

Focused on her, he looked unsure. "Because I'm your forever. I've got you. It doesn't matter who else doesn't or refuses to have you."

She said, glancing over at Cheryl. "I've got you. We've got each other, and that's never going to change Jared."

He looked at her with a half-smile. "Until the rims hit the muthafucking road," she said, kissing him lightly at first. Jared grabbed Diane by the back of the neck and deepened the kiss. Once he released her, he was more grounded.

Facing his mom, Jared took a deep cleansing breath, "Mom, I may not understand why you left and right now. I don't want to know. I came here hoping we'd develop some type of, I don't know something, but I see that was a mistake. I won't interrupt your life any longer, but I'm glad I introduced my forever. Unfortunate for you, you'll never recognize how amazing she or our future kids will be. And maybe that's how you want it. I pray that's how you want it, because I would never want you to experience what it's like to want someone to love you and never receive it."

They got up and left.

It was a quiet ride back to the hotel. Diane didn't want to say anything thing until they were alone. She wanted Jared in a comfortable setting to express himself, however he needed to after this fucked up ordeal. Once they arrived in the room, Jared walked to the shower and Diane followed. Both stripped out of their clothes in silence, Jared adjusted the temperature and stepped in. Again Diane followed. Under the spray, Jared turned to Diane, looked her in the eyes and asked, "Why doesn't she love me?"

She didn't have an answer for him, nor could she think of what to say, so she said nothing. Moving under the spray, she held him as he cried.

After the shower, Diane helped Jared in some pajama bottoms as she dressed in her boy shorts and tank top. She wanted him to have easy access if he needed it. He did.

Jared was on top of her as soon as she got in the bed. He pulled her shorts down as he kissed her. Once her bottom was half completely bare to him, he grabbed her by the throat and entered her. He was rough, but she allowed it, knowing it was what he needed. Jared fucked her hard as he tighten his grip around her neck.

As the night continued, they cried, fucked and sucked each other. By morning, he was much better. They sat and talk about what happened, shared pain from an absentee parent and the way it transformed them into who they are now. They connected on a deeper level. Diane's happy about the choice she made to stay with Jared over the holidays.

That day in the hotel room solidified that she would never leave Jared, no matter what he did. He was her forever.

Chapter 23

By the time they headed back to DC at the end of the week, Jared seemed back to his old self and for that, Diane was glad. They got back in the swing of things, preparing for Christmas and all that it entailed. Jared, Diane, his dad, and grandad decorated the tree as a family. Diane loved listening to the stories of Jared as a child and a semi-rebellious teen. It gave insight into something she never received. This holiday turned out to be a healing experience, and she was thankful in more ways than one.

Finally, reading and responding to Resto's text, Diane gave him the closure he was looking for. They conversed via text for about ten minutes, saying their goodbyes for now, agreeing to revisit a friendship in the future. Drained from the long day, Diane looked forward to a bath and a long nap, knowing that Jared's good mood would lead to good sex.

Upstairs, the sunken tub got nice hot with bubbles and rose pedals, lavender buds and citrus. She stepped in the tub, laid back and closed her eyes. Happy with the decision she made ending things with Resto. Diane enjoyed the time spent with Jared and his family. It was simply an amazing day. Today she experienced being in a familial home filled with love and affection.

Jared peaked his head in the bathroom and asked Diane if he could have her log information for the laptop. He wanted to check his grades. Settled at the desk, he logged onto the Bison web. Jared checked her grades first. She'd done well as he imagined. A's and B's meant the Dean's list for him and her. Just as he was about to close her laptop, a message from a chat pinged. Jared noticed it came from her professor, so he opened it.

Half asleep in the bath, Diane's eyes bulged when she felt a hand grip her tight as hell around the neck. She saw Jared's face filled with rage.

"So you were fucking your mutha fucking professor?!"

Diane said nothing. Jared literally tried to choke the life out of her. Diane grabbed his wrist, hoping to release some of the pressure he applied. The force had her rising out of the tub. Jared guided her movements with his hand. Naked, soapy and wet, he led her by her neck to the bedroom and, with a push, she fell onto the bed. Diane quickly got up in case he physically attacked her. She needed to defend herself if she couldn't calm him down.

"I saw the messages on chat and text! How long?! How long have you been fucking him? Are you still fucking him?!" Jared screamed so loud Diane was afraid his father would come up.

"Jared, please lower your voice. Your family is downstairs."

"I don't give a fuck! What the fuck?! Did you fuck that whack ass nigga?! Do you realize how old that mutha fucker is?! Huh?!" Jared grabbed Diane by the shoulders and shook her.

"What the fuck Diane? Mutha fucking talk now!

Diane started crying. Jared didn't care.

"Fuck them tears, man. Talk!"

Staggered breaths were the only sounds heard in the room. Afraid to tell Jared the truth, Diane thought being accountable would save their relationship. If she hadn't listened to Kim, he would've known before this and it wouldn't have been an issue.

"Jared."

He held up his hand to stop her from speaking. "Diane, I don't want to hear shit you have to say if you aren't answering my fucking question!"

A nervous Diane began rapidly firing her answers. "The week before Thanksgiving when I was sorting out my shit, we had a day date. He invited me to a movie, then dinner. I spent the night with him. It was hard figuring out my feelings. We bonded over parental issues and one thing lead to another. It just happened."

"So you fucked him once? Or.."

"Multiple times." Diane said, "It was multiple times the entire week. We had a kind of connection. I don't know, it just was different."

Pacing back and forth, Jared's anger rose to the surface. As he continued to pace, he wanted to smash her in the face. With so many unanswered questions, they didn't come fast enough.

"Diane, please tell me everything before I do something we'll regret. Please, baby, for the sake of us, tell me."

Shaky hands covered Diane's face as she told Jared everything from the night he came over to the night she returned to the dorms. Jared had in tears in his eyes. "Jared, please. It's over. I promise you it's over."

As he wiped eyes, it surprised him when he allowed her to give him a kiss. Jared wrapped his hands around her waist, gazing in her eyes with so much love. "One thing, lil momma. Did he have my ass?"

Jared thought she'd spaced out when it took a few minutes for her answer. "Diane?" He said, as he lifted her head with his index finger.

"Jared, I'm so scared. I don't want to lie to you. My feelings were all over the place, I promise. I love you."

"You gave it to him?" He whispered as the air left his lungs. The one question that was liable to break him, but he had to ask, "Protection?"

Diane dropped to the floor. She clung to Jared's ankles.

"Fuuuuck!!" Jared cried out.

"Get the fuck off me Lil Momma before I do something I can't take back."

Diane backed away from Jared and ran over to the closet to pack a bag. She decided it was best to leave before being tossed out. Hopefully she'd be able to get into the dorms even though they were technically closed. Diane sensed Jared behind her. She slowed.

"Diane, I don't want you to leave. You are my forever. One fight doesn't mean to leave."

His tear-streaked face came into view through hers. Diane hugged his waist. "Jared. There is no excuse for the choices I made, but when I tell you, I was so confused. I wanted to get away from feeling those unfamiliar feelings."

Their eyes locked. "I promise I'm all in."

"I know Lil momma. I know."

Jared and Diane got into bed and held each other. Closing her eyes, she seemed weightless.

The dreams started again, and Resto opened himself to them even more. Lost, he didn't grasp how much longer before being fully consumed by madness. Inebriated, he laid back on the bed, dick in hand, urging thoughts of Diane to the forefront. Both Diane and his mama were there while he stroked his dick until it fully erect surging a deep orgasm forward.

Weak from his release, Resto didn't bother with a wet cloth. He just laid in bed as a calm came over him. His phone pinged with a message.

"Diane."

Her: I hate the way we ended things, and I wanted to know if you can meet me in your office so we can get closure in person?

Naughty Professor: I'm been trying to forget you. It's been hard. The dreams are back and I can still smell you on me. I've missed you so much, but I'm trying to respect your decision.

Her: I'm sorry for hurting you. It wasn't intentional, we'll talk more at school.

Naughty: What time?

The next day, Resto made it to the school fifteen minutes early to prepare himself for Diane. The only reason he thought Diane wanted to see him again was for one last goodbye. He really missed the way she kept mama at bay.

Resto turned as he heard the door opening. He released a breath and stood. Halfway up, the bat came down on his head.

"Diane" put in work as the licks continued. The rage grew as each lick made contact and it pleased to release all the pent-up anger in him. The whacks continued until Resto's limp body covered in his blood hit the table. He repeatedly bashed his head possessed with pain.

The knife he found in Diane's jeans, he used to stab Resto repeatedly, only stopping when he retracted the knife and a piece of organ remained on the tip.

The assailant snapped out of his rage once he saw the brain matter sliding off the table on the floor. Not bothering to clean up, he left the building with his head held high. The school is a ghost town this time of year. He hadn't worried about getting caught. In his car, he eased into traffic for the twenty-minute ride home.

Diane woke up as the bedroom door opened. She noticed Jared. "Hey babe, where were you? Are you okay?"

Jared turned on the lights as he stood in front of Diane, covered in blood. Diane rushed to him. "Oh my God, are you okay?! What the fuck happened?"

They walked to the bathroom as she began unzipping his jacket. The bat fell from his waist and hit the floor with a thud.

She noticed all the blood and her name. "Diane? Jared, what the fuck is going on?"

He said nothing, just removed the rest of his clothing as Diane grabbed a bag.

Realization dawned on her. "Jared, have you been doing this all along?"

The shower started and, with shaky hands, Diane secured everything in the bag before tying it in a knot. Both stripped and stepped into the shower.

Under the warm spray, blood and brain matter washed down the drain. After a few breaths, Jared opened his eyes, focusing on Diane.

"Everything I did, I did for us. You are my lifeline. If I don't have you I'm dead anyway so..." Jared looked at her and asked, "So what you gonna do?"

Diane gently ran her hands down his face, lightly kissing his lips.

With a washcloth and some soap, she lathered it and began washing Jared. "So Beauty and Dreds? You did that?"

Nodding, he replied. "And that Eli nigga."

Diane slowed, then continued to wash Jared from head to toe. She didn't know what to think about what Jared had told her. Diane, in that moment, understood what being cared for looked like. She's slightly turned on, disgusted and impressed.

After the shower, Diane added the washcloth to the bag as well. "We have to get rid of this."

Jared watched as she took the bag and placed it in her suitcase in the closet. Back in the bathroom she cleaned it from top to bottom. She walked back into the closet, adding the cleaning supplies to the bag. Once done, she stood in front of Jared and asked, "What is inside of Diane? It's heavy for a mini Louisville Slugger."

Jared was sitting on the bed naked. He grabbed her waist, pulled her to him, and buried his head in her stomach. "Cement and lead balls. I did for you Diane. I can't have another woman I love and care about abandon me again."

Burying his face further into her stomach, he moved his hand to her ass, squeezing. Jared licked and sucked her stomach. He moved further, spreading her legs a bit as he slid off the bed to his knees and started sucking her pussy like his life depended on it. Her head fell back, Diane opened wider and grabbed Jared's head. He sucked and sucked until her knees buckled. She exploded.

With a pussy stained face, Jared reiterated, "You are my lifeline. I'm dead without you. Promise you'll never leave me?" Cupping his cheek, she met his eyes. "I'm your forever. I can't leave you."

The next day, Diane took the bag and disappeared for a couple of hours. Upon her return, she had a smile on her face and lunch in her hands. Professor Resto's death was all over the news. The school is now closed until February. The police interviewed all the students, past and present, that had taken Resto's class, Diane included. Jared's dad allowed the police to interview both her and Jared together. It seemed they didn't suspect a student. The questions were regarding visitors coming to the campus to see him. If he spoke of a girlfriend or boyfriend, etc.

By New Year's Eve, the death of Resto died down. Jared and Diane continued to focus on spending time with each other. Jared's dad attended a party the doctors on staff at the hospital threw each year and his Grandad spent his New Year's in church. Diane and Jared cuddled in the living area with candles lit, music playing, and smoking. Passing the weed to Diane. Jared looked at her as she inhaled and stared at the lights on the tree.

"What'd you do with the clothes and bat?" He'd been curious about what she did since Christmas but didn't have the courage to ask until now. Blowing more smoke out, she turned and kissed him deeply.

"There are a lot of homeless people in the city this time of year. I visited a few and donated some food that will tie them over for a few days along some fresh socks, underwear, and blankets. Since they have new items, someone suggested a fire for keeping warm. I believe people call them dumpster fires."

Diane face the tree again. Jared smile at the lights dancing off her face. "You're my lifeline, and thank you for being all in with me. Even when I wasn't able to recognize what I had. Since day one, you've given me everything I'll ever need."

"We are and forever will be an us." He smiled.

"Until the rims hit the road."

The End

Acknowledgments

Thank you to Tamara Whitlow and Petyton Banks. They offered me resources and encouragement to complete this book and press forward. Thank you to Rowdy Roosky, Sade Rena for joining my lives on TikTok and just being there.

Thank you to Evelyn Sola and Akyra Chiffon, who read the mess of a first unedited draft. That took guts!

Thank you to all my Beta Readers. You all pumped me up while being honest.

Last, a big thank you to all of my TikTok followers who came along with me on this journey. You listened throughout this entire process without judgement and continued to come back for more. I really appreciate all of all of you!

Black Authors Matter!

Black Readers Matter!

About The Author

Darlene Cunningham is an Indie author that writes beautifully flawed characters who challenge the traditional ways of living and loving. She is a graduate of Thee Illustrious Howard University where she completed coursework in Creative Writing, Poetry and Scriptwriting. She currently lives in Atlanta.

Rate Your Experience!

Sign up for my newsletter to stay informed about my upcoming releases and featured Authors!

Please take the time to go to Amazon, StoryGraph and Goodreads to rate and/or review my book.

Thank you in advance!

Amazon, StoryGraph & Goodreads

amazon

Coming Soon

Kayla is a fifty-year-old professor who'd lived most of her life afraid of everything. She rarely left her hometown of Tennessee. Gifted with an all expense paid trip to Loiza, Puerto Rico. Kayla decided it was time to stop existing and start living.

An age gap romance with a twist.

You know how his life ended. This book will explain how it started. Professor Resto from So This Is College... gets his own story.

Made in the USA
Columbia, SC
28 February 2025

54545226R00180